THE BODY ABROAD

BRIAN PRESTON

THE BODY ABROAD

BRIAN PRESTON

VOLATILE BOOKS

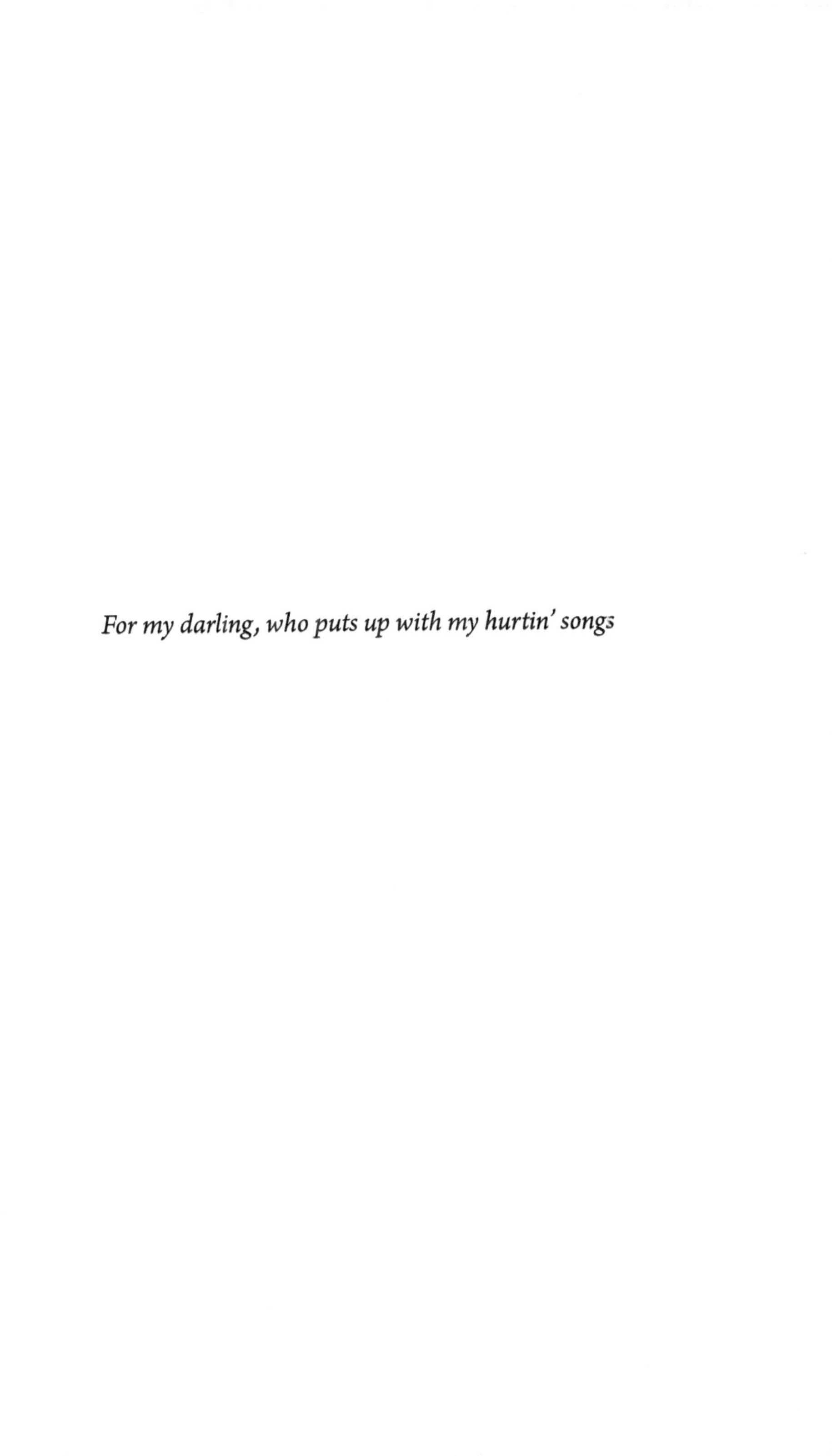

For my darling, who puts up with my hurtin' songs

PART I

CHAPTER 1

She had examined the body that lay broken in the roadside gravel, and now a State Trooper led her further back along the shoulder to something she hadn't noticed before—a Go-Pro camera sitting atop a tripod. Lilia had a fleeting thought that it looked lonely, like a faithful dog waiting for its master.

"Should it be dusted for prints before we mess with it?" she asked.

"I already handled it to shut it off—it was still running when I got here," the Trooper said. "I've never heard of a camera set up and running at an accident like this—you think the guy wanted to record his own death?"

"It's possible. Weird, but possible," she said. "To turn it off did you just touch a button, or did you really handle it?"

"I pawed at it pretty good. Couldn't figure it out."

"In that case we may as well rewind and take a peek."

"You're the boss, I guess," said the Trooper. "Coroner's not usually here this quick though."

"I was driving out to Spangle to buy cherries at a little orchard I like near there," Lilia said. "Then I came across you guys. And as fate would have it, I'm the Coroner on call this weekend."

"Cherries are awesome this year," said the trooper. He unscrewed the camera from the tripod. "I always go north for mine. Green Bluffs. The Picker's Trot is coming up—I came second in the pit spit one year. Now how do you rewind this sucker? I always get my kids to figure these things out."

"Give it to me," Lilia said. "I don't have kids, I'm used to solving things by myself." She took it from him and looked it over. "You press here, it's a touch screen." He stood at her shoulder as she pressed play.

"Good thing we've got this for ID, 'cause his face is scraped up real bad."

"Don't talk, just listen," Lilia said. She held the camera delicately in her hands like a little digital oracle, and they watched as the screen showed a teenage boy in a baseball cap riding in a car, framing himself in a video selfie. They heard him shout, "Here! This is perfect. Stop here. Stop!" The car slowed to a stop.

The video was jumbled as he climbed out and pulled a backpack from the back seat. He leaned through the passenger window and the camera settled on the woman at the steering wheel. She looked unhappy.

"Mom, I'll be fine," he said to her. "I've got my phone, you can reach me anytime. It's got GPS, you've got the app to track me. It's cool. Lemme go."

"Stop pointing that camera at me!" his mother said.

"Ma, don't cry. I can go if I want."

"The whole idea is crazy. You are not a filmmaker, Jordan, you are a teenager. Perverts cruise these roads looking to prey on kids like you—"

"Ma—I'm a high school graduate—"

"Barely! You haven't even started college, and—" The roar of a passing semi-trailer drowned her out. She stopped and waited for it to pass, but the kid shouted over it.

"You can't stay here, Mom. Just drive away! I love you Mom."

Turning away from his mother's teary face, he stepped back from the open window and walked along the shoulder.

"Is she gone yet?" he asked. The camera turned back and caught the SUV as it gripped the hardtop and pulled even with him. His mother gave one last unhappy wave before she accelerated away. "Yes!" he hollered. "G'bye Mom!" He turned the lens back to his face. "Whew—Holy shit, thought she'd never leave! Now it's just you and me."

A truck roared past. He waited for it to roll away into the distance, waited for quiet. "Hey there. Let me introduce myself. I'm Jordan Summerland, and welcome to my hitchhiking adventure, coast to coast across forty-eight great states! Are you set to meet and greet the real America, you and me? I'm super-stoked! It's gonna be awesome! I'm going to make a movie as I go along—kinda like Borat, remember Borat? Like that, only really real! The real America, posted on my blog, daily. I've got fourteen followers already, and by the time I've hit forty-eight states I should be famous—or dead! Ha! Now give me a sec to set up my tripod. This thing is going to have awesome production values!"

For a few moments Lilia and the Trooper saw jumbled images,

then the screen settled into a clear view of the road stretching into the distance. Young Jordan stepped into the frame at the edge of the road, with his rucksack slung on his shoulder and his thumb proudly raised for hitchhiking. "I'm doing this trip solo. Don't need no cameraman," he shouted.

Two vehicles passed before the third, a pickup truck, slowed down while the driver looked him over. The truck stopped thirty yards down the road.

"Holy shit! That took like, ten seconds! We're on our way!" He hurried to the truck, and talked to the driver through the passenger window. "In the back? Okay, great, let me just grab my camera!"

Tossing his rucksack into the bed of the truck, he cantered quickly back toward the lens, nearly skipping with happiness. Behind him the tires spun and spit gravel—the pickup suddenly high-tailed it onto the highway. "Hey! Hey hey HEY!!" Jordan sprinted after it for a dozen strides, but it was hopeless. It was gone. He watched it disappear into the distance, then walked dejectedly back toward the camera.

"Fucking asshole! What a fucking jerk! I can't believe that! Fuck *me*!"

A big semi tractor-trailer barreling down the other side of the road blasted its horn, either in sympathy or mockery. The passing truck kicked up a gust of wind that made the camera tremble and was strong enough to blow young Jordan's baseball cap off his head. It fluttered beyond his finger tips out onto the road, and on impulse he chased it—the last thing he ever did. A big rig coming the other way, unnoticed in the din made by the first, smacked him full-force.

"Nasty," muttered the Trooper. Lilia shushed him. On the screen the eighteen-wheeler shuddered and screeched into the middle distance, buckling to an emergency stop. Seconds passed before the driver came around the back end of his rig, looking tentatively to see what fate had wrought. He approached the body, then backed away, and began walking in small circles on the asphalt.

"He's still circling like that," said the Trooper. The two of them looked back down the highway toward the body, and beyond it the big eighteen-wheel rig. The driver of the rig was indeed walking circles in shock. A handful of other drivers who had stopped were sneaking peeks at the battered body and being shooed back by paramedics.

"Poor guy," said Lilia, shutting off the camera. "And poor kid." She felt a lump in her throat, and felt her shoulders tremble. She knew that later, when she was alone in her car, she would cry.

"I wonder if it's clear enough to get the plate number of that pickup," the Trooper said. "Charge him for stealing the kid's kit, and right on up to homicide."

"He didn't kill the boy," Lilia said. "What killed him was the wind blowing his hat off."

"Is that how you're going to write it up?"

"There's no way this death can be attributed to the guy in the pickup," she said firmly. Her cell phone rang. It was her work line. "Just a minute." She turned and walked a few steps away before answering it. "Lilia Chambers."

She heard her boss's voice. "Lilia, it's Pete. Are you busy?"

"Yeah, very. Quite by chance I came across an accident on 195 South. I was almost first on the scene. A kid's been killed by a semi. He set a camera up and recorded the whole thing."

"Like a suicide?"

"No. It's not like that. Just carelessness, I guess you'd call it.

Teenage inattention. I'm going to be here for awhile. Just a sec." Down the road she could see the paramedics were getting ready to move the body. She held the phone against her chest and shouted, "Don't touch it until I'm finished with it!"

She brought the phone back to her ear. "You're not wearing anything too revealing, are you?" her boss said.

"Pete, that is *not* appropriate."

"It is. When you're done there I want you to head over to State prison. Skyborne Heights. Ever been there?"

"Never."

"Then cover up."

"Pete, it's ninety-six degrees out here. I'm not exactly wearing a burka."

"I'm just warning you."

"I'm dressed as usual. Professionally."

"I figured that. You should be alright, then. If you have a sweater in your car put it on. Guys over there make a big deal of it when a woman appears in their midst. Especially a young one."

"Then why don't you send someone else?"

"You're the duty officer."

"I'm busy here," she protested.

"It's Fourth of July weekend. I don't have the heart to pull someone else in. They've got families, you don't."

"Don't rub it in."

"Sorry kid. Take your time, but get over there when you're done. They've got some kind of strange case going on."

"Really? What makes it strange?"

"They've got a body, they're not even sure if it's dead or not."

She turned her little Ford Fiesta off Highway 2 onto Strawberry Road, and in less than a mile came to a fork. To the right the road led to the Great Butte Casino, run by the local Indian Tribe; on the left it led to Skyborne Heights Corrections Center, home to twenty-two hundred minimum and medium security inmates. This is what America amounts to nowadays, she thought to herself—prisons and casinos, while all the real jobs disappear to China. She started to cry, not for America, but for poor dead teenage Jordan Summerland, whose body she had so recently knelt over. She hadn't cried at the scene, she'd made herself stay stoic and hardboiled, at least on the exterior, even as one of the cops who'd come out from Spokane turned away to vomit in the ditch. Jordan's face had been scraped by the pavement into a bloody mess, as if some God-like creature had passed his skull across a giant cheese grater. She'd seen worse, truth be told, but this time it was more personal. This time there was a video, and once she'd watched it she felt like she knew the kid—a big, dumb, happy-go-lucky guy starting out on life's grand adventure. Then bam, it was done. "I need to go home and think about where *my* life is going," Lilia said out loud, even though she was alone in the car.

At thirty-one she was the youngest of the five death investigators in the Spokane Coroner's office, and the only woman. Ranking lowest in the office pecking order, she was never surprised when the dirtiest, ugliest jobs were handed to her. She accepted that the joe-jobs go to any rookie, in any field, all part of an unofficial probation. She took these assignments without complaint, because whining about it would just confirm the prejudices of the Old Boys Club, as she called the four jaded men who were her colleagues. They were all ex-cops—when she was first hired, the Old Boys didn't believe a young woman with a nursing degree could possess the mental armor to go poking at the mangled corpses of the freshly dead, or inhale the rancid flesh of bodies that had decomposed a good long while. They enjoyed testing her mettle. So far they'd had to admit she was holding up pretty well.

She envied the Old Boys. They had learned not to take it on. But by the same token, by her measure they were all alcoholics, so maybe they did take it on, and blighted it, obliterated it, with substance abuse. She'd been working as a coroner for fourteen months now, and so far the work had not hardened her. Each death was still a tragedy deeply felt.

She pulled into the prison's vast parking lot, found a spot for visitors, and after she'd shut off the engine she looked under the passenger seat for a box of tissues. She wondered if she should put on some make-up so people wouldn't guess she'd been bawling her eyes out in the car on the way over. Her phone rang and she saw it was her mother.

"Hey Mom, what's up?"

"Just thinking of you sweetie. It's so beautiful out! Hope you're getting a chance to enjoy it."

"Not exactly."

"What's wrong? You didn't phone me yesterday, and I knew something was wrong."

"Yesterday was a whole other story."

"Tell me."

"Just a sec."

She found the Kleenex box and wiped her eyes and nose, and told her mother, "I'm the only one on call this weekend, and it's been crazy. Yesterday there it was a man named Norbert Hoogstra, who I think you might even know, he used to run a plant nursery on Ben Burr Road."

"Doesn't ring a bell."

"He's retired now. He was out behind his house—he has a few acres that back onto the creek by the golf course on Hangman Creek Road, a lovely spot with roses all over the place—and he was burning some grasses out of a ditch, and he had a heart attack. He fell over and died, right there on the ground, clutching at his chest— and he lay there in the way of the flames, and they passed over him and kind of licked at his body, and melted his windbreaker, and burnt the hair off his head—"

"Sounds horrible! You poor thing."

"It really was not pretty," Lilia said. She didn't tell her mother what had surprised her most—that human skin burned that way smells like barbecued pork. "The worst of it was, his wife was in the house making lunch, and came out to get him, and found the body. Poor thing—*she's* the poor thing. There was no one to call and come comfort her except a daughter in Seattle, so I ended up staying with her for hours, not wanting her to be alone."

"That's very sweet of you."

"But when I got back to the office Pete was on my case, telling me, That's not really your job, is it?"

"Then Pete's a jerk."

"Maybe you have to be a jerk to do this job properly."

"A woman is always going to do a job differently than a man. Don't let him dictate how it's done," her mother said.

"But if I do it my way, I get pulled in too many directions at once, and I get stressed, and tired, and I take on everyone else's pain—"

"That's called being a woman," said her mother. "You're stuck with that. We volunteer ourselves into a deep pit of never-having-guilt-free-down-time, and we feel responsible for the entire universe, then wonder why we feel overwhelmed."

"And feel guilty, that's the worst part," Lilia murmured. "Today I—well I won't even go into details, but a teenage boy died, horribly, horribly—I'm sure you'll see it on the news—and I'd just finished up at the scene, just as they were putting the body in the ambulance, when I saw his mother arriving—I knew it had to be his mother, I'd seen her on this video he made, and I almost got out of my car to go talk to her, and take care of her, but I didn't, because I've already got another call, that I'm on now, with *zero* down time between them. I just left the Troopers that were there to deal with her—one of them was a woman, and I just knew the job would fall to her, and she'd have to absorb all that pain, suck it up like a sponge and be fucked up for days, and I'm fucked up with guilt for making *her* do it, not me!"

"Oh darling. You really need to go home and have a bath."

"I'm in the parking lot at Skyborne Heights and I have to go in a prison right now," Lilia said.

"What?"

"Yeah. That's my next call. There's an inmate dead, or maybe not dead, they're not even sure, apparently."

"How can that be?"

"That's all I know."

"Well when you're done at the prison, go home and have a bath. With Epsom salts and lavender."

"Right mom. That'll fix me right up."

"I'm trying to help."

"I know."

"What are you wearing?"

"Jesus Christ. Pete asked me the same thing."

"Well make sure you cover your arms and have a high collar."

"I told him it's 96 degrees today, what do you think I'm wearing?"

CHAPTER 3

"The inmates call it Easy C, it's by far the most civilized wing in the institution," the deputy warden informed her. "But you should still be prepared for some pretty intimidating posturing by the inmates. Taunting, rude remarks, that sort of thing. And definitely avoid eye contact."

Lilia nodded. He led her through yet another heavily reinforced door, with only the tiniest of windows, bullet and bomb proof, she presumed. She was only half listening to what he was saying. She'd never thought of herself as claustrophobic, but this was the third door they'd passed through, and as each one slid shut and locked behind her she felt increasingly imprisoned herself. How did they stand it, these people? Not just the prisoners, but the guards?

"We haven't moved the body, on the advice of the medical officer here, who has pronounced the inmate in question dead. But there's definitely something strange about it—an irregularity that needs to be investigated," the warden continued. "I've never seen anything like it. Not that I can match your experience in these matters."

"And where is the prison doctor now?" she asked.

"The medical officer, you mean?"

"Is he not a doctor?"

"Well, not exactly. He has a degree in nursing. There's a doctor he can call on in emergencies, but that's frowned upon here. It costs our shareholders money, if you want to know. This prison is owned by a corporation, which means it's run like a business, and like any other business an unforeseen expense cuts into profit. In this case the man appears to be dead, so a doctor is not needed. But because of the suspicious nature of the death we called in the coroner."

"Or maybe coroners don't charge for their services, and doctors do?"

The deputy warden smiled tightly. "No comment on that."

"Where is the medical officer, then?"

"Oh he's gone home. He's pretty much a nine-to-fiver."

A final door opened and then slammed shut, and she was on the floor of the cell block, a long, brightly-lit hall of cages. She regretted immediately that she'd come straight from the blazing heat of Highway 195. It would have added no more than twenty minutes to swing by her condo and change into pants, instead of this sleeveless blue and yellow sundress cut just above the knee. She could have switched her open-toed sandals for trainers. The two inch heels on the sandals clattered like tap shoes across the polished concrete floor of the cell block and caused the hall to fall into a silence that frightened her, like a hush before a storm breaks.

She followed the assistant warden down the corridor, and suddenly men came forward to the bars, exactly like caged animals in a zoo, she thought later. Imprisoned primates. That's really what they were, after all. The only difference was they could speak, and they said things, lewd and shocking things, and the warden made no effort to quiet them. She kept her eyes lowered as she had been warned to do, but peripheral glances told her men were clutching their crotches. Some were thrusting against the bars. One prisoner shouted, "Look at me, damn it!" and she involuntarily made the mistake of meeting his eyes, and was unprepared for the hostility there, an urge for sex translated into hatred. After that she kept her eyes lowered, walking a gauntlet of taunts and catcalls.

One cell door was open, and the bars had been covered with a makeshift cloth screen, so that she couldn't see what lay inside. "Turn here," the warden directed, and she did, relieved to enter a tiny refuge of privacy. Inside the cell they were visible only from one other cell, directly across the hall, and the prisoner there was sitting back on his bed, looking on with passive curiosity, free of threatening body language or filthy talk. She felt grateful for that, but still she closed the cloth flap across the door to eliminate his gaze, hoping to create for herself a sense of safety, but feeling only the smallest comfort, as if it were night in the jungle and she was huddling behind the thin canvas of a safari tent, while wild beasts shrieked and baboons circled the campfire. She shivered involuntarily. The deputy warden, standing uncomfortably close to her in the tiny cell, whispered, "You should understand, you represent the most important thing they've lost. Therefore you represent *everything* they've lost. And I have to say, inside these walls or out, anyplace at all, I bet you turn heads." She glanced at him and thought, My God, he's leering just like the rest of them. He's getting a sick kick out of this.

She turned her attention to the body, which lay face up on the narrow bed. A fairly fit-looking male in his sixties, she would guess. There was something odd about him.

"How long has he been dead?" she asked.

"That's the million-dollar question," said the deputy. "We found him in this condition six—" he checked his watch—"no, seven and something hours back. No pulse, no heartbeat, no signs of breathing whatsoever. The medical officer tried to revive him with basic CPR. Mouth to mouth and plenty of pressure on the chest. And yet—"

"He was lying flat on his back like this?"

"No. He was sitting up cross-legged, in a kind of meditation pose. That's common for him. George here is quite the eccentric. Thick Polish accent—a scientist of sorts. He passes most of his days in deep meditation. From what I understand he even sleeps sitting up, in, um, I guess you'd call it a yoga-type position."

"Lotus position," she said.

"Uh huh. Some of the inmates call him Swami George."

"The skin is warm," she said, lifting an arm by the wrist to check for a pulse. "If he's been without breath or a pulse for almost eight hours, he should be well into rigor mortis by now."

"That's exactly what the medical officer said," the deputy confirmed. "If the man is dead, then the process of decay kicks in immediately. The temperature of the body should be dropping by, well I forget the precise amount he said—"

"One point five degrees Fahrenheit an hour," she informed him.

"Under normal conditions, at room temperature, that's what we'd expect to see."

"Right. But this guy seems to be in some kind of limbo. Dead but not rotting. Or possibly not dead. Hibernating maybe."

"I presume you have a morgue here, where I can examine him more thoroughly," she said.

"You may find it's not up to your usual standards."

"Whatever. We'll make do. Please take me there, and have the body brought down."

He nodded, and held the sheet open for her to reenter the cell block. Across the hall the prisoner came to the door of his cell. Forgetting herself, she met his gaze, and saw nothing like hostility, or sexual aggression there; instead she thought he looked troubled, or even frightened. Then the other prisoners came back to life, and the cell block rocked with catcalls and obscenities. Lilia tensed and dropped her gaze to the gray concrete floor, her sandals click-clacking through a taunting gauntlet of menace and male rage until she reached the end of the corridor and the sanctuary that lay beyond its steel door.

The morgue was poorly kept, and of late it had become an unofficial storage room for cleaning supplies. She had a guard move several boxes from the stainless steel work table, and asked for a cloth to clean the surface. The body was carried down by two guards on a green canvas army surplus stretcher that looked old enough to have done service in the Korean War. They laid him on the table and helped her remove his clothes. She hesitated, standing over the body, running a hand over the chest and stomach, surprised again at how it remained warm to the touch.

"Now what?" asked the deputy warden.

"Normally in this situation I'd have it in my head to perform an autopsy, but if we're not ready to declare him dead, then the best thing would be to try to revive him," she said. "We'll get the defillibrators to give his heart a jolt, see if that doesn't kick start his heartbeat. You have defillibrators on hand?"

"Defilli—what?"

"I guess that answers my question. Call an ambulance. They'll be sure to have a pair."

"Now wait a minute. An ambulance doesn't come cheap. Who's going to be billed for that?"

"Are you refusing to order me an ambulance?"

"No, but—"

"Then go do it."

He nodded and left, returning a short while later. She asked him, "Who first noticed that he wasn't breathing? Who notified you that he might be dead?"

"Another prisoner. The one directly across the hall. His name is Travis Pendridge. They're friends. They spend a lot of time together."

"And how did he know his friend was dead, and not just meditating, which was normal behavior? How would he have known the difference, without examining him closely?"

"I don't know that. I expect they talk each morning. The old man takes breakfast along with everyone else, and this time he didn't respond to the call for meal time. I'm assuming that's the way it happened. I don't know if you've ever dealt with prisoners, but I can tell you right now, no one saw anything, no one heard anything, no one remembers anything. It's the convict's code. Try to get to the bottom of anything that goes on among them, and you'll find they've all been struck deaf and dumb."

"Do you have an interview room? I should at least try to have a talk with this Mr. Pendridge."

CHAPTER 4

Good behavior got me this diary and this pen, but it's arbitrary. Anytime the guards sweep they can take it.

My cell is five foot by nine. Best part is it's all mine.

Before I got here I spent more than seven years (2678 days, but who's counting) down in Walla Walla—The Walls—on Block F. Maximum security. Seven years in a four-man cell.

It damaged me.

I promised myself I wouldn't let it damage me, but that's like promising your sweat won't stink. There were days down there when a muttered phrase drew blood. You shut up, but you can't stay out of the way. In a space that small there's no neutrality. You earn your space, work for it behind a grim mask and ready fists. Don't fuck with me, I'm crazier than you. And what if it comes true?

In the Walls I never slept well in the night. I'd wake up wound tight, feel my body rigid, frozen in ice. And in the day, never anything new to say—some days a fart passed as a major public pronouncement, an improvement over the shit that came out of mouths.

That's over. It's better here. I'm healing. I want to heal. A cell to call my own feels like a—well I can't say a luxury, there's nothing luxurious here. It's a reprieve, is all. A place to breathe. I am grateful for this tiny mercy. Count your blessings? I have only this one, but I am grateful.

I should write my memories. Make my case.

Let me say this. I regret what happened, and will regret it till the day I die.

This is odd. I'm speaking formally. Writing is not my normal voice. I don't know if anyone else will ever read this, but if it happens and it's you, I'm aware as I put the words down that I want your approval. The blessings of a stranger.

I find I have much to say, but don't know how to begin. I'm not a natural talker and anyway, there are few men in here you could describe as good listeners, so I'm out of practice. We're all reduced. Thoughts and feelings are trapped inside me like doves under chicken wire. I need to write them out. Let them flutter like loose pages. Let their wings carry them free.

I want to tell you about my wife. I loved her. I still love her. We met in the summer, when I was nineteen.

She worked in the pro shop of Terrapin Springs. That's a golf course. Just up the road from where I grew up, there was a little nine-hole public course that was my second home. By the time I was ten I probably made a thousand dollars prowling alone in the leafy woods that hugged the sixth fairway, a dogleg par-five, hunting up lost balls to sell in the parking lot. That's a perfect life for a ten year old: learning a few acres of oak, cedar and alder forest like the back of my hand, knowing where the snakes hide, memorizing every escape hole where a chipmunk could scoot to his bunker.

Then when I was older I started to play golf, and I lost my fair share back to that same patch of woods, that same damn hole, the par-five sixth. I never minded much, in fact I loved disappearing from the sun-baked fairway into the cool shade of the woods. Like passing through a door, or a portal. I miss driving a golf ball, that simple ordinary pleasure denied me now like so many others, all except this small pleasure of pressing a ball-point pen on paper, feeling the ink lubricate itself and leave a slippery, glistening trail. That's microscopic, the scale of it. In jail there are no grand vistas to explore, only tiny amusements. I get excited when a spider forms a web—there's one now down the leg of my bed, and I do my best to leave it undisturbed. It's nice to watch him carrying on with his normal life without any comprehension of what a prison is. He could crawl out of here anytime he likes, but he stays, because to him this place is as good as any other. Maybe I should sympathize with the flies he traps and turns into prisoners like me, but I still root for the spider, the fisherman casting his net.

Just now I've been sitting cross-legged on this tired old mattress, holding my hands before my own eyes, remembering how I used to grasp a golf club. Left thumb tucked under right fingers. Anticipation of impact. I had a wicked slice. Golfing with Dad and

Uncle Ronald. One day there was a new girl working in the pro shop. Though I'd only seen her a minute, I was haunted all day by the memory of a silver dolphin on a chain around her neck. It hung poised to plunge below the surface of a camisole of cotton, white as sea foam, just visible because she left the top two buttons of her shirt undone. She saw me peeking. A smile on her lips. Something more to our exchange than the $4.19 she handed me back in change when I bought some balls and tees.

Her name was Alison. I fell in love with her before I even knew what love was. What did I know? I was nineteen. Hot-looking girl smiles for me over a glass countertop, that's going to make me linger over my choice of balls. You could even get them monogrammed. Mine would be TIP. Travis Ian Pendridge. They called me Tip when I was a kid.

"Which ball do you suggest for a wicked slice?"

"I don't," she said. "Just swing softer. Don't overdo it. Firm grip but casual swing. Or is it casual grip and firm swing?"

"Hm," I said, flustered by her beauty. She answered, "Hmm," with just a little bit of mockery in it, but it was also almost like "Mmmmm," like the sound of someone eating chocolate fudge ice-cream. She leaned forward, elbows on the glass. Sexy. I wanted some of that. But how to get it? A man who knows what to do and say just goes and gets it, right? But a man at nineteen isn't a man, he's a mass of insecurity and ego, strutting like a peacock, but not sure if his plumage is beautiful or ridiculous. That's the way I was, anyway. Easily thrown.

This is what I believe happens: You play a role to woo a woman, and by increments you become that person, the person you want her to think you are. And it's for the better, usually. Women aim for a higher moral standard. Alison did anyway, and she's the only one I have to go by. She made me a better man. She made me want to win her love.

The first time we made love was in the afternoon upstairs in my parent's house. I remember me fumbling with my guitar on the edge of the bed, strumming clumsily through a too-obvious song of seduction. *Norwegian Wood*. It wasn't necessary, but it was right. She lay back and closed her eyes as she listened, then slowly sat up and went to the window, where she took the cord in her hand and let the blinds drop in one smooth, shimmering cascade. The room turned yellow gold. The blinds let the sun come through the way closed eyelids do. They *glowed*. She went back and lay across the bed again, without saying anything, or even looking at me, and closed her eyes. Venetian blinds have this little vertical line of holes that runs down each side where the cord threads itself through. Tiny pinprick beams of sunlight snuck through those holes, and left a trail of sun drops across her body. I took her hand and placed it along that shimmering path, to make a bracelet of sunlight droplets around her wrist.

Writing it down now, I don't just remember it, I feel like I'm there.

She untucked her shirt. That necklace of sunbeams fell across her belly, like a line of floats dissecting the surface of a swimming pool. Sun pricks on the cleft between her small breasts. We made love for the first time, which wasn't perfect, of course it wasn't perfect. My rudimentary technique lacked a way to express deep love. Plus I was a horny kid. I love you, hurry up and spread and take this aching thing. I didn't say that, but I could have. Let me drain myself into you.

And then years later, after her cancer came, after the cops came and what happened happened, and they took me away, leaving her to die with a five-year-old daughter by her side and no dad in sight, I knew exactly what she meant by sunlight droplets. Tell Travis sunlight droplets. Her last words to me.

We knew, just naturally, how to share a couch on a cloudy Sunday. She was a reader—she'd sit with her feet curled back, heels against her bum, totally focused on a book spread open on the armrest of the couch. I'd lie on my side, head on her lap, oblivious in my supple youth that the couch was too short to let me stretch out in comfort. I could lie for hours half hanging off it, watching football on the tube, completely absorbed with what to call on third and ten from the fourteen. Alison called it a male soap opera, padded gladiators on steroids fighting over a hollow ball. Whatever. I still loved it.

I remember her looking up from some brick-sized paperback and saying, "Women look at life as if it's a novel, and men look at life as if it's a movie. Do you think that's true?"

"I need more information."

"You know what I mean. Women are more interested in the internal, what people are thinking, and how they feel. For men it's all action, goals and objectives, getting from here to there."

"Bring your sweet little ass from there to here."

"That's definitely movie dialogue. A trashy movie, too."

It hurts to think about these things. Heart, cock, mind, they all ache. Even my hands ache when I think about how they once brushed the hair from her face.

She was stronger than me.

I remember it was early autumn, we were hiking in the hills that rise up from the coast north of town. The narrow trail snaking up into dark, intimate woods, cedars and hemlock closing out the brightness of day. Her skin tanned and pink and wet from her own sweat. Her smooth thighs disappearing into denim shorts. She couldn't have been more beautiful. Fuck we were young and fresh. The smile on her face when she turned to me, waited for me to catch up, climb up. A viewpoint. The trees parted enough to see the ocean to the west. We kissed and nuzzled, wanting to fuck. Looking for a private place, we bushwhacked down through the underbrush, skirting some prickly thickets of impenetrable wild blackberry until we came across exactly what we were looking for, a sheltered mossy gully we somehow knew would be there.

Unbuttoning each other. Sweet Alison wouldn't take off her tee shirt, just pushed it up over her breasts, and kept her socks and shoes on too, feeling somehow less vulnerable like that. I stripped naked (did I really? From this cage where I sit now it sounds impossibly free), making a show of it, nineteen years old and proud of the body I'd grown without even trying, proud of my taut flesh, and fearless in it, wanting to show her there is nothing to fear, that she can relax. I lay down so she could be on top, and the moss was cold, it tingled my back, my ass. She lowered herself to straddle me, the sweat of her thighs turning cold, she was like marble, not the fire I was expecting.

What was that?

Nothing. Nothing.

There are people up there on the path!

They can't see us. Alison, look at me. Feel me, let me rock you like that.

Shhh. They'll hear us.

Let them go past.

We held our breath like co-conspirators, our smiles like silent giggles. Passing voices faded, leaving us again to our private world, our mossy love nest, but now we were chilled, cold in the deep shade. "Let's move over to that sunny spot, where there's no moss, just smooth rock baking itself in the sun."

But to get there we needed to cross the damp folds of another mossy gully. Alison picked up her shorts and panties, and pulled her tee shirt down so it was like a short short mini-dress, but I left every stitch of my clothes behind, and I pranced on ahead, leading the way, purely naked and dancing around like a wood sprite for her delight and amusement, facing her and backpedaling, letting my backside lead the way, stumbling then righting myself, then turning forward and stopping cold in my tracks.

"What is that?" Alison stopped at my shoulder.

"I don't know. I think it's a deer."

"It looks like a *fawn*."

It was a blood-splattered carcass, its legs splayed, jutting bone, cartilage and fur. A pile of intestine spilled out, fly-covered. It was fresh. Suddenly I was freezing cold.

"Oh my God. We were making love next to that," Alison said in a soft, scared voice. "Travis, let's get out of here."

And we both looked into the trees and the brush, wondering if a cougar was looking back. Alison put on her panties and shorts.

"Get your clothes, Travis. It's making me feel very weird to see you naked near that. Poor little baby deer! It has to be a cougar, right? Let's go get your clothes."

I started shaking and couldn't stop. It was Alison who was stronger, who led me away. She told me later, "You were in a trance. I had to dress you. Really, like a child. Lift one leg, then the other, and even tie the laces of your shoes."

So I guess I was a soft kid then. Prison remade me. Parts of me have shut down. Nothing can reach me, nothing can make me shake. There's no one to hold me if I did, so I won't.

Within two years of meeting we were married. The decision was made for us by the unplanned arrival of the baby. I would have been happy with an abortion—we were kids, fatherhood scared the shit out of me—but Alison wanted it. To her it was alive. She knew how I felt but I never pushed it either. It felt like her choice more than mine. I figured I'd suck it up and grow up. You do what you must when life sneaks up.

I haven't seen my daughter in ten years. She's sixteen now.

I've never allowed her to come see me in jail. I refuse to inflict that on her—it would only give her nightmares. So no visits. None. Ignorance may not be bliss, but it can prevent the opposite of bliss. Pain and suffering. Do I want to give her that?

I do get letters from her. My parents make her write them, I'm pretty sure. They're never long letters, but I sympathize with that. When I was a kid I hated writing twice-a-year thanks to my aunts and uncles, for Christmas and birthday presents. My parents were old school that way. Nellie's obviously my kid—does the minimum, let's say—short letters that only hinted at her true mind or character. "Dear Daddy, I am fine. School this year was good. I passed everything." Brief and grudging.

As she grew up her handwriting for a while reminded me of her mother's. Those lazy loops with the *l*'s and the *t*'s, big enough to make smiley-faces in. Then they changed again as she left childhood behind. The loopy loops tightened like elm leaves curling up into hollow flutes.

This summer for the first time I wrote her a letter back. She's sixteen now, after all, maybe old enough for me to start having a dialogue with her. She can handle things, I hope. She can handle a dad in prison, I hope.

I didn't know what to write, and ended up writing questions, really, not answers. I wanted to know what she knew. I wanted to know what memories she had of me. And of her mother.

And she wrote me back.

"Dear Dad,

I remember we used to have a dog named Mustard, and we would walk him to the fields beyond our house. They were wheat or hay fields. And you would lift me up by the fence so I could see where Mustard was hiding when he went in the fields. He wasn't really hiding, just I couldn't see him, because I was short. Now I'm pretty much full grown I think, I've been five feet

seven since I was fourteen so that means I've leveled out. I used

to be taller than all the boys, who were shrimps but now some

of them are getting big. I'm much taller than Grandma, which

I like to tease her about. I call her shrimp sometimes. And for

other remembrances, I remember mommy used to sing to me at

bedtime and I think I can remember the tune but not the words.

But if I heard them again I'm sure I would. And mommy's face

close to mine but not what she looks like, that's from photos

only. I see her face by looking at old pictures you took. I still

have all those old pictures, lots of ones taken even before I was

born and in some of them you and Mommy look very happy,

like you are in love.

If you are wondering if I remember what happened that

night the police came, well I don't. I remember they came and I

cried, but more like a dream where you don't remember why."

When Nellie was three Alison got very sick. It came on fast. We knew there was cancer in her family—an aunt, a grandfather. But those were old people. Not twenty-four. Cancer of the liver. A virulent form. A killer. We could not accept or believe that. Chemotherapy, aching limbs, nausea, no respite.

I started to grow pot for her, as an appetite enhancer, to keep the food down, to ease the spasmodic urge to gag that went with the chemotherapy. She'd always been a sweet goody-two-shoes when it came to smoking pot, and at first she couldn't admit to liking the "high" part of it. But before long she realized that it was futile to fight the high. It gave her a goofy smile and her laugh came out more giggly than normal. That quavery smile made me feel so tender. A side effect that affected me, you could say.

Marijuana was a medicinal herb, that's how I saw it. She would smoke it and her suffering was diminished. She could enjoy a meal. She could keep her other medicines down. For a while the pain would stop.

Love and attention, that's what growing a crop of indoor marijuana plants takes. It's no different than orchids, or roses, or raspberries. It turned me into a gardener. I miss growing plants in prison. Prison should be a rural experience—instead of locking us away in a concrete fortress, why don't you give us a patch of earth and let us nurture life from it? So many men in here are in need of healing. There is no healing in here. There's no sunshine. Nothing grows.

We were renting a little house on the fringes of town, and I divided a spare room at the back. The windowless half I painted white, and wired it up for growing. It was about the size of this cell I now occupy. But that little room, so warm from the two metal halide lamps, served as my sanctuary, my refuge. Alison and I always referred to it as "the garden." At first that was a precaution, so that if Nellie ever mentioned it to anyone it wouldn't raise eyebrows. "Dad spends time every day in the garden." Sounds innocent enough. And I did spend time in there every single day, tenderly coaxing medicine from those female plants, so eager to blossom, so horny for pollen, so hungry for love. I called them my ladies. "How are the ladies today?" I would ask them that, each and every morning.

Have you ever (I hope for your sake not) felt what it's like when someone you love is dying and there is nothing you can do? Ever known what it's like to lose your own willpower from worry? The soul aches. To shield myself from suffering, to remain slippery and elusive, I had to keep myself busy doing *something*. This was something I could do. Make medicine. Grow medicine from a seed, and later from cuttings. Do it with love.

The cops didn't see it that way. I don't how they came to know about it. Couldn't have been word of mouth, I was too careful. Or I thought so. Some people knew, of course. I try not to imagine it was someone I trusted. Maybe police don't need an informer, they have high tech toys. Maybe they fly over in helicopters, take infra-red heat-revealing photos of whole neighborhoods. Under electronic scrutiny, my little indoor garden would have glowed like a super-nova. How it happened doesn't really matter. They found out.

It was an April evening, days getting longer, and the sun warmer, after a bleak winter. Alison lay in the big bedroom upstairs. She was dying. There was no doubt of that by then. Mere days left. Nellie was asleep in her little bedroom across the hall. She must have just turned five years old. It was Alison's birthday the week before, and for Nellie's sake she had tried to come downstairs and bake a cake, but she couldn't. She couldn't even drag her weary bag of bones out of bed. We had to bring store-bought cake to her bedside. Oh my God it was sad. Trying to add a little levity to the gloom, I had asked the bakery to write in letters on the cake, 'cheMOTHERapy,' just like that, because I'd noticed how one of the worst words contained one of the best. It was an idea I had, to celebrate her motherhood and also acknowledge the chemo, the reality of what was going on.

Stupid idea, I knew as soon as Alison saw the cake. She didn't cry, but I started to. She gave me a weak smile of forgiveness, and said, "That was the last thing I wanted to be reminded of."

Like any kid Nellie was focused on cake, but at five she already knew her alphabet pretty well, and looked at the letters suspiciously. She asked her Mom what it said, and Alison said, "Happy Birthday, sweetie. Now just blow out my candles and stop being a snoop." Nellie blew so hard that the candle wax splattered like tiny teardrops on the icing.

Later that evening I must have had a premonition, because I padlocked the garden, and put the key in my pocket. Usually the door lock was enough, the padlock was only for when I wasn't home. Not that it mattered. My world was about to turn upside down.

About eleven at night. I'm in the kitchen alone, when out of the blue there's a huge BAM! and a battering, splintering, explosion of the front door. The winter wind comes howling through the house like the devil's tongue.

I instinctively run to the base of the stairs that leads up to the bedrooms, and I take up a defensive karate-style stance. I know nothing about martial arts, but I'm ready to lay down my life to protect my wife and child.

Seven police officers ride that cold wind through the door, guns drawn, SWAT gear, black helmets, paramilitary swagger mixed with their own fear. I see it in their eyes.

"Get the fuck out of my house," I scream. But they don't break their charge. Two of them tackle me in a blur of fists and profanity, knocking me across the head so I see an explosion of stars, and then blackness for a second. I'm on the floor, face down, handcuffed behind the back, and they're searching my pockets.

A cop takes the key from me and unlocks the padlock to my secret garden, and that ungodly pure and bright metal halide light spills out across the living room carpet like a glacier in sunlight.

"Well now, what have we here? Someone's been a busy boy! Growing some real beauties, looks like!"

I say, "It's not like that," and a police boot comes down half-weight on my back, like a warning. I'm face down on the carpet, bathed in that halide glow.

"Who else is home?"

"My wife. She's upstairs. She's very sick. And my daughter's sleeping."

Two cops start up the stairs, guns drawn, held like prayer books, up and out from their chins. One of them is big, even for a cop, and there is something mean in him, you can feel that. He's the alpha cop, the one in charge. The staircase is bare wood, narrow, and steeper than most. I can hear every step of their boots.

"Daddy!"

"I'm down here sweetie. Everything's alright. It's just some policemen, come by to inspect the house, that's all."

The boot holding me down lifts from my back and a cop tells me to roll and over and sit up. "Nothing's going to happen to her," he says, but he doesn't sound certain.

I can hear one of the cops upstairs cooing, "What's your name, little girl?"

Nellie shouts, "No! Go away! I don't like you!"

"Don't you touch her. Don't you touch her!" I'm screaming it.

And then Nellie's little feet stutter down the stairway in a tangled drum beat, and she lands with a unsteady thump at the bottom. She barely takes in the half dozen cops before she locks her pale blue beautiful eyes onto mine. Me on my knees, struggling to free my hands from the cuffs, wishing I could reach out and catch her as she flies to me, her little arms wrapping around my neck and holding me oh so tight.

"It's going to be alright. Daddy says it's gonna be all right."

"He tried to touch my face!"

A cop behind me says soothingly, "He didn't mean anything by it. Just trying to be friendly." But that doesn't soothe Nellie, she's holding as much of me as she can in her fragile, shaking arms.

"I've got a girl that age myself," the cop says.

From upstairs I can hear a voice, sharp and interrogatory, coming from the bedroom where my wife lies dying. I hear only a male voice. I don't know if Alison is responding at all. I don't know if she can muster the breath to speak.

"Don't you fucking lay a hand on her," I scream.

Nellie cries out and clings tighter around my neck.

"Sorry, baby. Not you. Not you."

And then the unbelievable, the unthinkable. Those thugs, those monsters, they force my wife down the stairs. Alison, my sweet Alison, her gaunt face too weak even to show emotion.

"That's right, Ma'am," the big cop is jeering. "Never too sick for a trip downtown. Just put one foot in front of the other, and gravity does the rest."

A couple of cops bring her down, half-thrusting, half supporting her, keeping her upright, until the bottom step, when she stumbles. One cop lets go and she twists and slumps like a rag doll. The big cop curses and lets her drop. Poor baby. My poor broken baby.

"Mommy!"

"Get up, lady. Get up now."

"You leave her alone!" Nellie wails.

"She really doesn't look too good."

"Get up. Now!"

That big cop is bending over her limp body, pulling at an underarm like a scavenger picking at a corpse. He rolls her over and poor Alison looks into my eyes, dreamy, detached, and shockingly vacant, as if this final earthly humiliation can't reach her, she's already glimpsed what lies beyond. But then Nellie cries out to her mother, and in those empty eyes a flicker of fire ignites, sparked by hurt and shame that her daughter should see her like this. The cop tries to lift her by the arms and her head rolls back, and Nellie, five-year-old Princess of Rage and Fury, rushes at him from behind, catching him with his back bent, off balance, his big frame stumbling forward, arcing across my wife's prone body, his arm wildly grabbing at and catching hold of a lamp stand, a stick-like prop too trivial to support his great weight; it gets transported with him in free fall, and he's propelled down until his un-helmeted head strikes sharply against the corner of a table by the couch.

Nellie keeps raging and screaming, and he rises up like a bloodied animal, pulls his gun from the holster, thinks better of that, wheels and with his other hand grabs her skull like a cantaloupe and pushes her down to the ground.

"Bitch! Bitch bitch bitch—"

I'm on my feet, handcuffs or no, charging at him, a Kamikaze in house-slippers, wishing my feet were laced up in a pair of those black police boots, at least I could kick him, I'd stomp that fucker good. I still manage to land a good gut-busting kick to his ribs, and he brings that gun up to shoot me, or scare me, but I'm beyond fear, and charge at him a second time, and the strangest thing is, my handcuffs come free, without me even thinking about it or trying to understand it, the damn cuffs come loose and my arms come forward like they're jet-propelled.

My hands are free. I take that fucking gun barrel and twist it back at him, right up under that fat chin, and for one fleeting second there is fear in his eyes, and then an explosion and a spray of blood, and he staggers back and drops.

And Nellie screams again, and the rest of the men in uniforms descend upon me with fists and truncheons and gun butts, beating me raw until I can't remember anything anymore.

I killed a cop. And now I'm serving life. They'll never let me out of here.

If it weren't for a pair of faulty handcuffs, or police incompetence in putting them on me, that cop would be alive today.

In retrospect, I'm amazed the others didn't shoot me dead right then and there. Sometimes I wish they had.

CHAPTER 5

Now I've told you my story.

I hoped it would help me, to get it out.

Did it? I don't know. Maybe.

Maybe writing is good for me. It feels that way. Like I should keep at it. I should tell some other stories.

There are plenty of them, up here on Easy C. That's what we call my cell block, which is officially known as Wing 3 Block C. Fifty-three of us live here, mostly low risk, non-violent guys. Some I'd even describe as nice guys. Would you like to meet them?

Let's start with One Nut, directly across the hall. He got his name from an unfortunate anatomical accident a few years back— he broke into a house and lost one of his testicles to a Doberman. As One Nut likes to say, "Call it a Doberman, but don't use the word *pinscher*, that still makes me wince."

Next door to me is 'Throw,' short for Death Row Jethro, so-called because he spent six years on death row for the murder of a parish priest in a small Midwest town. He was cleared when the real killer, a former altar boy who'd been abused by the Father, left a confession in a suicide note. Straight out of prison and suddenly a free man, with a multi-million-dollar wrongful conviction suit in the works that stood to make him rich, Death Row Jethro, whose real name isn't Jethro, it's Sid or something, went on a drinking spree and got rowdy enough to get kicked out of the cave-like darkness of a suburban strip club for inappropriate groping of a dancer. He emerged into the parking lot's skull-numbing sunlight, the kind we never see in here, the kind that glints off car hoods and chrome, squinted his way to his vehicle, took out a knife from where it lay in readiness under the driver's seat, sheltered it from the sun under his untucked shirt, and headed back into the bar, where with one quick thrust he laid out the bouncer who'd so recently tossed him. Nice move, Throw. To this day he claims he can't remember any of it, the alcohol and UV rays messed up his head.

Then there's Doc, a few doors down the hall. We call him Doctor Stud, for good reason, although by appearance he's not in the least studly looking. He's tall, gaunt, blue-eyed, like a Nordic undertaker. Prison diet has made him positively skeletal. His case made the news a few years back, you might remember. He's a real doctor, he ran a successful clinic specializing in artificial insemination. Couples where the husband had a problematic sperm count came to his clinic, and Doc would find them sperm from an ideal donor, someone matching the husband's genetics, ethnic heritage, physiology, and even personality, as close as possible. He had hundreds of clients. He had a sterling reputation, at least until the parents of one of his perfect matches noticed their little boy was pretty much the spitting image of the good Norwegian doctor.

These parents were friends with another couple who had made use of Doc's extensive catalogue of sperm donors, and strangely enough, their kid looked an awful lot like their friends' kid. The two of them could have been siblings, right down to certain mannerisms that seemed to have come from nature, not nurture. Before long Doc was under investigation, and through the wonders of DNA testing it was confirmed that in the seventeen years he'd run his clinic, Doctor Stud had made a regular habit of substituting his own spunk for the promised goods. He had personally fathered more than four hundred children.

I shouldn't laugh. Shouldn't even smile. From the point of view of the families, it's a monstrous violation. Your beloved child turns out to possess and perpetuate the genes of a devious and seriously disturbed individual. On the other hand, in its own twisted way, it's pretty damn comic. Here in the jailhouse Doc's a bit of a hero, a celebrity who deserves a citation in the Guinness Book of Records.

I'm telling you about these guys, but don't think they're my friends. They share my circumstances, and suffer in the same way, but misery doesn't love company. Misery says leave me the fuck alone. I make only one exception to this rule—there is one comrade around here whose company I actually enjoy. That would be Swami George.

George Szymanski occupies the cell directly across the hall from me. He's an older dude. From Poland. Has a Slavic accent. He tends to mix up his v's and f's and w's in a way that's faintly comical. Watching tennis in the TV room, he'll say, "Nice surf and wally."

That's serve and volley to the rest of us. He's a large man, with a thick shock of white hair rising off his forehead like smoke from a forest fire. He looks like a cross between Santa Claus and a Hindu Guru. He really does act like a Swami—he spends most of his days on his mattress, cross-legged, saintly and silent, deep in some kind of trance.

Maybe because he is usually in that private, meditative pose on his own bed, in his own cell, he seems to move about in a state of grace here. George alone gives no outward sign of having inner demons to quell.

An example. Today a bunch of us were in the cafeteria, choking down another lunch of grisly ground round and macaroni. It was me, George, One Nut was there, and Throw. Colquitz, who happens to occupy the cell next to me, he was there too. George was saying something innocuous about how the Poles cook beef slow in crockery pots. Out of the blue Colquitz fixed George with these hard, remorseless eyes of his, and interrupted this harmless conversation to spit, "How is it that you always look so happy anyway, George? In case you haven't fucking noticed, you are trapped inside a prison."

"If you say so," George answered. He never seems fazed by Colquitz and his outbursts.

"Not if I say so! It is what it is, George. You and me and the rest of us are locked away to rot in a stinking prison. You're too old to outlive your sentence, Georgie-Boy, you'll die in here of old age if I don't get sick of your self-satisfied grin and kill you first. You act like you're above it all. This is a fucking penitentiary, and you treat it like it's gracious retirement living."

"The body is a prison too, Colquitz," George said evenly.

"What the fuck is that supposed to mean?"

"Think about it."

"No. I want you to tell me."

"If you escape the body, you escape the prison."

Colquitz allowed himself a full two seconds of consideration. "One of these days I'll help you leave your body, George. I'll finish you, motherfucker. Don't you smile at me like that!"

"I'm not smiling at you, my lad," George said softly, lifting his eyes to gaze at some high point between the florescent lights in the ceiling. "I'm not even looking at you. If I'm smiling it's at the whole universe, of which you and I are insignificant yet equal parts."

"Fuck you."

Swami George just shrugged one shoulder slightly, as if to shake off an invisible little bird.

Colquitz raised himself up from the table while the rest of us kept our eyes lowered. He's not a large man, but he's made of muscles, hair-trigger taut. Clench your fist hard as you can, now imagine your whole body sprung that tight. That's Colquitz, day and night. The rest of us turned away, waiting it out. He has eyes that can pierce metal, and they fell hard upon us. The man carries his demons around like a cabinet of torture implements. Polishing them, sharpening them.

Even on Easy C there has to be one goddamn psycho in the mix. It's not the time, the emptiness, the claustrophobia that makes prison so hard. That stuff is bearable. It's the sadists like Colquitz, taking up too much precious space.

Then without another word he left us, and we could breathe again, and Jethro said, "You're the guy who sets him off, George.

For some reason the man gets a hornet's nest up his ass every time he comes too close to you and your fucking, your Goddamn—well, what the hell is the word for your state of mind anyway, George?"

"Serenity," I said.

"Goddamn it, that is exactly right, Travis. The man is so *serene* I'm not even so sure he realizes where he is, either. Come to think of it, Colquitz has a legitimate beef about that."

Then he and One Nut and the others drifted back to their cells together, and it was just George and me, face to face across that table. I asked him, innocently enough, and not really expecting much in the way of an answer, "What exactly is it you're doing when you sit in your cell all day like that?" It's funny to think I'd watched him for months, and never really cared to know. Maybe I just thought he was wasting his time in his own way, a different way from the way I wasted mine.

"Is it for certain you wish to know, my boy?"

"Yeah. For certain, George."

"I'm traveling."

"Oh yeah? Where to?"

C H A P T E R **6**

For fourteen hours of the day our cell doors slide open electronically, and Easy C becomes unrestricted terrain. We are free to prowl between cells, or to the larger room at the end of the hall, which holds a tired, dog-eared collection of donated old books and magazines, and high on the wall, a television screen behind Plexiglas we can't control when it comes to channel selection. This is our tiny universe, and it is so under-stimulating that we turn to each other for entertainment, or at least diversion. We watch and are watched. There is no privacy here. Even on the toilet you are seen by all who pass.

This morning George was in his cell across the hall, in his familiar meditation position, cross-legged on the bed, and I went over to have a closer look at him. Not wanting to disturb him, as lightly as I could I sat myself next to him on the bed, and held myself still. I watched his chest, looking for the faint rise and fall of his lungs, and I swear to God, he was not drawing any breath at all. Ever so carefully I lifted his hand from his knee so I could check the pulse at his wrist. Nothing. Nada. Zip. Disconcerting, to say the least. With a rising curiosity I placed my ear to his chest. No breathing. No heartbeat.

A caustic voice from behind me broke the silence.

"Why don't you stick a thermometer up his ass, Pendridge?"

At the cell door loomed Colquitz, his sallow face a mix of puzzlement and arrogance.

"I was checking his heartbeat," I said. "I got worried about him. He doesn't seem to be breathing." I don't know why I blurted that out. I should have told him to fuck off and mind his own.

"You're not the only one around here paying more attention to George these days," he said coldly. "You're a step behind me." He glanced past me. "What's with Georgie?"

George had begun to twitch and shudder, ever so slightly, in fine vibrations that could be faintly heard, like the hum of a tuning fork, barely distinct from the buzz of fluorescent lighting. This strange hum somehow made me think that life itself, or some substance essential to life, was pouring back into the empty vessel of his body. The old man's mouth parted and drew breath, his eyelids began to flutter, and within a half minute his eyes opened to reveal that clear gray-green gaze of his. He didn't seem surprised to see me, but registered a slight displeasure at the sight of Colquitz in the doorway.

"Ah yes," he said, turning his attention again to me, with a hint of playfulness in his eyes. He whispered to me, softly enough to that Colquitz couldn't hear. "The student begins to show interest in what the Master can teach him."

"For awhile there I was more interested in whether you were dead or alive," I said.

"There is no point worrying about me," he said.

"I've got my eye on you two," Colquitz interrupted. "Anything you have worth teaching to him, you can teach me too, George."

"It is not possible," George countered. "The Master chooses the disciple, and some will never be worthy."

"But I've already taken my own initiative and helped myself to the textbook, George," Colquitz replied with relish. "You think that when you're deep in one of your altered states, I haven't come in here like Pendridge did today, and poked around a bit? There are no secrets from me, old man. I've seen your precious notebook. It didn't mean a hell of a lot to me, but I did my best to pay attention. I managed to commit a little bit of it to memory, just in case all your gobble-de-gook turns out to actually have a higher purpose. Does this sound familiar?" He paused to gather his recollection, then recited, in a soft, sing-song chant: "*The mantra can be written, the meaning cannot be guessed, the faith cannot be shaken, in the one who loves you best.*"

"Mongrel!" George shouted. I'd never seen him angry, never seen him lose his legendary Swami George cool, until that moment. His face quivered in rage. He tried to pull himself up from his cross-legged position, but stumbled forward as if his legs were asleep. "Those words are not meant for you!" he cried. "You are a like a filthy dog living on the streets, skulking in the alley, sniffing around a rich man's kitchen. Oh yes, the smell attracts your brutish nose, your belly is hungry, and you may find a few discarded scraps of bone, but you will never be invited to the feast."

"If you say so, George," Colquitz replied. "Sell me short if you like. But from here on in, I'm watching."

George began to work his fingers into a tiny crease along one corner of his bed mat. It was a slit sewn shut. Now he ripped it open, shoved his hand into the cotton filling, and extracted a thin blue notebook, a grade-schooler's exercise book. He curled it tightly in one fist like a relay-racer's baton, and shook it at Colquitz. "So you've discovered this document, my friend? You've been spying in my absence? That will not happen again."

He brought the coiled pages to his chest and then, with a sudden gesture flung them toward Colquitz in the doorway. For a brief instant they fluttered like doves' wings, and then burst into flame.

Colquitz fell back into the hall. "Be gone, vermin!" George shouted at him. An alarm sounded, warning prisoners to return to their cells. The fiery pages consumed themselves, leaving no trace. Colquitz backed away uncertainly.

"I'm watching you, George," he growled, then turned toward his cell. I got to my feet.

"How did you—"

"It's nothing," George said dismissively. "I'm no arsonist. The words themselves are combustible. They're the only thing in this world I can burn with mere thought. But I do have other powers." He grabbed my arm and held me back for a moment. "What is important is that I am in a hurry now to leave this place," he whispered. "The book was something I meant to leave behind for you, so that you could learn the secrets in the same way I learned them from my mentor, Tomas Czeslow."

"Who's that?"

"I'll tell you soon enough. Now I see the written word is too dangerous a possession in this den of thieves. It will be necessary to teach you with spoken words, only. To accelerate the process, tonight I will give you a demonstration."

After lock down, lights lowered, I lay sleepless in my bed. Across the hall I could see George in his yoga posture, back straight and legs crossed. I watched him expectantly for awhile, but gradually my attentiveness gave way to drowsiness, and I drifted into a fretful sleep.

When I was a free man, when I was a husband, when I was a father, my daughter Nellie used to wake me some mornings. She'd be up at first light, tread lightly into our bedroom, and watch us sleep. I remember waking to the feeling I was being watched, opening my eyes to see a cherub's face studying me. She never said a word until my eyes were open. God knows how long she must have stood there sometimes, waiting for me to open my eyes. Then it was "Morning Daddy, time to get up!" I was dreaming about that when I woke with a start—and there was George sitting cross-legged on the floor of my cell, peering at me, his face an arm's length away. He brought a finger to his lips to shush me before I could utter a word of surprise.

"Good evening, Travis," he whispered softly.

"George. This is—how'd you get in here?"

"I am only partially here," he replied, and with his eyes he directed me to look at his cell across the hall. There he was, sitting cross-legged on the bed.

"Do you know what the word bilocation means?" he said. "Perhaps now it is time you begin to understand the phenomenon. It should be quite obvious."

I looked at one George, then across the hall to the other. "Bi-location. Two places at the same time. But how? Are you split in two, or are there two of you?"

"Shhhhh. Softer on the voice. I'm going to take you out of here, to a place where we can talk more freely. Be forewarned: there is a risk of complication. What is important to remember is that you must cling to me at all times. Kneel on your bed and move back as far as you can against the wall."

I did as he said, and he rose up and sat on the bed with his back to me, his feet on the floor. "I want you to wrap your arms tightly around my chest, the way a child would cling to the parent. Piggyback, I think it is said in English—like I am carrying you on my back across a swiftly flowing river." I leaned forward and brought my arms around over his shoulders, holding him loosely. "Now Travis, do not be bashful at this moment, do not be inhibited by macho ideas of how close two men can touch. It is necessary that you place your body firmly against my back now, and hold your head firmly against mine. Cheek to cheek! Think this way: You are merging with me. You are pouring yourself into me. Will you try this?"

"Against my better judgment," I said.

"Judgment does not enter into this equation," said George. "In a few moments all doubt will be dispelled."

So I held him from behind more tightly, but still skeptically. He turned his head back toward me, and whispered a phrase which I was to repeat in my mind. It wasn't English, just a short jumble of syllables. "Is that Polish?" I asked.

"Something older," he whispered curtly. "Now concentrate upon these sounds, hear them in your mind, focus all your thoughts and energies upon them, which will be difficult at first, but should become easier with time. These sounds are very forgiving, they will work with you, not against you, so that even an amateur such as yourself can make use of them. This chant is ancient, it predates language. Now, practice."

I repeated the phrase over and over in my mind. At first it competed against a barrage of unbidden, random sensations: fear of what would happen if a guard were to catch us in the same cell like this, the absurdity of the position we'd assumed, even the scent of George's hair, and the nearly forgotten humanity of holding another person tightly in my arms. But very quickly that repeated phrase grew in strength in my mind, taking charge, overpowering and dismissing any other thoughts.

For a brief moment my mind objected, and I had an image of myself as a drowning man, surrendering helplessly as warm water filled my mouth and throat. I was sinking, and at the same time, I was angry with myself for drowning. *You give up too easily, Travis! Fight it! Fight!* But I couldn't. A flame flickered, then was doused. Warm water, womb water. A torrent. Curl up, hang on, repeat the chant, chant, chant.

Chant. Cling to George. Chant. I began to rise. I clung to him tightly now, the way a rider on the back of a motorcycle clings to the driver on a dangerous road. We were rising together. I could see the cell block, all of it. A glimpse of me kneeling on the bed with my arms wrapped tightly around nothing. The prison guards' lunchroom, seven of clubs led in a game of cards. They don't see me. We circle above them. Spin and gone. Freedom like a bird remembering flight. Chant. A world beyond. A strip mall, a woman hurries before the dry cleaner closes. Chant. A restaurant down the block, a guy at a window table orders the fish burger with slaw, not salad. Chant. George in charge, intangible trust. Chant. The world below. Cling to George. Two houses with a blue fence in need of paint, chant. An attic light bulb pops when a switch is flicked. Chant. A tree in a forest split fresh by lightning, chant, a river swollen with rain, chant, a highway, chant, chant, up a valley road, No Trespassing, chant, open the cabin door, chant, rest now, chant come to rest on the floor. Chant, *You can stop your chant.* Chant. *Stop your chant.* Chant.

"I said stop your chant! Travis!"

I heard George. My eyes were open, yet waiting for focus to come to them. I was not frightened. Where is George? There. Here.

"Oh my God."

"The deity has nothing to do with it, as far as I have been able to discern," said George. "Can you guess where you are?"

I looked around. A small, rustic, one-room cabin, with two draped windows and a single door.

"Looks like the Unibomber's place," I said.

"You've kept your sense of humor, at least. And in a way you are not far wrong. Guess again, please."

"I'm not in prison, I can tell you that much."

"Ah, but you are," said George. "You are both here and there. You are more *here* at the moment, certainly, for you are conscious, and communicative in this location. Back in prison, your body is a mere shell, a husk, kneeling on the bed, arms embracing me, except the body you embraced has left, it's here. To a guard passing by it would look like you were embracing a void. We must hope no one sees you, for you will stay like that until we return. Back in prison my body is in a meditative pose, just as I left it in the first place when I crossed the hall, picked you up from your cell, and brought you here. A miracle, is it not?" He smiled, but then quickly turned serious. "At this point in your apprenticeship you cannot be out of that temporarily empty vessel for long, not without terrible risks. And tomorrow you will be in some pain, I forewarn you. It will feel as if you have awoken from the dead. And in a sense you will have."

"I feel pretty sore already," I said, stretching my legs out on the floor in front of me. "Wobbly headed, too. I'm not seeing you in focus. It's a little off."

"Natural, all quite natural, I assure you. What you left behind in prison I refer to as the *corpus verus,* or *body proper.* You are experiencing at this moment your first stuttering baby steps in what I call the *corpus foris,* or *body abroad.* Probably your breathing is tentative?"

"I don't know."

"What do you mean, you don't know?"

"I don't exactly feel like I'm in this body at all," I said. "I feel like I'm still floating around the room."

"Close your eyes."

I did.

"Now imagine that you are completely centered in your body. Imagine your arms are capable of elongating, of growing outward, like the limbs of a supple tree, reaching for the light. I want you to imagine these long, willowy arms of yours ending in fingers like the tentacles of octopi, covered in suction cups. I want you to imagine these fingers sweeping around and about this room, encompassing every nook and cranny, sweeping up and collecting every single strand of cob-web or dust cloud that might conceivably contain some fragment of your essence. Are you doing so? There may be bits and pieces of you that failed to find their way from the body proper to the body abroad, and they are floating around you like tiny asteroids around the sun. These bits of matter you must pluck from the ether and pull back to their proper place. Are you imagining such a thing?"

"Yes."

"Keep your eyes closed. Are you feeling yourself slightly more whole than before?"

"I hope so."

"I hope so too. Take a few deep breaths."

The air that filled my lungs was unlike any I'd breathed in years. I wish I could tell you it was the pure air of freedom, but it was actually musty—the indoor air of a stale couch and carpet.

"Your lungs sound better. I think you will be fine now. Open your eyes."

I did. My vision was much better. George's smile had something of the show-off in it.

"You will come eventually to feel entirely at home in your body abroad. You may or may not find that the experience is slightly less complete than you are used to in the body proper. For example while emotions are still felt intensely there is a certain reserve, almost like a ghost might feel, removed from the physical realm. If one believes in ghosts, of course."

"Should I believe in ghosts, George?" On the whole right now I'm feeling a lot less skeptical about the paranormal."

"Good for you. Now, go to the window and take a peek outside. You will see a peak outside. You will be piqued by what you see, if you pardon my punning. And leave the curtain open, for I love the view."

I walked to the window, still slightly unsteadily, and pulled back the thick tarp-like curtain.

"Mount Shasta?"

"Correct. We are on the lower slopes of that lovely, famous, near-perfect, still-active, and potentially life-threatening volcano in Northern California. Now, why do you suppose we are here?"

"I'm afraid I can't keep up to you, George," I said. "That chant wants my mind back. It's lurking, like background noise."

"Fight it for now, but don't be angry with it" George said. "It's your friend. Think of it as an eager dog, the kind that forever demands to be walked. You are the master, but it knows it is needed. Later it will provide essential service, and get you home again. What I call the mindsoul—think of it as your essence—wants to return to the body proper, the same way an elastic band or a metal spring wants to return to a state of rest. Whenever you occupy your body abroad you will sense a faint impulse, a longing, like homesickness, to be reunited with the body proper. Over time you will find that it is not so terribly difficult to resist. You will become accustomed."

"For now I'm not. It feels strange."

"Don't dwell on it," George sighed. "Now, as to my earlier question, regarding the importance of Mount Shasta, and why we are here, I'll answer myself. Or rather I'll begin by asking: Do you know about chakras?"

"I've heard of them. In yoga, right?"

"Yes, yoga. That esoteric exercise from India, nowadays being taught in a watered-down form to middle-class North Americans, as an aid to reducing stress and improving blood circulation. You may recall that in Yoga there are seven chakras aligned along the spine?"

"If you say so."

"I do. A chakra is the most intense point of energy in your body. Now, not to be tangential, do you remember Tomas Czeslow? I mentioned him today. I said he was my mentor," George said.

"I remember that now."

"But he was not a *living* mentor, as I will be to you. He was long dead when I discovered his work. He was a Pole, like me, a brilliant alchemist of the late fourteenth century, working not so much like other alchemists with minerals and physical ingredients, but instead concentrating purely on the mind alone. His approach, you could say, was more like an eastern mystic. Tomas Czeslow discovered certain meditation techniques for a specific purpose. He was not in search of God in Heaven, or Nirvana, or enlightenment, or any such nebulous spiritual goals one might associate with deep meditation. Instead, his intention was to concentrate transformative energy in the brain, and use this energy to alter the physical world."

"Mind over matter," I said.

"If you must. Such a weary cliché. The matter I refer to is the human body. I will now share with you a short biography of Tomas Czeslow, a great man who was mocked and derided in his lifetime, whose tremendous accomplishments were revealed only after his death, and even then only to me, and me alone. And soon enough to you. The man left behind a handful of notebooks full of intense mathematics, and ritual incantations, which would appear to others to be nothing but the poems of a madman. The experiments these ravings were purported to describe were never duplicated by anyone. Did you know of this?"

I shook my head no.

"Of course not. No one knows of this. A man of great genius has been ignored by history. Tomas Czeslow claimed great successes in his experiments, but these successes could not be re-created by the handful of well-intentioned imbeciles who came after him, and naturally his claims were dismissed. The only existing record of his techniques, handwritten on paper, languished in a dusty undercroft below a church library in my home city of Krakov, in Poland. Do you know Krakov? You call it Cracow here in the West. It has been a center of great learning for many centuries. For example, do you know the *Jagiellonska*? The Jagiellonian University there is named in honor of Vladislav Jagiello, the Grand Duke of Lithuania, crowned King of Poland in 1386. Krakov was an important center of learning in this period, which represents the very tip of the tail end of the late Middle Ages. The Enlightenment that followed is portrayed by history as a great victory of reason over superstition. But some things are inevitably lost when others are gained. Babies get poured away with bathing water, I believe is the expression?"

"Close enough."

"In the heart of my beloved Krakov there rises a castle. It lies on a hilltop that has served as a defensive position for skirmishing bands of humankind since time immemorial, and has been fortified and re-fortified through the ages. Inside the fortifications is a church, with a lovely courtyard built in the sixteenth century. This courtyard was constructed directly on top of an earlier holy site, a place of great Pagan ritual. Now, why do you think I mention to you the Castle in Krakov?" He didn't wait for me to answer. "Because that place is one of those remarkable earthly chakras!" he exploded. Then he sat back, as if expecting me to be astounded. But it was all too new and fantastical for me.

"Where are the other chakras?"

"I tell you later, my boy," he smiled. "Be patient. Maybe you can guess one? All you need do is look out the window."

"Mount Shasta."

"Precisely. That perfect volcanic cone, always bathed in snowy white—there is nothing more beautiful in the moonlight. So as I say, there are energy centers on the body that also exist on the earth, and when the two combine and are properly ignited, they are like fireworks of the soul. They can cause miracles, my boy! I know these things to be true. I also wish to inform you, that on the face of this earth, which as I am sure you know is in reality a miraculous ball of red hot iron, covered by only the thinnest membrane of cooled rock, these seven geographical chakras are points of immense transformative power beyond the capacity of the human imagination."

He studied my face. "Travis, do you believe me?"

"I'm keeping an open mind," I said.

"Good. That is the most I can ask for at the present moment, I suppose. You may be wondering how I know all this?"

"Tell me."

"I come from Krakov myself, as I informed you. When I was a young man at the university I took up medieval scholarship with great passion, and became fascinated with the lives and achievements of several obscure Polish alchemists. Of course, this was during the Communist era, times of great suspicion when it came to the pursuit of knowledge, and on the other side of the coin, great defensiveness on the part of the Catholic Church. I was able to gain access to rare manuscripts held by the Church, but only by pretending an interest in obscure Polish Saints. I affected an impressive piety, so much so that I was even invited to join the priesthood.

"But I was really after the sinners, not the saints. I was attracted to the mad scientists of the ancient age, the alchemists who the church, more often than not, branded fools or heretics. Nevertheless, in its deepest vaults the church kept records of saints and sinners alike. In a long-forgotten crypt of decaying documents, I found the papers they had confiscated centuries ago from heretical alchemists, filed away and utterly forgotten. In the catacombs under the church I stumbled across Czeslow's notebooks, fragile pages written in his own hand. The man passed much of his strange, solitary life meditating atop that hill in Krakov, at the apex of that powerful chakra. Some of his trances lasted a month, without food or water. On a more humble scale, I set myself to replicating his methods, to see if I could achieve what he did."

Again he paused and studied my face. "I like you, Travis. You are a good listener. I can tell you are paying strict attention."

"You tell a good story. I don't know if I swallow it whole."

"This is not a story, my boy. This is a life! My life! And what is still to come will amaze you. Now, where was I? Oh yes. I set myself to experimentation, based on the notebooks of Tomas Czeslow. And what did this behavior garner me? Like my long-dead mentor,

I too was scorned as a freakish loner. Wasting my life, carrying on with crazy, impossible nonsense. I lost myself for days at a time in trances. I was a young man, maybe nineteen or twenty, and this was not normal behavior.

"My family were greatly concerned, but I cut all ties with them to avoid draining energy away from my chosen path. After initial puzzlement and concern over my behavior, no one at the university took much notice. In a subject as arcane as Medieval Alchemy, a certain latitude is granted to eccentricity. As long as I remained a student, and an obviously devoted scholar, I was free to experiment. No one cared if I locked myself away for a few days. No one knew I was leaving my body and traveling."

"And where did you go?"

"Here, there, and everywhere! I was experimenting, exploring. Mapping a new universe only I knew existed. In my youth, I even came here to Mount Shasta—I've told you already that this place is one of those seven sacred chakras, in fact the only one in all of North America," he said excitedly. "And like the six others, it is a hub, a mega-hub. Issuing from it, like the spokes of a massive celestial wheel, are a series of energy conduits, each one a supercharged superhighway of pure untapped power, crisscrossing this planet, connecting this hub with the other six chakras, and the hundreds and thousands of smaller hubs. I call this network the Terrulian Grid. You may be surprised to learn that the prison where our bodies proper wait patiently for us to return to them was built directly along one such energy line, which greatly facilitates travel to and from it."

"I do have a question for you George," I said. "If you have

this knowledge, this unbelievable skill and ability to transpose yourself—"

"Transpose is not exactly the word—"

"Whatever. To bilocate, is that right? If you can move around the planet like a fucking miraculous God, or like the patron saint of frequent flyers, and if you can bring me here on sheer mental energy, then what the hell are you doing in prison?"

"Prison? What is wrong with prison? In some ways it's a perfect place for a man of my interests and temperament. I do see the irony in it—that a prison should provide a haven for a man in need of freedom to do nothing."

"Don't tell me you deliberately tried to get yourself locked up," I said.

"No no. Nothing like that. Before you stands a highly moral person, Travis. Committing any sort of serious crime, or deliberately injuring some other person, either physically or financially, is an impossibility for me."

"I want to believe you, George," I said. "But you're serving a lengthy sentence, and you don't get those for stealing cookies from a jar."

"Yes, there is that. I was convicted of a crime. But the crime found me, my boy. The crime found me. Are you sure you want to hear this?"

I nodded.

"My status as a prisoner is unfortunately a direct result of, or should I say, an involuntary culmination of the life path I chose many years ago in Poland, when I was still a young man," George began. "You have to understand, I have devoted my life to the study of bilocation, which is essentially a study requiring near constant meditation. As I mentioned before, in my youth I courted the Catholic church, and cultivated a pretended interest in their dogma and ritual, in the hopes that I could become a monk, and pass my days in a quiet monastery. For a number of reasons, mostly due to rather prosaic political infighting in the Polish Catholic church, my dream proved impossible.

"In life, one must always be prepared to find a Plan B. Mine was the haziest of schemes: escape Communist Poland, make my way across the Iron Curtain, and settle in America, where I believed that anyone with brains and financial flair could play stock markets and quickly be a millionaire. And of course, I told myself, once I am a millionaire, I'll be free to devote myself to my research again.

"Well, the first part of my Plan B came to pass, and I freed myself of the yoke of communism, and made it here to America, but the legendary land of milk and honey was not as I had imagined it to be. The streets of America had no pavement of gold. One was expected to work diligently to make a living, especially a foreigner with no marketable skills. One is expected to slave just to get by. A wage slave is still a slave, after all. For example the job of driving people about in a taxicab pays sometimes fifty dollars for a twelve hour shift. Barely money to live! No, to make real money, one needs a business plan, and capital, and partners. For one does not succeed in business all alone, the way a gambler wins in the casino. In America I had to work harder than I ever had in my life, just to make the ends meet.

"Of course, my research suffered. I needed time to meditate daily. I began to wonder, where can I find a place to sit alone for long periods of time undisturbed, where nothing is expected of me, where everything is provided for me? No, the answer was not prison, but perhaps some men might consider it a form of prison. Have you ever heard the aphorism, I'm uncertain what great wit can claim responsibility for it, but it goes like this: 'Marriage is a contract between someone who likes to sleep with the window open, and someone who likes to sleep with the window closed?'"

"I don't know that one."

"Well I heard that expression as a young man, and somehow I took it to heart, and saw a great truth in it. While I enjoyed the company of women, I was never interested in making any particular female of the species a partner for life. How could I? My life's love was my research, my experiments, my travels. My patient reconstruction and coaxing to life of the lost art of bilocation left me no tender feelings to bestow upon a female.

"But I did come to learn that love between a man and a woman is an experience of the highest order, even if my path to that knowledge was motivated not by a romantic impulse, but nearly the obverse: cold, calculated self-interest. You see, what happened was, I was reading a magazine, I believe it might have been People magazine, and I came across a story about a Polish sculptor of some renown but little financial success, who had emigrated to America. I naturally took an interest in his story, because it so closely paralleled my own. By some happy twist of circumstance this sculptor found himself in the favor of a rich American woman, an heiress she was, and in short order he married her, thereby freeing himself from the burden of procuring the income that is required for subsistence in America. This lucky son of the Polish soil was financially stabilized to such a degree that he could pursue his own interests and passions without worry, and that in turn gave him the confidence and security to produce art for art's sake. And in general, art for art's sake is better than art for money's sake, at least as far as the critics are concerned. In the end this man was critically acclaimed and financially secure. The best of all possible worlds.

"Now, upon reading of my compatriot's good fortune, I came to the conclusion that such an arrangement would be ideal for me also. A woman, let's say one who was recently widowed with a sizable inheritance, would lend me all the time, security, and material comfort I would need to pursue my research. And you know Travis, the funny thing about it is, when one sets one's mind to a goal like this, one soon realizes that what seemed a flagrant fantasy is no such thing. The world is not abundant with rich lonely women, but neither is it empty. One must hunt for them, but hunting is hunting, not terribly different from one species to the next. The animals of the forest have their own routines, and the hunter learns, for example, that his prey habitually drinks from a pond at dusk. So he hides there and waits, camouflaging his true intentions. I did likewise.

"At the age of forty-three I began to take ballroom dancing lessons. I possessed to my advantage certain traits that have always served me well in life; it is my good fortune not only to be an intelligent man, but to *look* intelligent, to carry myself about with a certain air of authority. I'm handsome, or so I've been told. If I pick up a tennis racket I seem the kind of man who plays a fine game of tennis. If I step onto the dance floor I seem naturally to belong there. I know how to run my fingers gently through my own hair in a way that attracts a woman's attention, and gives her some premonition of how tenderly I might run my fingers through hers. Of course it is hubris for me to say these things of myself, but as one of your great ballplayers said, in that delightful American idiom, 'It ain't bragging if it's true.'

"In any case, I took my best Old World European charm out of its musty suitcase, had it cleaned and pressed, and wore it to the ball. And there I found my princess. Not a real princess of course, but an American one, which is the best kind. When it comes to love, American woman retain a charming naiveté all their lives. Or maybe I shouldn't generalize. All I know is that I met a woman who had lived a full life with her eyes open, had come through it all a little scarred but utterly unjaded, and with whom it was easy to dance, easy to chat, easy to share fondness each for the other, easy to marry. And while she did not possess anything so grand as a fortune in financial assets, she enjoyed enough of a bulwark of stability that I felt my ship had come in. My little sloop had escaped the uncertain seas and found safe harbor.

"Our marriage prospered. She had a career of sorts, and she was in no hurry to give it up. She ran a retail business specializing in upscale antiques. This suited me, as she was out of the house most of the day. I don't want you to think me so crass and calculating that I had no feelings for her. I loved her dearly. I also loved being free all day to conduct my experiments, to make tremendous strides. Does that not sound ideal?"

"Perfect," I said.

"What I've shown you so far is a fingernail's worth of what I'm capable of, my boy. And everything that I know is, in its turn, a fingernail's worth of what I suspect lies out there, beyond, still waiting to be discovered."

This last he said with a certain weariness. He rubbed a hand over his face and eyes as if pulling cobwebs free, and looked at me with an expression that was impossible to read. A blankness.

"And?" I said expectantly.

"And what?"

"Your life was ideal. Then what happened?"

"Of course. Quite right. I should return to my story. Well." He hesitated. "The fact is, I'm—let me—I'm just not at all accustomed to sharing personal matters."

"Tell me now. You've led me this far."

"I will tell all. I think it's important." He rose from his chair and went to the cabin's sink, ran the tap, and returned with two glasses of water. Offering me one, he said, "You might be surprised to learn that our bodies abroad also need the nourishment of food and water, and are capable of all the physical functions of our bodies proper." He took a long drink from his glass, while I sipped from mine. It tasted of sulfur.

"But back to my story," George continued. "We were happily married. Sincerely happy. In love, really. But of course nothing beautiful lasts. Events did turn, but not in the way you might expect. Our honeymoon days gave way not to bickering or disengagement, but in fact just the opposite. We became closer, ever more intimate, especially once I shared with her some of my secrets, which she expressed great curiosity about, and I encouraged this. I wanted a traveling companion, someone with whom I could share the wonder of what I was capable of doing. I wanted a mirror. I wanted to see that wonder expressed in the eyes and face of another.

"I was growing ever more cocksure in my opinion of my own abilities. Perhaps in my zealousness to make her truly my partner in all realms, I rushed things. We should have taken tiny first steps, baby steps, but instead I was like a teenage boy with a supercharged car and an open highway. There was no wariness, no prudence, no deliberation. 'Come with me, my dear! Hang on for the ride!' That was all.

"That first time—the only time—when I had made up my mind to initiate her fully into my realm, I simply grabbed onto her, much as I just had you grab onto me this very evening, and I tried to pull her, to *will* her out of her body proper and into her body abroad. Together our mindsouls left our bodies, and we journeyed into the ether, but she did not materialize out the other side. She was half there. Her body abroad was half present, but not enough of her existed to make an entity.

"I could see her faintly and in snatches, I could feel her pleading to be rescued. I was unable to communicate with her. I abandoned hope of pulling her further into the body abroad, and simply tried to return us both home, back into our bodies proper, but there were further complications—it was as if she were tangled in a parachute, moving at a speed I could not control. I had no experience to draw upon, no idea how to compensate for a situation growing evermore harrowing. She was plummeting, I was holding her, gripping her tightly around the neck, trying to pull her back to me, trying to make her eyes see me. She panicked, as if she were drowning. She could not be made to see me.

"I gave every ounce of my strength to pull her back with me. And I thought I had succeeded. We came back into our home. I came back into my body proper. I was still holding her, my hands tight around her neck. I kept waiting for a glint of life to come back into her eyes, some hint of recognition. I became aware of how very tightly my hands were gripping her neck, and I let them loose. She slipped to the floor. I could not revive her as she lay there. I could never revive her."

George slumped limply in his chair. The cabin was quiet as space.

"I'm sorry," I said.

"Yes of course. A tragedy, no? Not unlike your own."

"Worse, I'd say."

"Perhaps. You didn't kill your wife. I killed mine."

"Accidentally."

"Oh yes, an accident. But like so many accidents, preventable. A consequence of carelessness and overconfidence. I've always felt my conviction for murder was perfectly justified. If I hadn't felt that way, I might have fled. Instead, with my dear wife's body laid out before me, and through a flood of tears, I summoned up the composure to call 911, and I pleaded for an ambulance, in the hope that paramedics or doctors might magically revive her. The police also came. I presented an open and shut case, what with the marks on her neck being consistent with strangulation, and the bruises all around that area also consistent with my hands constricting, and me denying nothing, blaming myself, flailing about and threatening suicide. I pled guilty, in any case. So in the end I got a jail cell, a twenty-five year sentence."

"What was her name?"

"I don't speak her name. I have not spoken her name since that day."

"I have trouble saying my wife's name too," I said.

George gave no sign that he had heard me. "I still hold out hope," he said, "I have to admit to you that much of my research has been dedicated to the search for my missing wife. Yes, I consider her missing, not dead—I am convinced that her mindsoul failed to reenter her body proper on that day. I believe it became entangled, perhaps torn into fragments, in the ether, and even now lies waiting for me to attain the knowledge, the know-how, to pick up the pieces and put my wife back together again."

He paused to collect himself, and looked deep into my eyes. "Do you think that's a reasonable ambition? Sometimes I worry I'll go mad."

"George, you've just shown me the impossible is possible. No ambition feels unreasonable anymore."

"If nothing is impossible, then it's possible I'm crazy," he muttered, curling his lips in a battered, weary smile.

CHAPTER 7

Last night George materialized in my cell—I've come to think of it as him coming to pick me up, as if we're carpoolers—and whispered to me that we were going on a pilgrimage. I clung to him, wrapping my arms around him tight, just like I did on that first night, and every night since, and together we rose into the ether. The journey took longer than any we've taken before, and in the tumble of images and emotions, in the hypnosis of the repeated chant, for the first time I saw George with some clarity, and I could see that he was not floating freely, serenely, as on other occasions when I had caught glimpses of him in that realm, but seemed to be struggling, summoning and focusing all his strength, a frail swimmer fighting a brawny tide.

When finally we emerged out of that weightless ethereal realm, and I entered into my body abroad, I squinted against a blinding late-afternoon sun, and faced a bell-shaped edifice the color of red clay. There was no one around. Tall weeds and tropical forest appeared to encroach on the grounds around the building. George told me it was a Buddhist stupa.

"We are in the Kingdom of Nepal, the little country that sits like an epaulet on the north shoulder of India, and we are close, a bit north and slightly east, of the birthplace of the great Gautama Buddha himself," George said. "Do you feel something? This is the site of the first of the seven chakras that encircle the earth. In this very special location we are already situated on the vast Gangetic plain, which gently and ever so gradually carries all water south and east to the Bay of Bengal, in the Indian Ocean. On its meandering route to the sea, the languid Ganges passes many, so many countless sacred sites, including the holy city of Varanasi, revered by all Hindus. Oddly enough, the first chakra, known more commonly as the Kundalini, is the lowest on the human body, right at the very base of the spine. This situation makes it naturally associated in the human mind with the process of elimination, of excretion. This is the most earthy of the chakras, the most 'grounded,' if I may use that term, and an appropriate term it is indeed, for the Kundalini is grounded in the very dirt of the earth. The Kundalini emerges from the ground like the top of a tap root, surfacing from the deep clay that lies far beneath the soil. Can you not sense the especially fecund, living power, soaked up from the soil here, sent as energy through the soles of your feet, and up your legs, like two bolts of lightning that meet in an electrical charge at a special place, right at the tip of your tail bone?"

I closed my eyes and tilted my head back, seeing the orange of the sun through my eyelids. Then by increments I truly did give my body over to a surging force, two streams of tremendous power that rose up my legs and joined together when they met. It wasn't sexual. It was more pure than that. More fundamental. More raw.

"Now you feel it, I can tell," George exclaimed gleefully. "That is the energy Mother Earth sends to every living plant, and the energy every plant in turn gives to the animals. In this place we are getting a direct jolt, like milk straight from the breast of the Goddess. Let us walk around this stupa. Remember, it must always be done in a clockwise direction. The ancients who built this place understood. Even the local peasants who live here today understand."

We strolled around the stupa, which seemed to me to resemble a giant perfect breast, upturned with a nipple on top in the form of a tiny bell tower. It glowed in the sun like a red brick kiln. Wooden cow bells clanked softly in the distance, and soon a herd of bone-thin white cattle appeared, tended by a young boy, bare-chested and bare-legged, with just a simple swath of cloth wrapped around his middle. He carried no switch or stick to control his herd; the clapping of his small hands appeared to be enough to guide them. The cows knew exactly where they were going. The boy stopped dead in his tracks at the sight of us, and then broke into a toothy grin.

"I know him," said George. "His name is Radlal. The first time he saw me here he thought I was a ghost. He had never seen a white man before. He ran home to his village, which is about a mile away, and his mother beat him for leaving the cows untended."

Radlal shouted some greeting to us in his language, then turned himself to the search for small rocks to use as ammunition for a home-made slingshot he had brought with him. The cows turned their attention to grazing the thick green grass.

"Don't these beasts have an aura of peace about them?" George remarked. "They display such a contented air. They remind me of a cat I once lived with, my dear wife's cat, who spent most of his days curled up on a sunny chair. These cows eat the grass that grows so abundantly here without having to lift a finger—well, in their case a hoof—to cultivate it. And at night they sleep and dream on its matted, yielding stems. Don't you envy them the life?"

"Cows get slaughtered," I said.

"Not these ones. These are sacred."

"They must be bored here. I wouldn't want the life of a docile, coddled cow—there's no action, no suspense, no tension."

"I think you are wrong, my young friend. You think life needs adventure to be worth living, because you knew adventure once, and now suffer its absence in prison. These cows don't miss such things, because they can't imagine such things exist. They chew their cud and are happier than you."

"If happiness is the absence of pain and suffering, yes, they're happier than me, George. Some rich lady's lap dog is happier than me. Plenty of creatures are happier than me. But I know happiness is not just the absence of suffering. It's elation, a high. I've felt it, and these cows never will."

We watched them for a few more minutes. A bird sang a throaty, comical song in a nearby tree. Radlal the barefooted peasant boy began to stalk it with his homemade slingshot. Beyond the trees for the first time I noticed a distant line of hills. I asked George what they were. He said, "If we were to march north from here, we would soon come abruptly face to face with the staggering peaks of the Himalayas, which as you must know provide the highest natural vantage point on this earth. Did you notice them on our journey here?"

I said I hadn't. It had all been a great whirling blur.

"You really must get more accustomed to moving about in this manner, Travis. We passed directly over Mount Everest, I would like you to know. That was a detour I fashioned at the cost of considerable personal energy. Do you think I can just flit around the globe on some inexhaustible psychic power source? No! If there were a Fountain of Youth on this planet I would have located it by now. There is no such thing, there is only growing older and more tired. This work is tiring, especially if I go out of my way like I did today. That tangent, and no small deviation it was, I meant as a gift for you, intended for your edification and delight. And where was your *head*, boy? You weren't even paying attention!"

"I did see snowy peaks, I think."

"Did you notice all the various climbing groups making a run for the summit?" George demanded. "The weather was ideal, a rare blue-skied sunny day at Everest, after weeks of howling snow squalls and bitter winds. Of course all the groups of climbers had been waiting for days for the weather to clear, and they all decided they wanted to make a run for the top at the same instant. It really was quite funny. A Gore-tex traffic jam! The place was as bustling as Disneyland on a holiday weekend!"

"I'll try to pay more attention on the way back," I said.

"No need. We'll take a different route. We will make a circumnavigation of the planet. That will be a first for you, if I am not mistaken. And this time, try to stay in your mind on the journey. Tie down your brain! Think of your cranium as an officer's cabin on a storm-tossed ship. Certainly in such fierce weather a few personal items must come loose and roll about, but they are mere distractions from what is really happening. Focus on the power of the hurricane, not the empty soda can rolling crazily across the steeply-angled floor. That's a mere effect. Find the cause! Leave your little cabin and go out on the deck. Feel the winds that blow you this way and that! Feel the source! Feel its might!"

Little Radlal loaded up his slingshot with a handful of tiny pebbles, and fired a scattered fusillade at birds in the leafy trees. We left him without saying goodbye.

Chant and chant. This time in that weightless liftoff from the earth's surface I saw things with new, intense clarity. Passing over the great ocean of humanity going about their daily lives, I felt witness to a billion actions great and small, yet at the same time I felt myself to be above that petty world, in a kind of heaven, a vast dimension George and I had all to ourselves. And for the first time I saw someone else floating in our space, a woman passing by on her own journey, giving no sign that she had seen us. She had curly silver and black hair and was dressed in loose purple garments. Later I asked George if he had seen her, and who she was. "Astral projectionist," he said nonchalantly. "You should be prepared to come across them from time to time. They are mostly women, Wiccans if you like, well-meaning ladies who have chanced upon a trick or two in their study of the ancient art of sorcery. Once or twice in my time I have traded knowledge with these women, mostly in my search for information about my darling wife, but for the most part they are suspicious of me. I'm a man of power in their realm. They do not trust men to use power wisely, to use it only for good. Unfortunately history lends credence to their dubious opinion of the human male.

"As for astral projection, their discipline is much inferior to ours. The mind travels, but the body does not materialize in the new locale. We've gone them one better. We travel places not just in spirit, but in body as well." He looked at me very seriously. "Perhaps you don't appreciate it as yet, but you are being initiated into a very exclusive club. I'm the only extant member. Once you have fully absorbed your lessons, then there will be two of us, and I don't at all mind keeping it that way. I would have been quite happy to have remained the only practitioner of this science."

"Then why are you passing it on to me?"

"For my own selfish reasons, as you will see."

C H A P T E R **8**

ast night in the cabin on Mount Shasta, George glanced at the clock on the wall and said, "It's time for a little journey. For this one I am going to let you guide me."

"For real?"

"Yes, indeed. It is my belief that you are ready to lead."

"I'm not so sure," I said.

"Why not?"

"I don't even know where to go."

"I think you do. I'm going to remind you of a phrase you have heard before, though not from me," he said. "In the early phases of bilocation, it provides power that you will later learn to draw on from within. Now concentrate as you repeat this in your mind: *The mantra can be written, the meaning cannot be guessed, the faith cannot be shaken, in the one you love the best.*"

"Colquitz," I said.

"That is unfortunately correct," he said. "Our friend and fellow inmate Mr. Colquitz has memorized this phrase, from the notebook I kept in my cell, the one whose pages ignited into flame to prevent him from gleaning anything further. The fool has dabbled in a business beyond his capacity. Even his memory of this little verse is slightly askew, likely because he can only imagine taking love, not giving it. His mind has digested it like a stomach's bile, and instead of 'The one you love the best,' he regurgitates it as 'The one who loves you best.' Hopefully, whatever other scraps of information he has consumed have been digested in an equally garbled manner. Be on your guard against that man, Travis. He is like the oily little Gollum. Lurking, learning, plotting. A man driven by such passionate hatred is a threat to us all."

He stood by the window of the little cabin, watching the wind whip the darkened forms of shadowy pines outside. "But forget hatred for now. Love will trump hatred every time. Love is tremendously underestimated as a source of power. Look at all the men of history considered to have been powerful. What is the power of a politician or a general? A mere momentary inventory of armaments—that is all they ever amount to. These things like guns and cannons, ships and warplanes, they rust quickly, my boy. What are these toys compared to the eternal power of a Buddha, or a Jesus Christ?

"Christ was crucified," I said.

"So he was. He did suffer. We all do. But in the end he triumphed. His message of love triumphed. In any case, Travis, it's time for us to conduct a little experiment, to give you a test, to see what you're capable of. I am going to ask you again to lead me where you will."

"I don't even know where that would be."

"That's fine. You won't exactly be choosing, my boy. Repeat the chant and you will be taken where you must go. Now repeat after me, and then keep repeating it to yourself: *The mantra can be written, the meaning cannot be guessed, the faith cannot be shaken, in the one you love the best.*"

Chant and chant. I rose quickly into the ether, unfettered and free. I could sense George lurking somewhere behind me, watching over me the way a parent keeps an eye on a child in a swimming pool. The pool became a swift river, George in the water behind, riding the current where it took us. The river, the chant, the passage over water that is really air, lighter than air, flying there over a million lives happy and miserable, all of them touching me and yet not, the planet spinning and pages turning and quite suddenly I was descending into my parents' house, the house where I grew up, in a taut line of power, a cord of light turning from silver to gold, down into the very room I knew as a child.

It looked different. It had been repainted, redecorated, and all traces of me were gone. But the bed was still the same one I slept in as a child, and who should be sitting upon it but Nellie, my daughter, sixteen years old, nearly a woman, tall and slender with long straight hair. She was brushing her hair. I could see it all so clearly, as if I were in the room with her, and of course I was in the room with her, but I held myself back, I didn't materialize fully into my body abroad. I hovered there like an angel or a ghost, afraid to move forward or back.

"Who is this one you love the best?" George's question brought me out of my amazement, and there he was at my shoulder, angelic and unformed.

"My daughter," I said. "I see her plain as day—"

"As do I. We'll stop short—best not to startle her, and best not to startle you too. We'll wait for a few hours, until she is in bed and sleeping soundly, before we pay her another visit. Until you are a bit more comfortable with the process of bilocation, scenes of extreme emotion are wisely avoided."

I meant to leave. I started to return home, but some part of me was being tugged down to the room, to her presence. I felt the pull of my essence, an urge to materialize into my body abroad, pulling at me like gravity drawing salt down through a funnel, my body taking shape, density and weight. I looked at my body and saw an apparition, not all there, but visible, someplace between transparent and opaque. I looked up at her and saw her eyes grow large and frightened, and I knew she could see me.

"Daddy?"

I felt a pull toward her, and a counterforce pulling me away: George, in the ether retreating, tugging me with him, cajoling me to retreat. I fell back to safety, away from the pain of love.

CHAPTER 9

Two hours later, George let me leave Mount Shasta on my own. "You will fly there free, solo if you will, under your own mental power. I will follow at a discreet distance, and if there is some unforeseen difficulty I will intervene. But the bond of love between you and your daughter, I am confident, will prove strong enough to carry you straight and true to your destination. Are you ready, my boy?"

"I don't feel ready," I said.

"Don't worry. Relax with it. Love is an intangible, immeasurable source of power. Love will carry you there."

I began to meditate. *The mantra can be written, the meaning cannot be guessed, the faith cannot be shaken, in the one you love the best.*" Then my mind gave way to a jumble of bits and pieces of the strange unspoken mantras I've learned, flowing through my head until an overriding rhythm made itself felt, and I surrendered to it, and felt it lift me, like an unseen angel levitating a dying soldier from the battlefield, or a drowning sailor pulled from rough seas. For awhile I was alone, until at some point I felt George at my back, and turned to share with him my state of bliss.

"This is what I call the rapture, like what certain Christians pray for," George said, smiling benignly. "But this is not given from without, it is coming from within yourself. You carry yourself where you desire to go. Where you love and are loved. Go there, now."

And I felt myself carried through the weightless ether, and I saw the world below me as a grid of psychic power lines, pulsing with energy, connecting people everywhere, every time one thought of another. I saw them all, near and far, without effort or strain, those rare people among us who radiate energy like supernovas, while so many others live isolated and unthought-of, emitting only the weakest of psychic signals to the rest of humanity. I felt like a baby in his mother's arms, a dolphin born into the water of a giant sea, warm and safe and soupy as the womb.

And then I saw Nellie, asleep in the house where I grew up, and I drew close, and willed myself into that place, emerging from the world of no form to the world of form again, and found myself in that bedroom, where the window, slightly open, allowed a mild breeze that carried a hint of the sea, and there, under a fluffy coverlet, slept Nellie, my daughter. My child.

"I would strongly advise that we do not wake her, but leave her to enjoy her girlish dreams," I heard George say. Some part of me resented his presence now.

"I don't know what I'd say to her anyway."

"The first thing you would have to say is, 'Don't scream!'" he joked. "She caught a glimpse of you before, but the full sight of you would, for certain, be a shock to her. And right now she is looking so innocent and peaceful." We watched her breathe quietly in sleep. "Quite a lovely girl. You should be proud."

"I want to watch her for awhile."

"I'll leave you then," George said. "I trust you know how to get home." I nodded yes, feeling not the slightest doubt.

I lingered, just watching her sleep. I could have watched her forever, for she appeared to me to be so tremendously innocent and pure, dreaming dreams free of fear. My heart felt too big for my chest, thinking of all those lost years.

Then Nellie opened her eyes and she saw me.

"Daddy?" She was unafraid.

"Yes sweetie. It's me."

"I saw you tonight. Earlier, when I was awake."

"Yeah. You did."

"Are you real?"

"Yes. You're awake now, not dreaming."

"Huh." She sat up in the bed and looked at the red numbers of the alarm clock. "It's so late. Should I turn on the light?"

"If you want."

The flick of the switch made us squint against the brightness. Gradually she relaxed her eyes, and inspected me.

"You seem pretty cool. I thought you'd be shocked to see me," I said.

"Maybe I should. But I'm not. Or maybe I'm still asleep. You look old. Older than I expected."

"Prison's not a place to grow old gracefully."

"How did you escape? Are they looking for you?"

"I haven't escaped."

"But you're here."

"I'm half here."

"I must be dreaming."

"No you're not. I can't explain it. Just accept that I can be here."

"Why did you go to prison, anyway?"

"Don't you know?"

"I guess I do," she said. "Grandma told me, years back when I was still a little kid. She told me I was there, and someday I'd remember exactly how it was. But I don't remember, and I don't know if I even want to remember. Did I see a man die?"

"It doesn't matter if you can't remember."

She stared hard at me.

"It sucks not having a Dad. You know?"

"I know."

"You're too old for me to call you Daddy. Or I'm too old."

"Call me Dad."

"Mom died of cancer. That's what happened and no one could change it. But you didn't have to go to prison. That's what I figured out. You could have stayed out of jail. You could have stayed my Dad."

"It wasn't like that."

"You knew Mom was going to die. Why did you make the police come?"

"You do remember, seems like."

"I don't, except what I was told. The police came, and one of them got shot when you tried to make them leave Mom alone. But why did the police come?"

"Do you remember my garden? In that old house where we lived, that padlocked room in the back?"

"With the bright lights?" she asked. "You used to shoo me out of there, told me the lights would burn my skin."

"That's right." I told her about the marijuana, how I grew it in the back room. "Your mom was suffering. She was in such terrible pain. She couldn't even keep her food down."

She hugged herself in the blankets, as if suddenly chilled. "I wish you hadn't done what you did. Then at least I'd have one parent, instead of none."

"I wish I hadn't got caught," I said. "Your mother was so close to dying when it happened. A week later and that room would have been dismantled."

"Dad?"

"Yes?"

"Can I have a hug?"

"Yes."

I leaned forward and felt her weight, her mass, in my arms. I started to cry. She smelled of clean sheets, strawberry shampoo, warmth and sleep. I knelt on the floor, with my daughter held tightly in my arms. I'd imagined this moment so often in the infinite prison night. We stayed that way for a long time, until I felt something shift, a lightness take hold, as if we two had begun to levitate, and I could feel the two of us rising toward the lines of power, which glowed strangely, as never before, stretching out before us like a golden umbilical cord, inviting us to slip into its pulsating current, when I caught a glimpse in the ether of George's disapproving face, and I caught myself, came back into the moment, into her room, to the bedside, two bodies in an enfolding hug, until I was certain we were there together, and I gradually loosened my arms, and let her go.

She brushed back her long hair, lifting it from where it had flattened and matted against her face. She was flushed with color, her eyes wide and thrilled.

"That was weird," she said excitedly. "I saw a kind of golden cord, like a rope, all made of light, leading off somewhere into the night, like, right up through the ceiling! And it felt like we were going to ride it—we could ride it on out of here like a magic carpet or something! Like something off of Star Trek or Star Wars! That was awesome!"

"I know. It's really something." I felt strangely proud of my power, pleased that she'd had a glimpse.

"How do you do that? How did you get here, Dad? How are you *here*?"

"I can't even really explain it myself."

"Is it through drugs? Marijuana?"

That made me laugh out loud, and I worried I might have woken the house. I dropped my voice low. "No, drugs have nothing to do with it."

"I've smoked it. Nanna blames it for Mommy's death."

"Nanna is wrong about that. But don't overdo the smoking of it. Don't fuck up your schoolwork."

"You sound like Grandpa."

"As I should. He's my Dad."

"Was he strict with you, like he is with me?"

"Just the normal amount." A flood of memories filled my mind, of my teenage years—the years of freedom: racing cars, chasing girls, drinking, trying out drugs. "I did all the usual things," I told her. "But I kept it under the radar. If he caught on to something his face would get this wounded look I didn't like to be the cause of."

"Hmm. I totally know about the face," she said. "I've seen it when he doesn't like my clothes. Bare midriff, that's his pet peeve. My friends come over and he's like, 'What's the matter girls, can't afford a full blouse?' I tell him it's just a *style*, but he's old."

"You're making me feel old."

"You're not old. You're old, but not *really* old."

"Now I feel better."

We smiled at each other. Talking seemed so easy.

"I wish you'd been around, Dad. Are you going to visit me often?"

"I hope so. Yes."

C H A P T E R **10**

George was waiting in the cabin on Mount Shasta, looking very displeased. "Ah, there you are. What were you doing with that child of yours?"

"She woke up. We spoke."

"I saw that. You almost lifted her into the ether. Are you insane?"

"I'm sorry, George. Once she saw me there was no going back."

"This is not good, Travis. This is supposed to be our little secret."

"What could I do? I didn't tell her anything about how I got there."

"No, you merely demonstrated it to her. Practically gave her a test drive." He shook his head. "This creates all kinds of loose ends. I don't like uncertainty, things that are beyond my control. There is much I want to accomplish." He began to pace the room agitatedly. "I'm going to accelerate your education. For tonight our too-short window has reached its end." Five hours was all the time George and I got each night—between midnight and five in the morning the prison guards make no passage through Easy C, so by five we needed to be back in our bodies proper. "When we return to the prison I want you to be prepared for a little surprise," George warned. "Now let's go."

And so we left Mount Shasta. The golden cord stretched ahead, pulling me home, and I sensed another cord, a twin, flowing swift and sure alongside me. I took it to be George, staying parallel as he usually does, only this time he was closer than ever. The two lines drew close, then touched, and then intertwined like a tangled clothes line, and I felt myself drop in a frightening loss of control, only to be caught and carried against my will. This was not my path. I began to panic. Nothing felt right. I felt myself placed like a confused and crying child into an unfamiliar crib. Not my crib. Not my home. Not my own.

Then I came back into the body proper, down into Easy C, not to familiarity, but to intense strangeness. My teeth hurt like hell, for one thing. They hurt and they felt foreign—even the shape of them, and when I slid my tongue in a tour of inspection around the cavity of my mouth, they felt irregular and weird. They felt wrong. I brought my hand up to my mouth to further explore my molars, and I looked at my fingers in shock. These were not my fingers. These were not my fingernails. This was not—

From the cell across the hall came the sound of soft, stifled laughter. I looked up to see myself in my cell. Then I realized I was in George's cell. Then I realized I was in George's body.

"What the hell are you—"

"Never mind, Travis. It is merely temporary."

It's a very strange experience to look at yourself, full and whole, as others see you. Not a mirror image, not an image at all. The real thing. In my cell across the hall, I was looking back at me.

"Put me the hell back in my body!"

"Shhh! Shut up. In a minute. Relax yourself, my boy. I only did it as a demonstration. So. How do you like being me? Go look in the mirror."

My eyesight was worse. I had to lean close to peer into my eyes, or George's eyes. They were definitely George's eyes—gray-green, not blue like mine—but as I looked more closely I recognized myself in the expression. Bewildered, but me. I could see my true self in those eyes, my essence, or I guess you could say I saw my soul, and oddly enough, it calmed me. Even in George's body, I was still me.

I turned back and went to the bars of the cell to talk to George.

"I feel very sore in here," I said. "The teeth especially. Does your body give you a lot of pain, George?"

"Perhaps. I've grown used to it, as if it were normal."

"Your teeth ache. Did you ever try to get your teeth looked after, while you're outside?"

"I did try once. But I've discovered that changes made to the body abroad do not survive in the return to the body proper."

"It's not just the teeth. The eyesight is poor. And there's a severe ache in the lower back. And one hip." I could have kept going, the list was long. Now that I was paying closer attention, pin points of pain were registering from all over the body. "You're suffering, George."

"Yes, yes. I know I am not well, and that is why I am making plans to improve my prospects. That's why I'm training you to be my apprentice, my accomplice."

"Can I have my body back?"

"Yes. Meditate with the usual, the necessary incantations, and I will meet you in the ether. Be passive. Let me merge and reemerge."

I began the chant. As my mind and soul lifted out of George's body I saw our paths crossing and connecting, and felt the pull to that nexus. On my way up I had a brief glimpse of Colquitz, in the next cell to mine, out of bed, upright at the bars of his door. His body was rigid, alert, attentive. He could see me.

CHAPTER 11

"Why did you name me Nellie?"

"I didn't. Your mother did."

"Why?"

"Can't remember, exactly. She just liked it. Don't you like Nellie?"

"I always wanted something more elegant. Cassandra, or Dominique."

"But you are a Nellie. A west coast surfer girl. Long legs, and a bit of Tomboy, am I right?

"Maybe. Do I look like her?"

"Not really. From the looks of you, you got the Pendridge genetics."

"I got a book from the library, about Astral Projection."

"It won't be any use. No book can explain how I'm able to visit you."

"Can you explain it?"

"My teacher wouldn't like it. He doesn't want me to come here and talk to you. But he can't stop me, because I know how to get here by myself."

"I wish you could come in the daytime. Come tomorrow—when I'm on the beach with my friends. You could just wander past, and I could comment to them, sort of casually, on how you look like what I think my Dad must look like, and then see what they say. It would be so funny!"

"Not a good idea. I'd rather keep this under wraps for now, and the last thing I want is for a bunch of teenage girls to start putting two and two together, from little hints you couldn't help yourself from dropping."

"I've already told Jerrid about you."

"Jerrid? Who's that?"

"My boyfriend."

"Jesus Christ, Nellie! Don't be telling anyone about me! I didn't even know you had a boyfriend."

"I do, but it's messed up. His parents moved away last month, so he had to go with them, so he doesn't even live here anymore, and then in September he's going to college in Seattle, so I'm going to have to wait two years until I can go to college with him. That's how we've planned it out, but two years is going to kill me! Just to think about it hurts like hell."

"Don't be telling him anything more about me, okay?"

"I only told him once, after the first time you visited. I was bursting—I had to tell someone! And then he didn't even believe me."

"Good for him. Sensible kid."

"It's because he's far away and I had to tell him by phone. He didn't take it seriously at all. Just, 'Yeah right Nellie.' He said I didn't need to make up stories to get his attention. Made me so frigging mad! I wanted to strangle him."

"On this one I'm with him. I wouldn't believe you either."

"It's hard keeping a secret like this! It's great having a Dad but it also sucks, the way we have to meet, in the middle of the night, whispering like this, so we don't wake Grandma and Grandpa. And I never even know when you're coming, so sometimes I lie awake thinking you'll come tonight, and you don't."

"I know, it does suck. I'll tell you what. We should set times in advance. Every time we meet we'll set up the next meeting at a specific time. That sound good?"

"It'll work for this week, but next week things are going to get tricky. Jerrid's coming to visit. I'll be busy."

"Busy. With your boyfriend. In the middle of the night."

"You never know."

"You're too young for that."

"I'm sixteen, I can do what I like."

"I guess you can. But be safe."

"I will. I know all about it."

"Are you already, active?"

"Dad! Not yet. But I'm getting ready. Lots of my friends are doing it. It's overdue."

"What's the hurry? Are they happier than your friends who aren't doing it?"

"I don't want to be having this conversation, Dad. You're about three years too late for *the talk*. Grandma took care of that."

"Just be safe, and be careful."

"I will. I already bought condoms, in case Jerrid forgets."

"That's more than I need to know."

"Just don't show up Thursday night. Or the next few nights after that. Give us a few days privacy. He's here for two weeks, so when you do show up, can you please arrive out in the hall, and knock softly on the door? You shouldn't just barge into my bedroom unannounced, Dad."

"He's going to be staying in your room?"

"Not exactly. According to Grandma and Grandpa he's sleeping in the room across the hall. But there'll be some sneaky tiptoeing going on."

"Parenting is getting too fucking complicated."

"Don't sound all bitter."

"I never had the chance to know you as a kid, and now you're not even a kid anymore."

"Get used to it. If I can deal with the freakiness of a dad who flies in from jail, you can deal with a daughter who's all grown up."

n the line-up for lunch today, Colquitz sucker-punched One Nut right in the face. He dropped to the floor in a clatter of plastic dishes.

The guards didn't see it and did nothing. Colquitz walked away, still fuming; One Nut straightened himself out. "What was that all about?" Doc asked him.

"Nothing, really," One Nut muttered. "He called me a jack-off and I said, 'At least I can get it up.'"

"That's his soft underbelly," Doc said.

"How do you know so much about it?"

"I know the whole Colquitz story, start to finish."

"How's that?"

"When I was awaiting trial I was denied bail; they considered me a flight risk. They were right about that—I would have slipped away to Paraguay or some other place that's known to be tropical and corrupt, and once settled there I'd have lived out my days, selflessly working in medical clinics for the poor. A good doctor is easily for-given when the need is great."

"What's that got to do with Colquitz?"

"In jail I shared a cell with someone who knew Colquitz real well. Wallace was his name. I can't recall now if that was his first name or his last. He was a drug dealer from some minor-league town up in the hills. Hawks Nest. Ever hear of it? It's a coal town. A bunch of big open pit mines. They're really strip mines, they use giant machines to shave the mountains down, to get at the coal seams. Wallace told me Colquitz was the only son of the owner of the mines. He was a rich kid, heir to the wealthiest man in town. That gave him a cer-tain liberty with the police, who were in his Daddy's pocket, and Colquitz lived like a hell raiser. Booze and drugs of all sorts. By high school the he was dishing out so much cash for cocaine that the local cops went to his Dad and suggested he cut off the kid's allow-ance. They convinced him to turn off the money tap at the source, hoping the kid might straighten out.

"But that backfired. Colquitz started dealing blow himself, to finance his habit. He moved out of his Dad's place and into a big old ranch house that he'd inherited through his mother. The place was a long ways out of town, and before too long it was the party palace of the whole valley. Plenty of young dudes, miners making good money, would cash their pay checks Friday nights and head out there to convert it straight into blow. Colquitz still enjoyed immu-nity from prosecution, because of who his Daddy was. Once in a while his daddy would drive out there and beg him to straighten up and take an interest in the family business, but Colquitz just laughed in the old man's face.

"Wallace told me, the strangest thing about Colquitz was that despite the cocaine and money, he never had a girlfriend around, never had a woman. He was stunted in that way. Some people said maybe he was queer. A closet case. But if he was, he wasn't getting any of that, either. No, it seemed like Colquitz was completely asexual, or non-sexual. Which fits with the Colquitz we know, too."

"What do you mean?" I asked.

"Come on, man. Does he gotta spell it out? We're sharing a big ol' cage here!" This interjection came from Deathrow Jethro, who had joined our table. "Everyone strokes, everyone's seen it. You jerk off, I jerk off, we all jerk off, and it's live and let live. Then there's Colquitz, who if he sees you at it, will always yell out some stupid insult or interruptive fuckery to get under your skin."

"He's not the only one who says things."

"No, but in one aspect of his behavior, he's alone," Doc said, reclaiming the reins of the conversation. "Think about it. Have you ever seen him bring himself off? You're right next door. Ever seen him, or heard him late at night?"

"I never have. That's true."

"I'm telling you, the man is asexual," Doc asserted. "The man is incapable of getting an erection. And that's why he's a miserable bastard, and that's why he's in jail."

"What did he do?"

"Wallace worked for him as a mule, packing coke up from the coast by car, and living in a shack at the back of Colquitz's property, behind the main house. One night Colquitz shows up at Wallace's door, all messed up and edgy, he's got scratch marks on his face, blood on his clothes. He says to Wallace, 'Listen, I've got a girl back at the house, and I think I killed her.' He wants Wallace to help him to get rid of the body. They go look at the girl, who's definitely dead, and they have a couple of drinks, just to calm the jitters. Colquitz is chugging back rye until he breaks down and tells Wallace, 'She was laughing at me, and I couldn't stand it.'

"Wallace says, 'That can't be all there is to it. You don't kill someone for laughing at you.'

"And Colquitz tells him how he'd picked up this girl hitchhiking, a local girl working a summer job, she was hitchhiking from work just at twilight, you can do that in a town where everyone knows everyone. She knows him a little, she's been to parties at his house, she likes to party. She asks Colquitz to get her high, and he's only too happy to oblige, says come on back to his place, to his house in the woods. And then he tries to get it on with her.

"He tells Wallace, 'I just wanted to know what it was like, that's all. I had to *try*, for once in my life. Just try. She was ready for it, she was into it, she was into me.' The girl wanted to smoke weed, said it made her horny. So he gave her some weed and let her smoke it. Then she said she wanted to sit out on a couch on the back deck and watch the sun set behind the mountain, and he led her out there, and slid in beside her on the couch, and started to kiss her, fondle her, mess with her. She started getting into it, and then she took hold of his hand, and asked him where the bedroom was.

"Now, according to Wallace, when Colquitz told him what happened next, he started to cry like a baby. 'She knelt by the bed and unzipped me, and she started using her mouth on me. And I was ready for it, praying that my useless prick was finally going to get a jump start. But nothing. My cock let me down! It stayed all limp and lackluster. And then she started to laugh at me. She shouldn't have laughed. I put my hand over her mouth, just to shut her up, and she bit it, the bitch! I slapped her and she clawed at my face, and her fingernails blinded me, and I tasted blood, and then I lost it, I just lost it. I picked up the phone lying on the bed and it fit in my fist like a perfect fucking pestle. I swung it hard, once, twice, and the third time I heard a crack, an awful crack.'

Doc paused for effect. We'd all been quite spellbound. "That's what Colquitz told Wallace, and that's what Wallace told me," he said.

"Sad story for the girl," said One Nut.

"Yeah. You almost feel sorry for Colquitz and his useless prick," Jethro said. "Or you would if the man had ever shown a scrap of humanity around here."

"He never has, never will," Doc said. "As for Wallace, he helped him bury the body up an old logging road, helped him clean up the carpet and dispose of the bloody clothes. He did it grudgingly, knowing it wasn't right. The town was in a frenzy to find the killer. Everyone was a suspect. Now, Wallace started to get paranoid that he was next on Colquitz's hit list, or maybe good old-fashioned guilt weighed on his conscience, but he went to the cops. He settled up. He got a short sentence out of it, which he was just getting set to serve when I met him. Colquitz got life, and we got Colquitz, right here on Easy C, inflicting all his fucked up, unrepentant bitterness on us con men, card sharks, and assorted articulate, dishonest, but pacifistic wimps."

<h1 style="text-align:center">C H A P T E R **13**</h1>

Tonight I watched George meditate across the hall, and a moment later materialize in my cell. He seemed excited, agitated even, and that's unusual for him. He whispered that tonight would be the night of revelation. "Do you think I took you under my wing out of pure altruism?" he asked. "There is a quid pro quo, and tonight it's time for you to pay something back. Follow me quickly."

He had me sit on the bed in the meditative position, placed a hand on my forehead, and drew me with him. This connection by touch—it had been a while since we'd needed to do that. But tonight it seemed like he was leaving nothing to chance. Tonight he was all business, leading a quick ascent and descent, a short hop directly to a new destination. We came into our bodies abroad in a private room, in a hospital.

In the bed lay a young man, pallid of face, with a skin tone that was so sallow and waxy that intuitively I understood he was not just sleeping, but in a coma. "We are in a hospital in a Midwestern state," George informed me. "Tulsa, Oklahoma, to be exact. I found this boy on the internet, a truly marvelous invention, an electronic reading room for all the newspapers of the world. For many months on my bilocatory jaunts I've been scanning web sites of American newspapers large and small, waiting for the proper report to catch my eye. I've sought a headline such as *Local athlete in coma*, or *Youngster's bright future cut short by brain injury*. There were many false starts, stories with great potential, but usually there was some fatal imperfection of circumstances.

"But at last I've found a case that happens to be ideal. This fine looking young man, athletic and fit, is in a coma, as a result of an incident that occurred while playing ice hockey. Apparently a rather thuggish opponent whacked him with a stick, and the boy's helmet came loose, falling free just before his head cracked against the frozen playing surface. The result was severe brain swelling. It has now subsided, but the hemorrhaging that occurred after impact has made the prospects for recovery close to zero. The boy is brain dead. He is in this coma for life. Unless. Unless what? What do you think, Travis?"

"Unless you trade bodies with him."

"Exactly. I feel not a shred of guilt or remorse, nor should I. I am paying honor to this fine young man, allowing his body a second chance. He will live on through me. And he was a natural athlete, a road racer on bicycles in the summer, and a lover of hockey in the winter. That's how I found him. The headline that attracted me was *Local Cycling Champ In Coma After Hockey Incident*. He seems ideal for my purposes. I am finally ready to take Tomas Czeslow's work one step further. This is something I have largely developed on my own, something I call *corpus mutationis*, or body exchange."

The kid in question was a handsome young man, no doubt about that. He lay still, barely breathing, looking like some wax figure in a museum.

"His name is Dylan Podnovski, which is a wonderful bonus," George continued. "With such a name I will be able to return to Poland on occasion, on the pretext of tracing my ancestral roots. As for the name Dylan, I pray it is in honor of the poet with the surname Thomas, not that whiny-voiced pop star with the given name Bob."

"Bob named himself after the poet. And Bob Dylan is a better poet than you think, George."

"Well, it's immaterial. Only a name. It seems the family is literate at least," he said, picking up a library book that lay open, pages down, on a bedside table. "They are reading to him all through the day, in the hopes that the regular presence of a familiar voice might reach him, and rouse him, and draw him back to our world."

The book was *Tom Sawyer*. "A fine choice," George remarked. "Perhaps it was a favorite of the boy when he was younger. Let us play a game, let us just see if we can't randomly select a passage, and find some meaning for us there, the way religious Christians are fond of doing with the Bible." He flipped a page or two and scanned down, until some word or phrase caught his eye, and began to read: "But the elastic heart of youth cannot be compressed into one constrained shape long at a time. Tom presently began to drift insensibly back into the concerns of this life again. What if he turned his back now, and disappeared mysteriously? What if he went away—ever so far away, into unknown countries beyond the seas—and never came back any more!" He closed the book with a sharp snap that filled the silent room and the sleeping ward with sudden sound. The noise startled him, causing a guilty, childlike grin to cross his face.

"In this case, it is the old man who will disappear mysteriously," he suggested, grinning even more broadly. "Perhaps not mysteriously, for it will be made to appear that my corpse has suffered a death typical of prison. And far away, in freedom, this young man will be the center of local attention, blossoming back to life." He placed the book carefully back on the table, at exactly the place and angle it had lain before.

"Pay attention to the newscasts, Travis, or read the papers over the coming weeks. In this town a story will emerge of a local sports hero who spontaneously springs out of a coma. A full recovery, in record time! This kind of heart-warming tale will make the magazines. You will be hearing plenty about the boy who miraculously awoke, at the end of all hope, who astonished the medical establishment, not to mention friends and family who knew him before. Of course I will take it slow at first, play dumb if you will, but I'm not going to play-act all my life. I'll have the same mind I possess now, and of course I will make use of it in that new body. This young fellow will show significantly more intellect than anyone formerly gave him credit for."

"Sorry to rain on your parade, George," I said. "But you need to be careful here, and think it through from every possible angle. In life there are always consequences no one sees coming."

"If they are unforeseeable, there is nothing I can do, my boy. Of course there is risk." A thought made him smile. "Who knows? I may manifest some inexplicable behavior, for example, it could be that once I begin to speak in that young body, the words will come out with my Polish accent. Wouldn't that be amusing?"

He stood, and placed a hand on the forehead of the dormant boy in the bed. "I'm sure this is all quite sudden and shocking for you Travis, but the moment has come for transfer. Here is hoping that all goes well."

"And what am I supposed to do?"

"Just wait. I will tell you."

Keeping his palm on the boy's head, George closed his eyes, and quickly entered into what I presumed to be a trance-like state. At first there was no outward physical indication that anything was taking place, until after a few minutes his knees began to wobble, and his body slumped.

He began to swoon, to fall. I reached out and caught him in my two arms, and set him carefully in a nearby chair.

"Forget about him."

The words came from the boy on the bed. His eyes were open. A huge grin broke across that broad, youthful face, and he spoke again.

"Perfect! Ah, Travis, this is perfect. And what do you say, is there an accent? Polish accent?"

"Say something more."

"The rain in Spain falls mainly down the drain."

"No accent."

"Perfect, my boy!"

"Careful now George," I warned him. "You'll need to readjust your world view. No nineteen-year-old would be calling me boy. Sir is the word now."

"Ah yes, of course, Mister Pendridge, Sir. You're absolutely right! Never too soon to start adapting to the new reality." A thought struck him. "One thing I never checked, until now." His hand disappeared under the sheet, and rummaged exploratorily at his crotch. "Travis! Fantastic! I am hung like a giraffe!"

"We usually say horse, in English."

"I know that. Giraffe is even better! A greater distance to hang."

Footsteps approached down the hall, and we fell silent until they were well past.

"We shouldn't waste time," he whispered. He gestured to his former body, slumped in the bedside chair, gray hair hanging limp over the forehead. "He is brain-dead now. No time for pity. You must take that tired old carcass, which served me so well, really a lifetime of service, that ugly bag of aches and pains I will not soon forget—you must take it home with you, back to Easy C and the cell it knows so well. And Travis, I have one final favor to ask of you."

"What's that?"

"In my mattress you will find a metal blade, an excellent prison-made shiv. It is about six inches long, with a needle-sharp point. When you have reunited this body abroad back into my body proper, when the two are again one, when that sterile mind has been returned to the vessel of flesh that awaits it, I want you to take this blade and make use of it."

"George, I can't—"

"Now no objections. One clean stroke. Plunge it into the heart. I want you to make sure—"

"I can't do that," I said.

"You have to! I want to make my transfer to this body absolute and final! To do that I need my old host terminated. Travis, you must do this for me. It's mercy killing! The soul in that body is absent. It lives here now! The brain in that body is dead. The body itself is nearly dead, you felt that when I placed you in it. It won't be a living, breathing entity. It's just meat. It'll be like poking at a corpse!"

"Why can't *you* do it then?" I asked. "Come back with me in your new body, finish the job yourself."

"I'm afraid to. I'm barely moved into my new home, and I don't want to take chances with it yet. What if there is a complication? What if a guard sees me? He'll see a young man who does not belong there. I have to protect my new identity, but you and he—" he gestured to the old body, the old George, slumping ever more precariously, corpselike, in the chair—"will be in their rightful environment."

"George, I'm just not the kind of person—"

"This is no time or place for protracted negotiation. Sir. Please. I beg you. After all I have done for you, all I have taught you, grant me this small favor."

"Alright. I'll try. I'll do my best," I said finally. But I wondered when the moment came, would I have the stomach, or the courage, to shove home that makeshift knife?

In the hall we could hear voices, and the rubber wheels of a cart on linoleum. I ducked out of the line of sight of the small window in the door, and prayed that whoever was passing would not see George's carcass, clad in prison clothes, slumped in the chair. They passed by.

"Take it home with you now," George pleaded. I lifted the limp body just enough to slide myself into the seat under it, and let it settle back heavily against me. "Squeeze it in your arms, fasten your mind to it. That's it! Wrap your thoughts around it, and carry it home with you, back to Easy C, which I intend never to visit again."

"I almost hate to leave," I said. "I'd like to be here just to see the look on the nurse's face, the first time you open one eye and start chatting her up."

"No no. I told you, I will start slow." Then he gave me a little demonstration: eyelids fluttering, voice quavering, he breathed a sickly sigh: "Mo-omma. Wh-wh-where am I?"

"Goodbye George."

"Not goodbye, Travis. This is a time of new beginnings. One door is closing, but many others wait to be opened. We're the only members of a peculiar and distinctive association, you and I. We two are Masters of the Art of Bilocation, and I'm sure we'll have a reunion someday, if only to compare notes. Don't forget my name. Dylan Podnovski. Look me up sometime. If you need any help or guidance, look me up."

"Sure. For sure I will."

"And stay out of trouble!"

I began the rhythmic meditative loop that initiated the first phase of the transition, chanting my mantras and searching the ether for the golden cord. I was carrying an extra load, another mindsoul, and its emptiness, its incompleteness, weighed heavily upon me. Normally in the early stages of my meditation I'm used to feeling my mind brush up against George's feverish mind, which by sheer magnetism seems capable of lifting me up and out of my body. I've learned to operate separately from George, but almost always in tandem with him. He has been there for me, and I only truly realized how much that meant when he was suddenly no longer there. This time I was linked to nothing, just a fallow crackling void, like a radio tuned to an unused wavelength.

I could hear George calling out last words to me, an echo slowly fading to silence. "It's up to you, my boy. Don't let me down. Carry him home and make two into one." I really did feel transformed into a big old vulture, a bird of prey, lugging a carcass home to the nest. My talons clutched my cargo, not the mind of George, but rather a strange, sterile, derelict mindsoul, the once-vibrant mind of an athletic boy, reduced to a vacant husk.

We made a sweet, soft descent down into George's waiting cell, where his body proper waited in a posture of meditative repose. I settled on the bed beside him, and placed a single palm against his forehead, just as George had instructed. He'd told me the transfer would be seamless, that his waiting body was an empty vessel wanting to be filled, that it would suck the boy's mindsoul like a sink drain sucks a whirlpool of water. But it didn't happen like that. I'd carried my cargo to this point, but now I felt it slip from me, and slither back into the ether. I was losing it, and I began to doubt. I lacked the skills to bring it back, to corral it—it was like collecting smoke with a butterfly net. It was scattering, not gathering. It was gone.

I tried to chase it, but which direction to go? I felt like a child lost at a busy intersection. I came into my body abroad in George's cell, wondering what to do next. His body proper sat waiting for me in unbreathing stasis. I'd promised to kill it, to finish it off. I tore a seam at the end of George's bedroll and found the shiv. Duct tape for a handle, and a thin prong of metal sharpened to a point. I brought it up to his unmoving chest.

My orders were to kill the body, but only after the brain-dead boy's mindsoul was placed within it. That hadn't happened. I had an out, a good reason not to shove in the blade. And I was happy for that, because I knew I couldn't do it. I couldn't do it.

PART II

While she waited for the prisoner named Pendridge to be brought down to her, Lilia went back to the morgue to take another look at the body of George Szymanski. Laid out on an old army surplus gurney in that dusty room half-filled with cleaning supplies, the old man still somehow managed to convey an air of serenity, of peaceful repose. She'd seen enough corpses to know that once life leaves the body so does dignity. A mortician's artifice might render a facsimile of peace, or contentment, but a dead body in its natural state invariably struck her as looking sad, empty, and finished. George on the other hand looked like a living man at rest. She put her ear to his mouth to listen for his breath, and took hold of his wrist to feel for a pulse. As before, she found neither, but touching his skin she felt a body that retained the warmth of the living. The sound of doors opening brought her out into the hall, and she saw Travis Pendridge being led toward the interview room. Of all the men she'd encountered on his cell block he was the only one who had dropped his gaze when he saw her, and now he did it again when she looked at him, just before he turned and entered the room.

She followed; he was already seated when she entered. She had to squeeze past him to take her seat behind the desk. When she was seated and their eyes met he stared at her deeply, until she turned away from the intensity of his gaze.

"Forgive me," he said. "I don't mean to stare. But I haven't sat down with a woman like this, eyeball to eyeball, in a long time."

"I understand," Lilia said. "I want you to feel comfortable here. I'm hoping for some answers from you."

"What should feel natural feels unnatural," he said.

"Yes. I get that," Lilia said. "However. I've called you here for a specific purpose, as I'm sure you know. So why don't we try to get down to business?"

He nodded.

"There's an inmate named George Szymanski, lying on a gurney just down the hall, a seventy-seven-year-old man who is no longer breathing, has no pulse, seems to be completely without vital life signs, and yet cannot be declared dead. You, I'm told, are his closest friend."

"Friendship is a relative term in here."

"You knew him as well as anyone, let us say."

"I suppose."

He had lowered his gaze to the desktop, and seemed to be transfixed by her hands, staring at them so intensely that it made her self-conscious. She folded her hands together on the blank legal pad in front of her. "Upstairs, you didn't seem like the others," she said.

"You were hiding in the back of your cell, keeping to yourself, while the rest of your friends were behaving like complete animals."

"They don't get out much."

"And you do?"

"I'm not saying."

"What does that mean?"

"I'm not saying."

"I'm really at a loss to explain what's going on here, and I hate being at a loss," Lilia said. "According to people around here, you were his closest confidante. On top of that, you were the last person to talk to him. So rather than me grasping at straws, I'm wondering if you have any theories for me?"

"None that are credible."

"At this point, Mr. Pendridge, I'm ready to entertain the incredible. Give me something incredible."

"I wish I could. It's something I can't … share."

She stared hard into his eyes. He turned away.

"Are you messing with me?" she asked.

"No. I'm messed up. I like talking to you."

His lifted his eyes to her face.

"How long have you been locked up here?" she asked.

"Here? Three years. Nearly eleven years in prison so far."

"Eleven years." She said it with a certain sympathy.

"Too long, isn't it?" he said. "It's not surprising that I want to mess with you. To keep you talking, I mean. I can't help with your case but I'd sit here all day, if I could."

"Well, unfortunately, I don't have the luxury of time that you do."

"Oh, time's not a luxury here. Time has a whole other meaning."

"Yes, I guess it would," Lilia said. "I'm sorry if I've reminded you of that."

"It's okay. You don't have to be sorry, although it's nice to hear you say the word. It's been years since I heard someone say they were sorry."

Lilia took a long, hot shower. In the warm damp fog of the bathroom she shaved her legs, then rinsed off again, dried herself, and wrapped a big blue terrycloth housecoat around her warm body. She went to the kitchen and took some Thai take-out from the fridge, emptied the carton onto a plate, and tucked it in the microwave. It was vegetarian Phad Thai: since the incident a few days back when she'd inhaled the pork-like smell of poor Norbert Hoogstra laying burned in the ditch, she hadn't been able to face a meal with meat in it.

She was supposed to have gone out this evening, to a gallery opening with her friend Heather. She'd begged off. Sometimes it's too much effort to look right, she'd told her. Even in sleepy Spokane, population a quarter million, an event at an art gallery called for more than run-of-the-mill style—you were expected to pull off an artsy, hipster twist. Black tights, black boots, you'll be fine, Heather had said.

"I'm just not a Bohemian. I work as a public servant, Heather."

"Give yourself more credit, you're a Coroner, for God's sake. They make movies about people like you. You're very glamorous."

"From the outside, maybe, but not from in," she said. "It's hard—every case revolves around death, but when you show up you're always too late to prevent it. I'm really starting to think I'm better suited for nursing. You get to help people. Save people. Bring them back to health."

She had spent much of her time the last three days at Providence Holy Family Hospital, the city's largest. Normally she'd expect to be down in the morgue with the corpses, but this case was different, it had gotten her up out of the basement and onto a private ward, among doctors and nurses who devote their effort to rescuing the living, not puzzling over the lost. She owed her change of scenery to the strange case of George Syzmanski, the prison inmate and medical curiosity she'd admitted to hospital. In the three days since she had first examined him, George still showed no sign of a pulse, no sign of brain activity, had not been observed to draw a single breath. Yet somehow he continued to exhibit not the slightest sign of decay or any other physical transformation associated with death. Most strikingly, his blood had not given in to gravity, had not pooled in the lower extremities, as one would expect when the heart stops pumping. A series of thorough tests and state-of-the-art MRI and CAT scans showed a body indistinguishable from a living specimen.

This phenomenon had drawn some of the best medical minds to the scene, first locally, and now, as word spread, attracting the interest of neurologists and pathologists across the country. Lilia had grown extremely protective of George, and had come to think of him as *her* patient, before anyone else's. Today her boss, the Chief Medical Examiner, had ordered her to leave the hospital and return to her regular duties, and she had felt something close to heartbreak over it. "I'm having to face the fact that what I like about this case is there is *hope*," she told Heather over the phone. "There's a chance he'll suddenly snap out of whatever this strange stasis is that grips him, and he'll come back to join the living. I'm more of a rescuer than I realized. I miss that in my job. I'm sick of arriving too late. I thought I'd get used to it, get jaded about it, but instead it's affecting me more and more."

"That's why you need to go out, look at some paintings, sip some wine," Heather cajoled her. "As I remember, last time we went to one of these affairs you spent the evening flirting with some handsome, mysterious guy in a well-cut leather jacket."

"And a ring on his finger."

"God. You are depressed. If you change your mind text me. I could swing by and get you. I could even phone you if it turns out to be fabulous."

"Then I'd have to be dressed and ready."

"Just throw on some clothes and screw it. That's bohemian, isn't it?"

"Nah. Blizzard and I are staying in."

Blizzard was her cat, a pure white Persian. After Lilia had sated herself on phad Thai and Blizzard had licked the bowl clean, the two of them headed to bed. A couple of weeks back when she was sick with the flu, she'd dragged her television from the living room to the bedroom. "That's a dangerous precedent," Heather had said when she'd come over and seen it. "You're crossing the line from couch potato to bed potato." But Lilia wasn't really a couch potato, she seldom turned the tube on. She turned her attention to the pile of books haphazardly arranged on her bedside table. An Annie Dillard lay on top, half read. She picked it up, found her place, and settled in.

On the bed beside her Blizzard let out a low moan. Then the cat suddenly jumped up and went rigid, hyper-alert. "What is it, Blizzy?" Lilia murmured. Out of the corner of her eye, through the French doors, she caught a glimpse of something in the living room, a glimmer, as if an image were being projected. It looked holographic, three dimensional, faint and translucent at first. A seated figure slowly materialized. A man. He opened his eyes and seemed to be uncertain. He stood up, and looked through the glass panes of the doors at her.

"What do you want?" she called out. Then she recognized him—the prisoner Travis Pendridge.

Sitting cross-legged in his cell, Travis began the song-like cycle of incantations that George had taught him. "*The mantra can be written, the meaning cannot be guessed, the faith cannot be shaken, in the one you love the best.*" It was his charm, his talisman, his special code; he had the intention of visiting his daughter Nellie, and it brought him quickly into the ether, to the golden cord. But suddenly there was something unfamiliar in the flight path. He felt as if he were looking from the window of a speeding commuter train and not recognizing any of the stations. Suddenly he felt himself descending, pushed and prodded like a toddler made to prove he can walk. Warily he felt himself materialize into his body abroad.

He was in a place he'd never been before.

A strange apartment, modern, clean, and well furnished. An off-white couch flanked by matching arm chairs in a spacious living room, with drawn shades covering large windows. One wall had a pair of French doors, mostly glass. Behind the glass narrow blinds with their horizontal strips open revealed a queen bed with a huge white comforter heaped like a cumulous cloud. A cat jumped from the bed, leaving a woman, holding a book, looking at him wide-eyed in amazement.

He knew her. The coroner.

"What do you want?" she asked.

"I'm—I'm not sure," he said. "I didn't come here on purpose."

"Then go. Get out of here."

"All right. I will. I'm not supposed to be here. I'll leave."

She got up from the bed and moved quickly to the glass doors. A lock clicked quietly.

"How did you get in here?" she asked through the glass.

"Same way I'm going to leave," he said. "Give me a few minutes." He sat down on the carpet and tried to focus his bewildered mind, but couldn't. He had followed the exact incantations and techniques that had always taken him to his daughter. *The one you love the best.* Now there was a complication. He'd been pulled here, into this woman's life. Into her private place.

He knew she had affected him during their brief meeting at the prison. He'd stared too long at her hands as a way of avoiding looking into her face. He found her beautiful, and he'd thought of her often in the three days since. In fact he'd thought of her almost constantly. But *love the best*? He felt her eyes on him as he tried to will himself back into the ether. He was glad she wasn't screaming blue murder, or calling 911. Or pulling a gun from a bedside table.

"I'll leave you," he insisted. "I'm trying to get away, as quickly as I can." But it was impossible for him to concentrate with her eyes on him, making him self-conscious, preventing him from disappearing into his mind, from losing himself in the rhythms of the incantations needed to lift him from this unfamiliar place.

"Don't look at me," he said.

"What?"

"I'll leave peacefully, don't worry. But I have to meditate into a kind of trance, before I can disappear. And I'm having trouble meditating, with you staring at me."

"Is that how you got here?"

"Yes."

They locked eyes for a moment.

"That makes no sense," she said.

"What's the alternative? I escaped from prison, snuck miles across town without being noticed, got into your building, and now your apartment, just to sit down and meditate here on your wall-to-wall."

"I should check online and see if there's been an escape."

"If you want. There's been no escape. Now I'm going to shut up. Let me meditate, and I promise I'll leave. Don't stare at me, it's *throwing* me."

"I'll turn the blinds," she said. The slats gradually shuttered to a blank white, first one door, then the other. Now they couldn't see each other. He looked at the blinds and thought she might be peeking at him through the little holes where the strings run through the slats.

"I should be reporting this," he heard her say. "I should be calling 911."

"Don't. Things are happening that are beyond my control right now. I'm begging you to keep this to yourself."

"How can I possibly do that? You're in my *home*."

"By accident! Let me leave. And don't tell anyone—you'll look like a fool if you do, because I'll be back in jail and no one will believe you."

She was silent for a moment. Then she raised the blinds so they could see each other. "Is this about George Syzmanski? Is this connected to him, somehow?"

"Yes. How is George?"

"Oh, he's the same. Dead yet not dead. He's being well tended to. For the moment I'm more interested in you. Explain to me how you are here."

He paused a moment. "I'm going to take a chance with you. I really have no choice but to trust you, now. I've left my body behind in prison, my body proper as it's called, and I came here in this body, my body abroad. So back in my cell I'm sitting cross-legged on the bed, looking for all the world like I'm at one with the universe. But in fact I'm at *two*, one is there, and one is here with you."

"Now you're getting less easy to believe."

"I know. You know too much now. There are only three people in the world who know about this: George, me, and my daughter. Make it four—there's a guy in jail named Colquitz who knows too much. You're number five. I need you to be on my side, because if you're not, everything will go to shit. Can I trust you?"

"If you have such amazing powers, what are you doing in jail?"

"Good question. George is no longer there, obviously. He left his body behind, and I was supposed to kill it, dead. But I couldn't bring myself to do it. And that's why you have him now."

Lilia shuddered. "It's too creepy," she said.

"I'm not dangerous or anything like that. I was taking a trip, an astral journey, you could call it, to visit my daughter. For some reason I touched down in this place instead of her place. I can explain everything, except for why I landed here, of all places, and not where I wanted to go. I wanted to see my daughter. Really."

"All I know is, you should leave now."

"Let me try."

Travis sat on the thick carpet, closed his eyes, and tried to steady his mind. It was unsettling, knowing she was watching through the glass. A worry hovered in the back of his mind—that he was losing his touch without George around to guide him, to keep him on the right path. He did his best to relax, and gradually, finally, to his great relief, he was aloft, disappearing back into the ether, into the Terrulian Grid, and on his way back to Easy C.

Blizzard accepted Travis before Lilia did. The second time he showed up at Lilia's place the cat was all over him, even before he had fully materialized, nuzzling against his legs and purring a playful welcome. Lilia watched from a safer distance. This time she could see he hadn't jimmied the door, or broken in through a window, but had in fact appeared out of thin air. Seeing is believing, especially when you see the unbelievable. This time she did not hide behind the French doors.

Travis rubbed Blizzard's belly. "Good evening," he said, with a faint, uncertain smile. He surveyed the room, as if looking for a conversation starter. "White cat, white couch. You seem very fond of white."

"Not exactly. I didn't choose Blizzy here—taking her was charity, for a friend who moved overseas. And then I saw the couch on sale incredibly cheap, because no one in their right mind wants white furniture. But I did—it hides all her hair." She spoke casually, as if he were just some friend who had dropped by in a normal way, and he was grateful to her for that. She said, "Excuse me a minute, I'm going to change." She was wearing a sky-blue terrycloth bathrobe, and got up and went to the bedroom. He felt a flicker of worry that she might phone someone from there, but decided he needed to trust her. In a moment she returned wearing a t-shirt and yoga pants, with the bathrobe over it. Double-layered, she sat on the far end of the couch and tucked the bathrobe over her knees. On the floor Travis was getting cat hair all over his prison orange, and looking into Blizzard's intense purple eyes. He could feel Lilia's eyes on him, but didn't meet them. He let her study him.

"How's George?" he asked.

"The same. I'm not looking after him like I was. I'm no longer central to the case, the high fliers of neurology have taken over—I'm just a backwater coroner with a nursing degree. Is that why you came here? To ask about George?"

"No, actually. I wanted to bring you this." He pulled out a slender notebook from under his prison shirt and held it out to her. She made no effort to take it, so he set it on the floor beside him. "It's a diary. I don't think it's safe for me to keep it in jail anymore. Remember I told you about Colquitz?"

"Remind me."

"He's in the cell next to mine. I caught him reading it today. I had to fucking fight him for it, excuse my language. It was quite the scrap. He knows way too much."

"And now I'll know too much."

"I trust you."

She considered this a moment. "I've done a lot of thinking about you," she said. "I'm a coroner, as you know—I'm very grounded in cause and effect. Everything happens for a reason. But this is different. This is beyond reason. It's like the occult—"

"I don't consider it occult," Travis said. "However bizarre it is, there's a real-world explanation."

"Well then explain it to me."

"I can't. I just know it works. It's like computers. I know it's all ones and zeros, but I couldn't begin to explain to you how that means you can stream a video. This diary will tell you pretty much everything I know. It's all there, except the chants. The chants aren't in English. They have to be learned aurally."

"Why give the book to me?"

"I'm not sure. In the ether, when I'm between my two bodies, emotions can have tremendous force. I'm just learning that. I seem to be pulled here, almost against my will."

"You're here against your will?"

"Against my better judgment, maybe."

She stood up abruptly. "Would you like some coffee?"

He was surprised, and pleased, that she seemed to accept him. "Tea, actually. Coffee in jail has turned me off it for life. I'll help you make it. That'll be a thrill for me—first time in years."

He followed her to the kitchen. While the kettle boiled she told him there might be some ginger snaps in a lower cupboard, and he got down on his hands and knees to dig around for them. It gave him a close-up view of her feet and calves, which he thought were perfectly proportioned. She caught him lingering too long, his eyes soaking up the sight of her. "Dear diary: A strange man appeared out of nowhere in my home, and now he's fixated on my feet," she said.

He loved her for that.

"Your toes are very cute," he said. He turned back to looking for the ginger snaps. "Here they are."

When they were settled back in the living room, she said, "This is all too weird. It almost feels normal that you're here, and yet it has the potential to get very unsettling and creepy. If you turn out to be a stalker or something, then it's doubly creepy, because you can appear anywhere, anytime, through locked doors and windows. You can just zoom in on that mental magic carpet of yours."

"That's true. You have to trust I'm a gentleman."

"I don't even know you!"

"I'm a Pisces," he said.

"Oh, that helps."

"And what are you?"

"Gemini."

"Pisces-Gemini. All we need is Linda Goodman to see if we're compatible."

"How would you know about Linda Goodman?" she asked.

"I read it once. I did have a life before prison."

"I know. I checked up on you, after your last visit."

"I could have saved you the trouble. It's all in the diary," he said.

"I know what happened. I went the courthouse and photocopied documents."

"You have them here?"

"Yep."

"Can I see them?"

She brought him some files, and he sat on the couch, flipping through them, looking for one in particular. There it was, almost the last. A witness statement from Alison Pendridge, handwritten from her hospital bed.

> *"Whatever Travis did he did out of love. He grew the medicine out of love. He defended his child out of love. I'm leaving this world very soon, I know. It could be days or hours it feels like... I don't have the strength to tell the whole story. They dragged me from my sickbed, they drove me before them like an animal down the hard wooden stairs. I wish I could have been stronger. I wish I hadn't fallen so easily. I wish I could have spared him seeing that. Seeing how they treated me. He is a good man. It was a terrible accident. It was a terrible way to end. Tell him I love him, and I'll always understand."*

An addendum at the bottom of the page, in a different hand, read: *She died seventeen hours later.*

Travis set the paper down on the couch. A lonely tear showed itself at the corner of his eye. He smudged it away and stood.

"I should go," he said.

Lilia came close to him, close enough that if he wanted to reach out to her he could take her in his arms and she would console him. She was offering that to him. He took it. It felt good to hold her close. He looked into her eyes afterward and he could tell that she had accepted him. That she felt something for him.

Words don't matter—nothing was said in words—it started with a movement of her body, the way she turned to face him. It was a little later by the kitchen sink, when they'd brought their empty cups there, and he was rinsing them out. He was telling her again how good it felt to do something so domestic, so cozy, after eleven years deprived of small pleasures. He'd squeezed out way too much dish soap for a couple of plates and cups, and as she stood next to him at the sink she reached out to skim some soap suds from the underside of his arm, lightly brushing his wet skin. Her neck showed itself as she lifted her face toward his, a little gesture of acceptance, and willingness, and invitation. He felt trusted.

He leaned to kiss her. From there, no turning back. Lovely kisses.

"Eager boy," she said, mockingly.

"More than eager. Eleven years. Horny doesn't begin to describe it."

"Horny—that's a horrible word anyway. Sounds like teenagers."

"How about aching? Hungering? Lusting?"

"Down boy. I get the picture."

They kissed in the kitchen for a long time. Her lips felt to him as tender as little pillows. She led him to her bed. They shed their clothes, and she was beautiful in her flesh. Two bodies hot and eager, and she lay back to take him, took hold of his cock with those fingers he had found to be so beautiful and delicate to look upon the very first time they'd met, and she rubbed a little button of oozing pre-cum around the head—

And he lost it. He came in great gasping spasms all over her hand. She milked him, his body curved like a dolphin leaping from the sea, his pleasure sweet and strong as torture, coming in her grasp, until it was over, and he made her loosen her grip, telling her to go easy, it's over, I'm spent, and thinking, let me subside into the empty calm that comes after, let me finish, and become myself again.

"Didn't mean to explode like that." He wanted to laugh—it would have been funny if he hadn't felt so stupid and it didn't now need wiping up.

"Quite the gusher," she smiled.

"Sorry."

"No, it's fine. Just means we can take it slower now, knowing you won't be in such a rush." She reached for some tissues on the bedside table and mopped her hand, and wrist, and up her forearm, and got more from the box to dab his belly.

A little bit later they did take it slower. And she was right—this time it was tender and fine. She gave him her body as a gift.

C H A P T E R   **5**

The next night when Travis returned, Blizzard again picked up on his arrival first, mewling and yowling long before Lilia had any sense of his presence. The cat sat in the middle of the carpet and rubbed herself happily against him when to Lilia he was still little more than a translucent apparition. When at last he became whole, she said, somewhat coolly, "There you are. I was getting anxious. I couldn't get settled."

"There was a cell search on the block. Took forever. I couldn't leave till it was done."

"I felt like I was just waiting."

"Now I'm home," he said.

"Very funny. I need to talk to you."

"Sounds ominous."

"Not ominous, but serious. Important, to me. What happened last night is—well, it's very, extremely, out of character for me to do that with someone I just met. I felt swept away—like you had some tremendous energy, like an aura emanating from you, as if maybe you picked up some special power from the cosmos on your way here. I don't know how to describe it. I've read your diary. It sounds amazing and intense and life-changing to be able to travel up in the stars like that—and some of that energy clings to you when you're here. It was super intense and it sucked me right in."

"You're regretting it?"

"Yes! I mean, Jesus Christ, Travis—I made love to a convict who magically appeared in my bedroom. Does that sound in any way normal? Does that sound like a *thing*? I mean, what was I thinking?"

"We got caught up in the moment," he said.

"Obviously. In all that intensity I had a moment of weakness. Seeing you cry over your wife, it touched me. I felt like I needed to comfort you—and it just snowballed from there, and got out of control." She was trying not to cry.

"It wasn't so bad," he said.

"I like to be in control."

"Fine," he said. He was at a loss.

"What do you mean, fine? You appear here out of nowhere, anytime you like, and that's fine?"

"You want me to make an appointment?"

She wiped at the wetness in her eyes, and said, "We need to back up. We need to start from square one."

"Okay," he said. They looked at each other. "You want me to go first, or you go first?"

She smiled but then looked serious. "There's no one I can talk to, you know."

"Me."

"You know what I mean. I haven't told anyone."

"Tell me."

"I have feelings for you, obviously. But this is so weird, the circumstances are so bizarre. Not something I would have chosen. I'm very picky."

"You picked me. Not exactly a catch."

"I didn't pick you. You picked me. You penetrated my defenses."

"You could still kick me out. I'd go."

"We're past that," she said.

She'd been standing over him the whole time. Now she sat on the couch. He got up from the floor and sat on it too, at a distance from her. They were quiet for a moment.

"What was your wife like?" she asked out of the blue.

"Don't ask that."

"Sorry. I can't help it. I'm curious."

"It's not something I'd like to talk about, just now. I'm really happy to be here, I'm so glad I met you, I just don't want to be dragged to an unhappy place. I'll always be unhappy, thinking of how it ended. I never said a proper goodbye to her."

"I am sorry," she said.

"You can ask me anything else."

"Aren't you curious about me?" she said. "You hardly know anything about me."

"I do."

"Like what?"

"Like, I bet you were a jock in high school."

"How do you know that?"

"You're very fit, and athletic-looking. So I just figure."

"That's not knowing, that's surmising. But you're right—I was captain of my high school volleyball team, and we made it to state finals. I wasn't the best player, but I was a good motivator, and leader, and I got a scholarship to college out of it. Once I was there all the girls were awesome athletes—they had skills and reflexes I could only dream of, and they didn't need motivation and leadership from me. So. That was the end of that." She looked him in the eye. "Now let me ask you something," she said.

"Fire away."

"What is your goal in life?"

He laughed out loud. "I guess the same as every prisoner. Survive my sentence with my sanity intact."

"You seem sane enough."

"I'm damaged. I know it."

"How?"

"I can't define it. But I'll have post-traumatic stress when I get out, I'm sure."

They were quiet for a moment. Blizzard jumped up and settled on his lap. He nuzzled her behind the ears and cooed baby talk to her.

"But what are your long term goals, now that you would seem to have more options?"

"I don't know. But what I do know—I remember this from being married—is that when a woman asks you a question like that, she wants you to ask her the same question back."

"Sneaky," she replied.

"So tell me."

"Well. My long term goals. Like all thoroughly modern women I got my career in gear first, because that's what we're supposed to do. I've got where I wanted to, and now I find I'm not that thrilled with it, with being a coroner. I might go back to nursing. That's kind of a decision to be made in the short term. Long term, the other part of my life? I'd like to be married."

"Happily married, you mean. Marriages can be good, or not. They can go either way."

"Right. Happily married. I'd obviously have to feel no doubt it was the right person."

"These days you can be with the right person without marrying them."

"Maybe. But marriage proves something, I think," she said. "It proves the man isn't just acting, that he's sincere. A man could live with a woman because he can't figure out something better. But he wouldn't get married insincerely. I hope not."

"So a woman wants marriage to prove the romance has been genuine, and not a waste of time?"

"In a way. Then there's kids."

"You don't have to be married to have kids either."

"Yes you do. Realistically. Marriage anchors it. It lets one parent stay home, if that's what it takes. I'd want to be a stay-at-home Mom until they're school-age—otherwise they're getting all their values from their peers, the savage little tribe at day care."

She moved close enough to him on the couch that she could pet Blizzard on his lap. He rubbed the back of her hand tenderly.

Then a strange feeling came over him.

It started as a tingling, a restlessness, and he felt his skin crawl. He felt constrained, as if he were being pinned down by some malevolent power.

"I've got to go." He could barely choke out the words.

"You've got to go? Why?"

The sensation of restriction grew stronger, sucking the air out of his lungs. He was suffocating. A tightness around his rib cage felt like tentacles pulling him under. "Just let me—let me concentrate."

"What? Because we're talking about—"

"It's got nothing to do with that! Let me concentrate!"

He dumped Blizzard from his lap and let himself slide from the couch to the floor. He felt an intense need to get away, to get back into the ether, and tried desperately to hurry into the essential trance. It was not easy with Lilia's eyes burning holes through him.

"I tell you I have feelings for you, we have our first real talk, and suddenly you just have to go," she muttered.

"It's not like that."

He shut his eyes tightly. Not even a goodbye. A struggle to start the journey. An urgency. Up into the ether, a tangle of power lines, the golden cord trampled and indistinct, like a muddy path on a battlefield. But he found it, and followed it, and felt a burden weighing him down, like a soldier carrying a wounded comrade from the front. Overburdened and frightened, he willed his way onto the grid, and followed the golden cord back home. He saw the prison, Easy C, his cell, his body proper waiting on the bed, and dropped down into it, exhausted.

He was not alone.

Emerging out of his trance, and back into focus, he felt a stranger's head on his chest, foreign arms wrapped around his body.

Colquitz.

Travis struggled to twist himself free, Enraged and repulsed, he brought his hands up to gouge at Colquitz's eyes.

"Don't hurt me! Don't hurt me!" Colquitz pleaded. "Travis! The guards. They'll hear us!" He fell back onto his haunches against the wall, and brought his open palms up in a defensive posture. "Easy, boy. Easy," he muttered softly. Travis let his mind clear. Colquitz rubbed at an eye where Travis had gouged him. He swore a blue streak, softly, in the dim silence of the cell block.

"What the fuck are you doing in here?" Travis demanded.

"Trying to hitchhike," Colquitz answered. He looked awestruck. "That was amazing! I almost made it! You didn't know I was there! That woman. The coroner! I was starting to feel it, the room, her couch, her cat, I could smell her cat—I could smell her!—fuck man, I almost made it—"

Travis knew it was true. He had felt gripped by the choke hold of a strange power he now knew to be Colquitz. The thought of it made him furious.

"I should kill you right now—"

"Please, Travis, don't be angry. I just wanted to know what it is you know, go where it is you go. I didn't know it was going to be a private affair like that. You love her! I felt that! I didn't mean to interrupt. I'm out of here. I'm out of here!"

He fell to his hands and knees and slid along the floor to the cell door, and ever so gently slid it open. In the silence the ears of the other inmates pricked up, heads cocking like ferrets. Travis's cell door should have been locked. Colquitz slithered quickly out into the corridor, and pulled the door to his cell open, then shut it behind him. "Fucking bastard," Travis hissed at him. He couldn't figure out how two cell doors could be left unlocked. Colquitz must have an in with a guard, Travis thought, but there was no way to know for sure. He took small solace in the knowledge that Colquitz still needed to piggyback out of jail, and wasn't capable of bilocating on his own. He told himself that from now on he would have to be more careful, more attentive, and be on the lookout for an unwanted stowaway.

C H A P T E R   6

The next morning in TV room, while Travis sat staring vacantly at the Price is Right, Colquitz came and leaned by his ear, muttering contrite bullshit. Travis swatted at him to make him back off. "Don't ever come near me like that, motherfucker," he growled. "And wipe the smirk from your fucking face."

"Don't be angry with me, Travis. This isn't about you at all," Colquitz said. "This is about sharing knowledge. The late great Swami George was kind enough to share his esoteric art with you. All I want is a share too."

"You're not getting anything from me."

"Not willingly, no. But pretty soon, my friend, I'm hoping to progress to a point where I won't actually need you." A fault line of nervous energy twitched across Colquitz's face. "I read your diary, remember? There were some tasty tidbits in there, for sure, my man. Thanks for those. Swami George had a book, too—he was writing it for you, remember? He threw it in my face and it burst into flames, remember? He thought that was the end of it. But he was wrong, Travis. I did more than sneak a peek at the thing before he destroyed it—I was copying out all those meditations and ancient incantations as best I could. I know more than you think, and I'm getting close, Travis! I know exactly what George was pulling to get himself out of here. I know he's in another body somewhere on the outside. It was in his book!"

"You're crazy."

"Yeah, I'm crazy. I piggybacked you last night, I rode on out of here with you, saw the power lines and the swaddling grid connecting everyone with everyone. I rode along in the wake of your own golden cord. The Terrulian Grid, I know all about! And I've had a taste now, I've glimpsed the life outside. Next time I'm going to take a big ol' crazy bite right out of it!"

"Stay crazy," Travis said.

"Why can't you help me out?"

"Because you don't deserve to be out there, Colquitz. You're the last person who deserves to be out there."

"You can't say that," he spat. "You don't know the first thing about me."

"Don't I? I know you killed an innocent girl for no greater sin than she giggled at your shriveled little dick."

"Who told you that?" His voice took on a dark edge.

"I think his name was Wallace. Ring any bells?"

"Wallace," he repeated. His eyes narrowed to slits. "He's the reason I'm in this hole."

"No. You're the reason. You killed a girl."

"Yeah, and then Wallace ratted me out. Once I do get out of here—and I will, I promise you that—I've got one clear-cut fucking goal in life—to end his."

PART III

Nellie was thrilled to have her boyfriend back.

He'd driven down late that afternoon, and put his suitcase in the spare bedroom, and then they had eaten dinner with Grandma and Grandpa, and Jerrid had behaved in precisely the right way for the occasion—he'd been civil and articulate and ate extra helpings, and carried his dishes to the kitchen over Grandma's protests. Then he and Nellie made their exit and headed to the beach, to connect with their friends around a driftwood fire encircled by guitars, surfers, and barefoot girls dancing in the sand. There was a keg of beer, lots of vodka coolers, the smell of reefer, and talk of mushrooms, although no one offered Nellie or Jerrid any. He would have been willing if they had. He already felt high—back in his old hood, but away from family, drinking but not drunk, ready for something new to happen, high on the promise of a starry August night.

Nellie took his hand and led him away from the fire to a cooler, more intimate place, out of sight among the undulating dunes. They kissed. Her skin felt cool on the exposed surface of her bare arms, but warm beneath her clothes.

"I have a surprise for you," she whispered.

"I have a surprise for *you*." He pulled her against him so she could feel his hardness.

"That's not a surprise. That's totally normal for you."

"Are you going to use your hand?"

"That wouldn't be a surprise." She had done it before sometimes to give him pleasure, but that was as far as they had gone. She had felt a strange, thrilling power over him in those moments when he surrendered to his release.

"Your mouth?"

"More than that."

"More?"

"I'm going to let you do it."

He let out a low purr of delight and pulled her against him, kissing her lips, face and neck.

She giggled, pulled free, and said, "Not here, silly. Not in the dirt—"

"It's not dirt, it's sand—"

"We don't even have like a blanket or anything. You'll get sand all over your thing, and then it'll get sand all up inside me, and totally not feel nice," she insisted. "The first time should be nice, like a memory to cherish. I want to be cozy in a nice big bed. Let's go home, we'll do it in my room there. You can sneak from your room into mine, and that's how we'll do it for the very first time."

"Your grandparents, sleeping right next door—what if they wake up?"

"We'll do it quietly. Slow and gentle is the best way at first, from what I've heard."

"The bed's gonna creak like hell. Remember we were rolling around on it? I thought the damn thing was about to break."

"We'll have to do it super soft."

She giggled and felt her body tingle, a minor tremor that hinted at some ecstatic sexual spasm. She was all nerves and excitement.

"Let's go get it done," he said eagerly.

As they crossed the low dunes in the moonlight, and made their way toward the car, she said, "You know what else about my bed?"

"What?"

"I was conceived in it."

"*What?*"

"My Dad told me I was conceived in that bed. When he and my Mom were staying at my Grandma and Grandpa's, before they were married. I was the little accident that made them get officially hooked up for life."

"I don't even want to think about my parents having sex," Jerrid said.

"That's different," she said. "You live with your parents. I never knew my mom, really, I just barely remember her. I just have photos to look at. She looks young and beautiful in them, so to me she'll always be young and beautiful."

"My mom just got Botox," Jerrid said.

"Yuck!"

"All the little wrinkles around her eyes got erased. But the rest of her looks the same old saggy way, so what's the point?"

"Too bad people couldn't just stay preserved at the perfect age.

Like, twenty-two maybe. That's kind of like my mom. She's preserved in photos, at sixteen, eighteen, twenty-two, then there's nothing after twenty-four. My Dad's been telling me lots about her—"

"Don't start on the Dad thing," Jerrid said. It was a sore point between them, the only one. Her dad flying out of prison at night? It was too weird. He didn't buy it.

She dropped it. This was not a night to pick a fight.

Twelve thirty at night. The house was dark, but as they made their way up the driveway two spotlights, tripped by a motion detector, bathed them in a mercilessly bright halogen-white glow, like the cold blinding light of God driving Adam and Eve from the Garden. Jerrid shielded his eyes and swore, and Nellie shushed him. By the door she fished around for a key in a potted plant.

"When we get inside, I'm going to go to the bathroom, and then I'm going to go to my room and slip into bed," she whispered to him. "I want you to wait in your room until you hear me finish up. Then I want you to strip off your clothes. Wrap a towel around you and tiptoe down the hall to my room."

"I have to strip? What's up with that?"

"I don't want you dumping your clothes in my room, in case there's some interruption from Granny or Grandpa. I don't want any evidence."

"*I'll* be the evidence," he protested. "Clothes will have nothing to do with it."

"Just do it my way. I've thought it all through. The less I have to worry about, the better."

She kissed him playfully on the mouth, put a finger over his lips to cut short any further comment, and started up the stairs in the near-dark. Jerrid followed obediently, excited and a little apprehensive. Nellie believed him to be sexually experienced, but at eighteen he was, in fact, a virgin. Early in their relationship he had lied to her about that, and claimed to have had sex with not just one, but two other girls in the months before he'd met Nellie. He'd wanted to seem more worldly than he actually was; he had invented a swagger that had no substance. Now he worried that he should have come clean, that his clumsiness and uncertainty in the act would reveal him for what he was. Not just a virgin, a liar too.

At the top of the stairs they parted; he went to his room, and she went to the bathroom. She inspected her face in the mirror, and smiled slyly at her own image. She was pleased with the way she looked, giddy and thrilled and horny as hell. It was finally going to happen.

She made her way to her bedroom. The window was open a crack, and she closed it against the sea breeze. Quickly she stripped off her jeans and top, and slipped under the covers. She was still wearing her bra and panties. It would be more fun to have Jerrid take them off. Somehow she felt it wouldn't be right to be completely naked and waiting, it would be too final, and she couldn't be sure yet—a last-second change of heart was a possibility she hadn't ruled out. She could still back out of the whole deal if it didn't feel right.

The room was lit by a single bedside lamp. From the drawer below it she pulled out a single condom in its little plastic pouch. Jerrid likely hadn't even thought of being prepared. She would take pleasure in giving him a whispered lecture on the subject of sexual responsibility, and how it should fall equally to both partners. She would make him promise to take it seriously.

She tucked the condom under her pillow and lay back under the covers. She thought about lighting a candle for added romantic atmosphere, and climbed out of bed to look for matches, but couldn't see any on the dresser or bedside table. The bedside lamp would have to do. Or maybe just the streetlight and moonlight through the gauzy curtain. She climbed into bed and turned out the light, listening for Jerrid, waiting for the door to slip open. After a moment, as her eyes adjusted, the moonlight seemed to fill the room.

In the colorless light, she noticed a hazy figure start to appear. She knew instantly what it was, and who. The meditating posture, the prison clothes. He was sitting with his back to her. She pulled the covers up around her shoulders and called out. "Daddy!" But he hadn't completely arrived yet. She waited and tried again. "Dad! Go away!"

His image grew sharper, and then the moment arrived, that moment when for certain he existed in the room, in her presence. He was smiling, until he saw the unwelcoming scowl on her face.

"Get out of here, stupid!"

"What is it?"

"It's Jerrid, that's what! My boyfriend's here and he's going to be coming in here any minute."

"Oh. Shit. It's Thursday. I forgot. But what the hell. I thought you wanted me to meet him, eventually."

"Not right now!"

There was a thump in the hall, like a body falling.

"That must be him. Go!"

"I can't go that fast. I have to meditate. You know that."

"Then meditate."

He tried. It was hard to relax into it, what with his daughter glaring at him. He was making small progress when a soft discreet knock at the door brought him back fully into the room, in to his body abroad, and then the door opened. A teenage boy stuck his head in, and then his body, naked except for a small towel held at the waist. In the moonlight he saw Travis, and looked utterly confused.

"Jerrid. Hi. I'm Nellie's Dad."

"Oh. Really?"

Travis felt bad for the kid. Must have been quite a shock.

"Now do you believe me?" Nellie asked.

"Uh. Yeah."

"Jerrid, can you go wait in your room for a minute?" Nellie asked. "Dad dropped by totally unannounced, and he's *just* leaving."

"Uh. Okay."

He retreated out the door, closing it softly behind him. In the next moment there was a loud thumping noise that sounded like a body falling to the floor.

"Great!" Nellie muttered. "Now he's tripped over something, and probably woken up Grandma and Grandpa. Get out of here!"

"What are you wearing under there?"

"None of your business. Now get lost!"

"All right, all right. I'm going. You have the right to your privacy. But you better be safe."

"We had that discussion. Don't you think I've thought of that?"

"Did you get on the pill? You should get on the pill."

"I've got protection!" she hissed.

"I'm gone."

"Good. Sorry. Bye."

CHAPTER 2

Jerrid had followed the script precisely. He'd stripped naked and wrapped a white towel around his waist. He'd opened the bedroom door and listened to the sounds of the house. The ticking of a clock. A faint hum of the refrigerator downstairs. He'd stepped out into the hall, and tiptoed to Nellie's door. As he'd opened it he caught the sound of a male voice speaking softly. He'd stuck his head in and found himself looking into the eyes of Nellie's dad. Fucking unbelievable. She'd been telling the truth.

They'd exchanged awkward greetings, and then it was a relief to be excused from the room, and told to step back into the hall. He padded barefoot back toward his room, and was reaching out to push the half-open door. He never saw what hit him.

In the hallway Colquitz crash-landed. The trip had been as wild as any from his acid-eating, drug-bingeing misspent youth. He was dazed and rattled, yet dazzled by his own power, his own self-reliance—he'd meditated in his own cell, linked himself to Travis through iron bars and concrete walls. He had been pulled through a bizarre cosmic soup, along lines of immense power, like jet plumes crisscrossing the heavens, carrying him over the weighty earth below, overwhelming him with strange glimpses into deep and shallow lives, corks bobbing on cresting whitecaps that were not waves but the surface of life itself, and ahead, in this unreality, he could make out his unwitting guide, Travis the Good, Travis the too fucking Good for his own Good, leading him on, pulling him to this place. What was this place? Not the coroner's apartment he had glimpsed last time, that trip had been a short hop compared to this one. He had expected to find himself in some radiant mystical Sun Palace, suitable terminus for a trip along such a golden path. Instead, he had come back to earth in a house. He was lying on a narrow runner of a carpet. Had he fallen there? He remembered a thump. He felt the side of his head and found a painful lump.

He rose unsteadily to his feet. He could hear faint voices through a door. It sounded like Travis, talking with a girl. He moved closer to the door, but couldn't make out the words. There was tension in what was being said, though. Shrill whispers on the part of the girl, or woman, he couldn't tell. He thought he heard her say goodbye, and then there was silence. What to do? Wait a minute. Maybe Travis has left. Maybe that's his girlfriend, another one. Fucker's getting it from that coroner chick, why not more than one? Listen. He put his ear right up against the door. No sound at all. Travis has left? Wait. Be sure. You're out, you're free, he told himself. Don't be in a hurry.

He forced himself to listen to this voice. It was part of a thoroughly practiced protocol he'd thought out for himself. You can't imagine where you'll end up, so be prepared for anything. Don't act on intuition, gather as much information as you can.

A door opened and a young man stepped out into the hall, wrapped in a white towel, like an athlete headed for the showers. It was dark, and Colquitz could barely make him out in the gloom. He stepped back into the shadow and the boy walked right past without seeing him. He went to the door where Travis and the girl were, knocked softly, then opened it. Colquitz could hear Travis's voice, then the girl's. The boy stepped back into the hall, closed the door gently, and retreated toward his room.

Colquitz came out of the shadows and grabbed the boy by the throat, pulling one arm tight around his neck, the other gripping him by the hair, and shoving him quickly through the half-open door of his room. Jerrid was no match for the fighting skills of the older man. In the scuffle his towel had fallen off. On some level he was more worried and self-conscious about his nakedness than with being manhandled by an unknown intruder.

In the bedroom Colquitz spun the boy around to face him, wrapping him in a crushing bear hug, pinning his arms to his sides. Face to face like that their foreheads touched, and he could feel the boy's fright.

"Get ready for an adventure," he muttered softly. "And hang on to me for the ride."

So much for his protocols. He was a creature of impulse, and in the lightning-quick instant when he'd reached out and taken this young man hostage he had effectively thrown all caution to the wind. He was going to go for it, all in one shot. This was a gift from the Gods—this kid was perfect. The full plan, to emulate Swami George, to eventually inhabit another body, someone young and healthy, would be attempted right here, right now.

He concentrated his mind on the rhythmic chants he had learned by heart. His body rocked with convulsive tremors. The boy had gone limp in his arms, as if he had fainted. Colquitz felt an odd lifting sensation, a great God-like force granting him buoyancy, so that his mind and body floated skyward. Then the great power lines pulled him and his cargo together, and he felt two minds, touching inwardly and outwardly, pulled up and into the celestial power grid, cigarette smoke sucked into a giant's mouth, then expelled into the sky. This is easy, he thought, I'm not doing any work at all, just being carried back to where I belong, the trip homeward like the rebound of a rubber band returning to a state of rest. He knew this was Travis's route, he was just free-riding on Travis's golden cord, rising out of the house and above the world in a perfect undeviating line all the way back to the prison, and down into the cell block like a welcoming celestial yellow brick road, no need to blaze a trail, just follow this perfectly safe, power-packed path. No detours, no confusion, no mistakes.

He felt as if he had always known this process existed, had always been ready to tap into it, from the first time he'd seen old Swami George blissed out on his prison bed. He had never felt so euphoric, as he came down back into the prison, and he could see Travis's body proper at peace in his cell, and his own body proper likewise waiting for his own return. He had successfully brought the boy with him; they hovered a moment in the ether like hummingbirds of light, and then Colquitz made a sudden, clumsy descent into his own body, and felt again doubt at his incomplete knowledge and skill. The boy was only half formed, resisting in his body abroad, wanting to go home. Through sheer will Colquitz pulled him into the world again, into his cell on Wing 3, into Easy C. Colquitz in his prison garb was back in his body proper, clutching a naked, trembling teenage boy. The kid wasn't putting up any kind of struggle. Colquitz clutched a hand around his neck, and held him at arm's length. Jerrid made soft choking noises and his eyes overflowed with terror. Colquitz loosened his grip slightly.

"Let go of me," Jerrid managed to say. "I'll give you anything."

"Shut up, you little shit. You're my guinea pig. Part one has gone off without a hitch—get ready for part two."

He tightened his grip on the boy's throat and looked him in the eye. He chanted a series of incantations and felt his body fall into a synchronized rhythmic dance, and felt Jerrid match it, and join it, until they were like the pistons turning in an engine. Colquitz felt an unspeakable elation, felt the two of them transported, momentarily merged and blended yet still defined as separate minds, and knew the transfer was working. There was a sudden explosion in his mind, and then it was over, and he was looking into the same frightened teenage eyes, but now they stared out from his face, his body, the body he had lived in for forty-three years, the body he had inhabited until seconds ago.

He noticed that the world had lost the blurred edges that for so many years he'd accepted as normal. His new eyesight was sharper than he'd ever known. A bonus of his new teenage body.

"I'm going to do you a favor," he said to his former self. It felt like talking to a mirror. "Your name is Colquitz now. Randall Colquitz."

"My name is Jerrid," was the answer. "I didn't do anything and I shouldn't be here. I don't know why I'm here." His eyes went wide with fright. "And why are you *me?*"

Colquitz hit him square in the face. It felt good. This young body was agile and strong, and could throw a punch. He saw his former self take the blow, his hands coming up way too late to prevent the fist from making crushing contact with the cartilage of his nose. The snap was audible.

The kid in the older body saw stars, and stinging tears filled his eyes. Blood flowed from a nostril, trickling down over his lip. He brought a hand to his mouth and looked in horror at the crimson that coated his fingers.

"I'm not going to hurt you anymore," Colquitz said soothingly. Jerrid watched himself speaking, and grew more confused.

"Let me go," he pleaded. Someone a few cells down muttered a sleepy protest at the noise. The cell block fell quiet again.

"I'm leaving you now, but I'll be watching," said Colquitz. "Jerrid, listen to me. Like I told you before, your name is Colquitz now. Randall Colquitz. Keep your mouth shut and eyes lowered, and with good behavior you'll be out of here in nine years."

Jerrid started to say something but Colquitz threatened him with a fist. "No more noise now, or I'll come back and kick your ass."

He sat his youthful new body down on the bed, and began to meditate.

Jerrid wiped the blood from his face with his shirt sleeve and watched himself, his former self, his body, his rightful body, sitting cross-legged and naked on the bed. The body began to lose definition—it took on an opaque, ephemeral transparency, and then it seemed to evaporate, until there was nothing left to see. It was gone. He was alone in the cell.

For a few minutes he just sat on the bed, nursing his aching nose. He lay back to stop the blood flow. When it subsided he sat up again and rinsed his hands in the tiny sink above the toilet. In the stainless steel mirror, a face looked back at him. It horrified him. It was the face of the man that had dragged him here. How was that possible? He wiped the blood from his nose and mouth, and licked it off his fingers. Then he went to the door of his cell, gripped the bars tightly in his fists, and began to sob. He looked down the dimly lit corridor, seeing in each direction nothing but a long series of cell doors.

In the gloom he called out, "My name is Jerrid Grierson and I've never done anything bad in my life! And I shouldn't be in here!"

He waited for an answer, but none came.

"Excuse me? Excuse me! Anybody? Is there guards or something? Can I see a guard? I need to talk to someone. Something's happened!"

From the other cells came sleepy grumbles. Someone muttered, "Colquitz, shut the fuck up."

He repeated it again: "My name is Jerrid, and I shouldn't be in here! Guard! Please, can I have a guard!"

The whole of Easy C began to stir into waking, a chorus of curses telling him to shut his mouth. He did for a moment, but then started back up, shouting out his name and his bizarre predicament. He tried pounding the bars and then kicking at them, but the heavy iron absorbed the sounds, reducing them to ineffectual pitter-pat. He started to cry, but caught himself, and wiped his tears, then shouted out with new vigor.

"I'm Jerrid fucking Grierson, I just finished high school and I'm registered at UW for pre-med sciences starting in September, my mother is Bonnie and my Dad is Carl, my girlfriend is Nellie and my car is a Honda Civic which my Dad just gave me for getting into the pre-med program. I'm supposed to be in Oceanside, Oregon, visiting my girlfriend and now I'm here and I don't know how or why!"

There was a deep rumble as heavy doors unbolted.

"It's Colquitz, shut him up."

"Cold-cock that motherfucker."

"Colquitz, shut the fuck up."

Heavy footsteps came down the hall, and two men in uniforms faced him through the bars of his cell door.

"I shouldn't be here," he said, trying to sound calm and reasonable. "I don't know who you are or why I'm here—"

The cell door slid open, allowing one of the guards to step forward. He wore a helmet and some kind of padded vest. "What's the deal? We've been good to you lately, Colquitz," he said in a low voice. "Keep your end of the bargain."

"I don't know what you're talking about," said the terrified boy. "I'm in the wrong body, somehow. My name is Jerrid Grierson—"

The guard's arm came up and Jerrid saw a black truncheon in a blur, crashing down on his skull just above the ear. He felt himself falling and brought his hands up to protect his face. "Stop!" he screamed.

"You shut up, we stop."

"I'm shutting up. I'm shutting up!" The single blow had made him see strobes of black and white, feel a pain so intense he thought he would lose consciousness. The beating had stopped, but not the pain. The pain would last a long, long time.

CHAPTER 3

Travis remembered how, once upon a time in another world, Nellie used to stampede across the carpet to greet him in a prolonged, luxurious hug. That was eleven years ago. Now she was about to give herself up to some boy. He didn't want to think about it.

He felt stung. He'd told her he hoped Jerrid was a decent, trustworthy kid. Yes, yes, yes, she'd replied impatiently, and under her annoyed gaze he'd focused, chanted his incantations, ascended back into the Terrulian Grid, and headed to Lilia's place.

She wasn't home. Depressing. There was only Blizzard, the pure white cat, and a note on the kitchen table:

Travis. Make yourself comfortable. I'm on call, got a call, had to go. I'm hoping I find a note from you when I get home. This is what I do not like—I can't even call you or connect with you to figure out what's up. Totally dependent on your whims as to when I get to see you. Which I hope is soon.

Lilia

He wrote he was sorry on the bottom of the note, and hung around and played with the cat—it felt fun and therapeutic after eleven years in a cell. Rejected by his daughter, stranded by his lover, what's a man to do? He turned on the television, and fell asleep on the couch, the first time he had ever slept in his body abroad. It was dreamless and deep. He woke with a start at four-thirty and headed back to prison for cell check at five.

He came into his body proper, feeling the senses reactivate as always in strict order. Smell first—the smell of sweat and toilets, of the eighty men who live in Easy C's cramped cages. Next came hearing: the hum of florescent lights and snoring in the night. This time the sounds told him something out of the ordinary was going on. Dim shouts, then clear words: "Colquitz! Shut yer fucking mouth!" The voice of Colquitz sounding strange, lacking the usual menace and bullshit bravado: "I—I shouldn't be here. I don't know why I'm here or—" The other prisoners drowning him out.

Travis came fully into his body proper and found Easy C awake and restless. Next door he could hear Colquitz, sobbing softly. Across the hall, One Nut called out derisively, "Enough, Colquitz! One more word about fucking Jerrid, and I'll rip your arm off and beat you over the head with it. I've had it!"

Travis felt a cold flicker of dread run through him. He called out urgently though the bars of his cell door.

"One Nut! What's going on?"

"You heard me."

"But about Jerrid? What about Jerrid?"

"You slept through all that?"

"Yeah, I guess I did."

"He's gone off his motherfucking head. Squawking shit about how he's named Jerrid and he has a girlfriend and a hot car and this is all some horrible mistake and he's really a college boy—"

"Did he say the girlfriend's name?"

"Can't remember."

Travis called out, "Colquitz. Colquitz." There was no answer, just soft whimpering from the cell next door. He tried a new tack. "Jerrid, listen to me."

A timorous voice answered, "What?"

"What's your girlfriend's name?"

"Nellie."

Travis couldn't swallow. "What happened, Jerrid? Tell me what's going on."

"Are you going to hit me if I do?"

"No, I'm not going to hit you. I believe you."

"Travis! What the fuck? Don't encourage him," said One Nut.

"It's none of your business," Travis growled. "Jerrid, wait a minute. Give me a minute."

Travis sat back on his bed and, quickly as he could, left his body proper. As his body abroad took form in the cell next door he found Colquitz on the floor in the back corner with his knees against his chest. His face was bloody.

"Where's Jerrid?" Travis demanded.

"I'm Jerrid," was the whimpered response.

"Then where's Colquitz?"

"Gone somewhere. He's *me*!"

Across the hall One Nut looked back and forth from Travis's cell to Colquitz's. In one cell Travis was meditating on the bed, in the other he was standing over Colquitz.

"What the fuck is going on? There's two of you, Travis!"

"I'll explain it sometime. Now shut up."

"Doc! Jethro! Look at this! There's two of Travis, or else I'm losing my fucking mind!"

Travis grabbed Colquitz and pulled him to his feet. He stood behind him, using him as a shield to block One Nut's view. They were face to face.

"You're Nellie's Dad! I'm Jerrid! I met you tonight. You know me! You know I don't belong here!"

"Yes. That's right. I believe you," Travis said. One look into his eyes told him it was true. Colquitz's cutting glare had been replaced by the beseeching eyes of a timid kid.

"It all started when I met *you*!" Jerrid said. "You can get me out of here!"

"Shhh. Softly. Don't say anything." Travis peeked over his shoulder and saw One Nut straining against the bars of his cell, trying to make out what was going on. He ducked down out of sight again and said, "Whisper to me. Tell me what the hell happened to you, Jerrid?"

"No one in here believes me," Jerrid whimpered. "I told them my name is Jerrid Grierson and I'm eighteen years old and I've never done anything bad in my life, and I kept trying and trying to tell that to the people, and the guards came and hit me and it feels like my skull got broke." He brought his hands up to feel the soreness.

"Before that. How did you get here?"

"I'm—it was—there was a guy. He grabbed me, right after I saw you. In the hallway at Nellie's place some guy grabbed me by the neck in a headlock, and he dragged me back into my room, and all of a sudden we were flying through space together! It was fucking insane. I don't know what it was, but it was crazy, and it lasted I don't know how long. Maybe forever, or maybe just a minute." He went quiet, reliving it. "I could see people below. Like if I wanted to go into their brains I could've, I could've known every last thing about them! But there was no time. He was dragging me—we were following a golden thread of golden light. And it led us right down to here. He dragged me into this cell, and he held on to me, forehead to forehead, I don't know what he did, but then all of a sudden I was him, and he was me. I'm in his body, and he's in mine, and he's gone."

"Okay, Jerrid. Listen. You know I believe you. I'm telling you straight up though, no one else in this rat hole will buy a word of it, so don't waste your breath. Don't be begging. You understand me?"

He nodded uncertainly.

"I'm going to try to put things right," Travis said. "To do that I'm going to have to leave the prison. My body is sitting next door in my cell, in a kind of a trance, and I'm going to meditate from here and leave you, but that body next door will stay in the trance—fuck it, why am I explaining this to you? I'm telling you, Jerrid, the important thing is just keep your mouth shut, keep your eyes lowered, and answer to the name of Colquitz, and I'll be back as soon as I can sort this thing out. All right?"

"That's what the other guy told me, keep my eyes down and I'm Colquitz now," he muttered. His lower lip trembled and he bit at it to stop himself from crying.

"I'm coming back Jerrid," Travis said. I'm going to help you out. Now sit tight, and I'll straighten it out."

"What choice?" he asked. He started to sob softly, like a lonely child.

"None. Don't cry. Be a good boy." Travis found it strange to look at Colquitz's ugly mug and feel pity. "Don't linger in front of mirrors, kid. And don't lose hope. I could be gone awhile, but I will be back."

CHAPTER 4

Colquitz had repeated the incantations zealously, with an unwavering hunger, and immediately had felt himself lifted up, leaving his cell behind. He felt a strong pull like a homesickness, a longing, and was reminded that he was in a body abroad, not his own, but Jerrid's. He was being drawn back to reunification, to unity. The uplift to the Terrulian Grid came much easier than he expected. Then the body abroad was absorbed into the ether, and he was only a mindsoul.

The planet was beautiful in its complexity and connectedness. He was riding lines of unfathomable power and couldn't help but be awed. He saw cities and towns and tiny private moments in their millions, he saw everything and all of it made exquisite sense. This knowledge came to him as a feeling, an emotion, not a thought. Soon he saw the house near the beach where his a new body—the boy Jerrid's body—waited for him, like a suitcase ransacked and hollowed, lying splayed upon the bed. He aimed himself toward it as best he could, but it seemed that little was required of him, his mindsoul yearned for a home, yearned to be made real, and doggedly pulled him there. He felt himself lowered into that fine body, that naked frame, filling it with mind and soul, almost bursting with the pleasure of coming home.

Yes. Yes. I have done it! He wanted to shout it, to test out his new voice. But he subdued that instinct, and muttered instead to himself, Protocol, Protocol, Protocol. Place yourself in the context. Make yourself at ease. Fit in so you're not found out. These were all part of the check list of self-admonishments he had prepared himself to remember in this moment.

First things first. He was naked. He needed clothes. There were clothes scattered on the floor around the bed, and more in a duffel bag in the corner of the room. He picked up a pair of pants and began to pull them on, then stopped and looked in the bag for a pair of underwear. He slipped on a pair of boxers. Nice. He stopped short of his crotch to examine his new kit. Looked okay. Could be worse. He hesitated handling it, constrained by a sense of taboo, a sanction against touching an unfamiliar cock. It didn't look like the one he was used to. He prayed this one would work, not like his old tackle. This cock was all untested potential. He tucked it away. He pulled on the pants, felt keys in the pocket, and pulled them out. Some house keys, and one for a car. A Honda. Out the bedroom window, parked just down the street, he could see it. Nice-looking Civic, dark blue. The kid had yelled something about it back on Easy C. That was as he was leaving, when he was only half there. How did he remember that? Had he seen it in the ether? Not important now. That kid was a silly fucker, asking for a shit-kicking.

He pulled a sweatshirt from the pile of clothes on the floor. In the moonlight it looked blue or dark green. It slipped over his head easily.

"What are you doing?"

Startled, he turned to see a teenage girl in the doorway. She was wearing a light summer dressing gown, cut short across her thighs to reveal long, coltish legs. Stepping quickly inside, she closed the door gently behind her, and stood facing him, her arms folded unhappily across her chest.

"Well hello there," he said. Even in the gloom he could tell she was a pretty thing.

"Jerrid, what the fuck are you doing?"

"I'm getting dressed."

"Five minutes ago I poked my head in here and you were lying on that bed like a fucking zombie. Like in a coma. I couldn't wake you. And you were naked!"

"Uh huh."

"You're supposed to come back to my room. My Dad has gone, and he won't come back tonight."

"Well, what was he doing here in the first place?" Colquitz demanded. Another of his protocols: when you don't have a clue what to say, ask questions.

"I explained all that to you before," she said testily. "But you didn't want to believe me."

"I believe you now," Colquitz said, trying to sound gracious. Then he added, experimentally, "Darlin.'"

"Darlin'? You sound weird. Like an old man."

Something in the way he was staring at her made Nellie pull the dressing gown more tightly around her shoulders. He was leering.

"Are you coming to my bedroom or not?" she demanded.

"Not," he said. "I'm getting the fuck out of here. And you're coming with me."

"Why?"

"Because I have business to attend to."

"Do you know what night this is? Do you know what we're supposed to be doing right now?"

He didn't, exactly, but he had a pretty good idea. He said, "Let's do it somewhere else. Let's take a little road trip in my nice car. Let's make it memorable. You coming or not?"

"It's the middle of the frigging night, Jerrid. Can't we go in the morning?"

"No. I'm in a hurry," he insisted. He felt an antsy, jumpy eagerness to bolt, to get far away from here fast. He knew that once Travis was back on Easy C, it wouldn't take him long to figure out what had happened, and come looking for him.

"Come on, let's go," he said. He could see she was wavering. This is too fucking delicious, he thought. Not only do I get to evict Master Jerrid from his fine young bod, I get Pendridge's fucking daughter as a bonus. He'll be fucking insane over it! She'll come in handy, too, as a sidekick. A hot blonde on my arm will open all kinds of doors. Not to mention other things she can do for me. "Grab your stuff and let's go, gal."

"*Gal*? Since when did you call me gal?" she asked. "You are acting *so* weird. Where are we going and for how long?"

He caught an edge of excitement in her voice. She was up for an adventure. "It'll take us twelve hours of driving, at least. And once we get there, who knows what will happen? Get dressed. Pack light. We're going way up into the mountains. A little town called Hawks Nest. It's beautiful this time of year."

Travis was frantic to make connection with the grid, but he faltered, and the more he consciously *willed* himself to make it, the more he flailed in space like a severed power line, twisting out sparks. Stress was breeding more stress, until something George once told him came into his head: *Remember who is Master, who is Servant. The Lines do not serve you, you must serve the lines.* He made himself go soft, and supplicating. Asking, not begging. I give up: Please grant me the power. My urgency is not arrogance; I appreciate this miracle, more now than ever. I need to see my daughter. He repeated his mantras, letting them overwhelm thought, and began at last to sense the familiar feeling of weightlessness, of consciousness outside the body. He entered the ether, looked down from above the cell block, saw Jerrid in Colquitz's body, and heard One Nut across the hall, shouting, "Where the fuck did Travis go? There was two of him, and one just *vanished!*"

He rose higher, saw the guards in their safe room, ignoring One Nut in favor of a card game. He connected into the grid, the golden cord waiting to carry him like a trusty chariot of pure thought. No diversion, no hesitation now, he was all purpose and focus. He knew where he needed to go.

He came back into his body abroad in Nellie's bedroom, his childhood room. It was empty. There were signs of hasty packing—drawers open, clothes and lipstick and toiletries scattered on the bed. Nellie was gone. Colquitz was gone.

From downstairs came noises, the sound of voices. He tread softly down and peeked into the kitchen, expecting to see Nellie and Colquitz, but instead saw his parents, up early. It was the first time he had seen them in eleven years without a glass partition between. He knew his Dad had taken a disability pension, after a serious fall shattered his hip, but he was not prepared for how frail he looked. An artificial hip had repaired him, but not restored him—he needed to hold the edge of the kitchen counter for balance as he watched his wife make coffee. He was speaking to her adamantly, emphatically, but the force of the words were undercut by a rasp in his voice, the tremor of the aged. "I wouldn't say this behavior is completely out of character, when you consider how she's been acting lately," he was saying. "That crowd she's been hanging around with, it's as if they've all gone weird and anti-social together in some mass teenage psychosis! They think the world is just a giant playpen and they have no duty to anyone but to amuse themselves in it. To just up and run off in the middle of the night like that! That's not the values we tried to put into that girl's mind."

"We taught her best we could," his mother replied. He stepped away into the shadow of the dining room, uncertain whether to show himself to them. "She's received her values from somewhere else. They all do now."

"Let's not start blaming others," his Dad said wearily.

"I'm blaming the internet. And TV and texting and all those things we have no control over and come across as old and tired and useless compared to. Do you think we should phone the police?"

"What for? They'll laugh at us. A sixteen-year-old girl runs off with her eighteen-year-old boyfriend? Cops have more pressing concerns than tracking high school romances."

"Maybe she'll walk through that door in a couple of hours, and tell us the two of them just took off to watch the sunrise, and now they're eager to tuck into a plate full of bacon and eggs. I'll tell her I love her—after I give her a good piece of my mind."

"You can tell her that when she calls, which will probably be soon. Maybe Jerrid wanted to get back to the city, and she went along for the ride."

"I hope so. But I have a terrible, sickly feeling," his mother said. At that moment Travis stepped into the kitchen.

"Good morning," he said softly.

A coffee cup fell out of his mother's hands and clattered against the floor, spinning on its side like a wonky top.

"Travis! Oh my God."

She rushed into his arms and hugged him.

"Mom. Mom. Dad. Don't get—it's alright. No one knows I'm here, and I can't explain exactly how it is that I'm here, except to say I haven't escaped from jail, I've figured out a way to be in jail and here at the same time. And I'm really worried about Nellie, I need to find her—"

His mother was crying. His Dad clutched even more firmly to the countertop. He looked shell-shocked. "We're worried too," he said. "She's run off with that boy of hers."

"Run off how? In a car?"

"Yes of course, in a car. His car."

"His car. What kind is it?"

"It's a Honda Civic," Dad said. "Dark blue."

"I saw them go," said his mother. "I heard them rustling around and got up to see what the commotion was, and they were just about to head downstairs with backpacks and bags. I said where are you going, and Jerrid said, 'Nowhere,' in a rather rude voice, which shocked me, because I'd never heard anything rude from that boy, not ever. And I said, 'Well you must be going somewhere,' and Nellie said, 'Apparently we're going to a place called Hawks Nest,' and Jerrid said to her with a real nasty growl, 'Shut up.' He used the f-word to curse at her, which was another shock, because I'd never heard that boy be anything but sweet."

"Hawks Nest," I said. "You're sure that's what he said?"

"That's what he said."

"Dad, I need to ask you something."

"Anything, son. You name it."

"Can I borrow the car?"

C H A P T E R **6**

The first light revealed the world beyond two beams of light and an infinite asphalt path. They saw the fields of the flat-lands, filled with August-tall corn, and grain turning from green to gold. Then they began to climb into forested, evergreen-clad foothills, and the weather turned foul. The blue light of dawn had hinted of brightness to come, but the sun never showed itself through a cloak of mordant gray clouds. By nine o'clock a cold wind swept rain against the car's windshield. Colquitz fiddled with the switches on the steering column to figure out the windshield wipers, cursing under his breath as the proper setting eluded him.

Nellie watched his face closely. The curl of his lip gave her a funny feeling. She couldn't remember ever seeing that expression on Jerrid's face. There was a meanness to it, an anger out of scale, too deep and dangerous for an everyday frustration like groping for a switch on a dashboard. She shivered slightly, but put that down to the change in weather. Because Jerrid's eyes were required to stay focused on the road ahead, she could study him carefully and at her leisure from the passenger seat. She realized she had no idea what he was thinking.

"What's with you, anyway?" she asked. "You keep muttering things."

"Nothing. And what's with this fucking music? What's this thing hooked up to the CD player?"

"That's your Nano, silly. Why are you acting so ignorant?"

"Huh. Nano. Like an Ipod-type thing? How many songs can it play?"

"I don't know. Why are you testing me? Thousands."

"Huh." He was silent a moment. "If you think about it, that's pretty fucking amazing, kiddo."

"What's amazing about it? It's normal."

"Ten years ago they didn't have them."

"Ten years ago I was six," she said. "And you were eight." She looked out the window at a derelict farmhouse, the roof bowed in the middle as if a giant had sat on it. "I do remember our old car when I was a little kid—in the CD all I ever wanted was Raffi over and over."

"Fuck Raffi. And fuck this noise. What is this shit?"

"It's not shit, Jerrid. This is your favorite. Kanye. I loaded it for you, in case you've forgotten."

"Not my favorite anymore," he spat. He glanced over at her. She looked distrustful. "Maybe I'm growing up," he suggested. "My tastes are growing more sophisticated as I mature. What I'd like is some ol' time country. We got any of that in here?"

"Ha! Very funny."

"I'm serious. Next truck stop I'm buying some decent shit to listen to."

"Jerrid—"

"And don't call me Jerrid. I hate that name. I've decided I want to change my name."

"Since when?"

"Since now."

"But Jerrid's so good," she protested. "I fell in love with you when you were Jerrid."

"You'll still be in love me."

"Not if it's like, Clyde, or Moe, or Jethro or something."

"Jethro. That's funny," he was silent a moment. "Deathrow Jethro. I used to know a guy called that. Dumb motherfucker. Huh."

"What the hell are you talking about?" Nellie exclaimed. "You're getting weirder and weirder."

"Call me Steve. I wanna be the good guy for once. Like Steve McQueen. He was good. When I was a little kid I watched Bullitt all the time, my dad had the video. I loved that movie. Steve. Yeah, call me Steve. That's all I'm asking, babe. Baby, babe? What do you want me to call you?"

"How about my name?"

"Which is?

"Don't be funny?"

"I'm gonna call you babe," he said. For a moment he took his eyes from the road to scrutinize her, and for the short flash of time that they locked eyes Nellie saw the strangest glimmer there. Something feral, wild, desperate, lurked in his eyes, and sent a stronger shiver through her.

"Where exactly is Hawks Nest?" she asked.

"Why?"

"I should phone my family. My Grandma will be worried sick. And my Grandpa will probably be totally disappointed in me." She took her cell phone from her handbag. "I'm sick of trying not to disappoint people. But I don't want my Grandma to be worried over nothing, either."

"Think she'll be worried enough to phone the cops about it?"

"I don't know. Maybe."

"Fuck 'em," Colquitz said. "You'll be back before they know it. Relax. We're on a road trip. We're fucking free as birds." Then he startled her with a sudden scream—earsplitting, unbridled, the lung-busting holler of a sunburned drunk in the ballgame bleachers. "I am finally fucking free!" he exclaimed. "You have no idea what that means, do you?"

"Don't shout like that," she answered. "You scare me."

"Don't tell me what to do, girl," he growled, his voice suddenly menacing. "Don't ever tell me."

"Jerrid—"

"It's Steve now!" In a sudden fury he slapped an open palm against the steering wheel. To Nellie it looked ridiculous—punching an inanimate object like that. But it was frightening too—it suggested he'd rather be slapping her face. The rain had stopped, but the windshield wipers were still making a dry, squealing sound like a hound with his tail stepped on. He turned them off. Nellie said nothing for a moment. When she spoke, the words came out with clarity and conviction.

"Jerrid, I'm not calling you Steve. I'm calling you Jerrid. You can either stop the car and let me out, or you can get used to being called by your real, actual fucking name."

Colquitz looked her over. She sat defiantly, staring back at him, with her arms crossed. Then he turned his attention back to the road.

"Round one to you, kid," he said. "Round one to you."

They pulled into a gas station that had a little country roadhouse attached to it. From the outside the place suited his tastes. It looked like a biker hangout. He checked the wallet in his back pocket for cash, but when he opened it his attention was drawn to the driver's license, visible through the plastic inner window. Jerrid Grierson. Lame name, but he was stuck with it. Eighteen years old. Other than that the wallet held one credit card, a bank debit card, and seventy-three dollars in cash. He worried the cards would leave a paper trail, so he decided to stick to cash. To get where they needed to go, gas was going to eat up a good chunk of that money. Screw buying some country CDs. They could wait.

The gas jockey was a pimply kid with freckled arms. "Nice wheels," he gushed. "But what's 'premed' mean?"

Colquitz looked blankly at the boy.

"Your license plate, dude," the kid pointed. "What's it mean?"

Colquitz glanced at the plate. PREMED. A vanity plate. He hadn't noticed it until now.

"Premeditated," he growled.

A few hours later, on the fringes of a town called Eldorado, Colquitz pulled the Civic off the highway at Grant's Gun and Tackle Shop, a single-story concrete bunker, surrounded on three sides by a puddle-dotted, unpaved parking lot. The drop in speed and the car's bumpy traversing of the lot woke Nellie, who'd been dozing.

"Where are we?" she asked sleepily, stretching her arms toward the windshield.

"Wait here."

Just inside the gun shop door a stuffed black bear reared up on its hind legs, snout open, its massive teeth bared in a terrifying growl. As an example of the art of taxidermy it was a work of the highest order, but Colquitz barely gave it a glance. He strode straight to the counter, which was made of heavy duty Plexiglas. On two shelves below were a collection of new and used handguns. He surveyed the lot intently, barely noticing the clerk who came over to serve him.

"I call this display case Handgun Heaven," the clerk drawled. He was dressed like a Mormon missionary in a short-sleeved white shirt and a subdued blue tie. "You won't find a better selection of pistols within eighty miles, I promise you."

Colquitz just grunted, and continued his fixated analysis of the choices at hand. After a suitable silence, the clerk asked gently, "Looking for anything in particular, son?" That last word brought Colquitz to attention, reminding him who he was now. He met the clerk's eyes, and knew there would be trouble ahead over proof of age. He heard the store's door open, triggering the bing-bong of an electronic bell, and turned and saw Nellie wandering in. He cleared his throat, put on his most charming smile, and turned back to the clerk.

"My name is Jerrid Grierson, and I'm looking to purchase a weapon from this vast and beautiful array of yours; it's for personal protection of home and castle, most especially the princess in the tower over there." Across the store Nellie was lingering over a display case of colorful feathered fishing flies. "I want her to sleep sweetly while I work the night shift," Colquitz continued. "I want my mind to rest easy, secure in the knowledge that she's in possession of satisfactory firepower, safely tucked underneath the pillow where she lays her sweet hair."

The clerk looked from Colquitz to Nellie and back again.

"How old are you two?"

"Don't you worry about that, I'm well above the limit required by law. Now show me something by way of a handgun, small and lightweight enough to be manipulated with ease by that sleepy girl's nimble fingers. These two over here look like they fit the bill."

The clerk opened a glass case and removed a couple of handguns of modest proportions. "I'm afraid I need to see some ID before we proceed any further," he said.

"Sure, I got ID," said Colquitz. He pulled his wallet from a back pocket, opened it, and dropped his driver's license, twirling it so that it spun a few times before coming to rest. He slapped his hand down to turn it the right way for the clerk to read.

"Says here you're eighteen," the clerk said, looking straight into the boy's eyes.

"And?"

"Gotta be twenty-one."

"God damn it, no way! You're telling me a person under twenty-one ain't even allowed to defend himself around here?"

"Sorry. Law's the law."

"Don't tell me about the law. I know all about the law." In a softer voice he said, "I know laws can be got around."

The clerk didn't say anything. Another store employee poked his head out of a back room to see what the fuss was about.

"Need some help?" he asked.

The clerk said, "No. I'm afraid we can't help this gentleman. I'm afraid he's underage."

Colquitz grabbed the license from the countertop. He spun around and marched to the door. The bing-bong sound kicked in again as he opened it. "Girl! Let's go!" he barked.

Nellie hesitated. The clerk in the shirt sleeves met her eyes, and she saw that he was sending her a warning. Be careful, girl.

"Let's go," Colquitz barked again.

＊

By two in the afternoon they stopped for lunch at a roadside truck stop. Colquitz was sullen and untalkative, and Nellie was quiet too, after a long restless night in the car. When they were done eating she went to the ladies room while he paid for the meal. At the cash he bought a pack of Marlboros and a lighter, a black one with a Harley Davidson crest on it. By the time she returned he was outside leaning against the car, lighting up.

"Oh my God," she exclaimed. "What are you doing? Since when did you smoke cigarettes?"

"You don't know me at all, do you?"

"I know you don't smoke. I know you've never smoked cigarettes in your life. You're the one who gags whenever there's tobacco in a joint. In case you've forgotten, you made me quit."

"So we've been smoking joints? You got any of that shit?"

"No."

He threw the pack of cigarettes toward her, and she caught it with two hands.

"Have one. Enjoy yourself."

She took one and brought it to her lips. He offered her a light, in the same instant inhaling a deep drag. As the smoke hit his lungs he began to cough violently, sputtering for breath. This made Nellie laugh.

"It's like you're in seventh grade or something."

When he'd finished wheezing and was able to speak, he said, "The mind is willing, but the body's not yet acclimatized to its new lifestyle, let's just say."

"I can't wait to see what you pull next," she said.

"Watch me."

Back on the highway, after about half an hour of driving, he took a sudden turn up a gravel side road. It was poorly graded and narrowed suddenly from two lanes to one. Scrub aspen grew right up to the edge of the road, and in places the low branches slapped against the side of the car.

"Where now?" Nellie asked.

"Your guess is as likely as mine," he said. "Mine is that someone lives up here."

Ten minutes later a series of small tracks splintered off from the road. Up a couple of them they could see trailers set back in the woods. They slowed at a lane that veered off to reveal an isolated double-wide trailer, set back from the road in a grove of tall pines. Colquitz turned the car and headed up the lane, a driveway of two rutted tire-tracks with grass growing between.

"This place looks good," he said.

"Looks like there's no one home."

"Exactly."

He climbed out of the car and she watched him hurry across the trailer's weathered wooden patio to a pair of sliding glass doors. He tested them. Locked. He peered through the window a minute. He came back and prowled around the car until he noticed a row of rocks arranged as a border along the edge of a neglected flower garden. He picked up a jagged stone the size of cantaloupe, approached the doors again, and hurled the rock.

In the car Nellie braced for the sharp shattering crash, saw the glass splinter and fall in jagged sheets, and watched Jerrid reach through the door to release the latch. He slid the door open carefully, and disappeared inside.

Nellie had never felt so alone, so far from safety. The keys were still in the ignition, the motor was running, and for a moment she thought she should just switch seats and drive away. They were supposed to be partners in an adventure. Everything was getting too crazy. Jerrid was getting totally crazy.

A wind had come up and was whipping the tree-tops wildly about. The crazed dance of their leafy branches did nothing to calm her. She made up her mind to get out and yell to Jerrid to get the hell out of there. He had no right to be smashing windows and trespassing into some stranger's lonely house, and she wasn't going to be an accomplice to that kind of shit. She glanced down to locate the switch to lower her window, and in that instant she heard him yell, "Score!" She looked up and saw him scampering quickly back across the patio and down to the car, waving something above his head, punching his arm in the air like a celebrating athlete.

A shotgun. In the other hand he held a box of shells, and a roll of duct tape. He put it all in the trunk and slammed it shut. When he opened the car door a blast of cool fresh air hit her. His face was flushed and triumphant, and he leaned across clumsily to try to kiss her.

"People are so fucking simple!" he crowed. "The underwear drawer. Every fucking important thing in the house is in the underwear drawer." Before he sat down he pulled a small handgun and a dozen bullets from his pocket. "You like it?"

He dropped the gun in her lap. She picked it up carefully.

"Don't worry, it's not loaded." He dropped the bullets in one of the car's drink holders and climbed into the driver's seat.

"And check this out!"

From his shirt pocket he produced a wad of bills held together by a thick blue rubber band.

"Where did you get that?"

"Where d'you think? Underwear drawer! The great unlocked safety deposit box of the dumb-ass American working poor."

"Why are you stealing?"

"Because we don't have any fucking money. Next question."

"Why the roll of tape?"

"Never know when you might need duct tape. Plus it was in the drawer too."

"Where are we going?"

"I have some business to take care of. An old score to settle. And once I do that, I'm gonna take you away somewhere and fuck your brains out, girly girl."

"Girly girl? What kind of bullshit is that? Jerrid—"

"Shut your fucking mouth," he shouted. He brought up a clenched fist, but seeing the fear it caused in her face, he caught himself and let the fingers loosen and fall to the steering wheel.

"Jesus, don't go postal on me," she said softly.

"Go postal? What the fuck does that mean?"

"You know."

"No I don't."

"You use it all the time. I probably learned it from you."

"Go postal," he said experimentally, weighing the phrase for meaning.

"Yeah. You know, like postal workers go nuts all the time, bring a gun to work and blast away at their bosses and everyone."

"You think I'd do that?" He laughed in a constricted way that sounded completely unnatural to her.

"It's just an expression," she said.

"Yeah, well. I promise I won't kill anyone. Unless they really fucking deserve it."

"That makes me feel a lot better."

He started the car, backed it to a turnaround, and they were under way again, back down the country lanes. Neither one of them said anything for a long time. When they were back on the main road he said out of the blue, "You're a fucking babe, know that?"

"Shut up."

"You're like all the girls I could never have in high school. The long-legged girls in cute dresses who studied art and music, and wrote poetry. All the dumb fucks like me got herded off to machine shop learning to cut sheet metal. It was a small town school, nothing else to do."

"You never took shop."

"Yeah I took shop."

"Shop was a pre-req for pre-med?"

"Pre-med? Oh, Pre-med! Yeah, whatever." Suddenly he laughed. "Surgery, sheet metal—sawing is sawing, right?"

He glanced over to see her looking at him like he was insane. "Pre-med," he said. "I love the license plate."

"No you don't. You hate it."

"Do I?"

"Your Dad chose it, and put it on when he gave you the car. And you were going to get rid of it as soon as you could afford it, because at college it would be, like, a total embarrassment."

"Yeah, there's that. Tell me more things I told you."

"Why?"

"Tell me why you like me."

"Why?"

"I want you to like me."

"The way you've been acting? You've gone psycho. You're scaring me."

"Okay. All right. I can understand that. But I promise, it's going to be different from here on in. I'll be able to relax a little. All the prereqs have been met now: I've got a decent weapon and serious coin. I've got a good car and a hottie riding shotgun. What more does a man need? I've even got a destination, and a plan. Everything's in place, so now I can relax. Let the plan unfold."

"And what is the plan?"

"You'll see. You'll love it. I got a little score to settle, is all."

After thirty miles the four lane highway narrowed to two as it entered the mountains. Travis was sticking close to the speed limit—not having a driver's license, he was worried about cops. He had a single credit card—his dad had lent it to him, along with a pair of jeans and a flannel shirt to take the place of his prison orange.

Hawks Nest. He had found it on a map in the glove compartment and was on his way. The car was a fifteen-year-old Ford Taurus, not exactly a muscle car. Colquitz and Nellie would need to be making plenty of pit stops and detours if he were to have any hope of catching them. He drove for hours, and as the miles slid past he began to feel at last that Nellie was close.

In the basin of a broad, forested valley he passed the turn-off to a pulp and paper mill, marked by a colossal billboard that said, "We use forests to make families grow." Some feeling like a premonition told him that Nellie had passed the same landmark only moments before. He would catch her soon, he was certain. Her closeness made him push the car to its limits. Around a downhill bend that doubled sharply back on itself he realized he was driving crazily, and forced himself to reduce speed. It didn't matter. A sweeping curve led down onto a long bridge over a river, and at the far end he could see the blue Civic that contained his daughter.

After two minutes he was right on their tail. Nellie looked to be asleep, resting her head on a bunched-up coat against the side window. The road reached the end of the valley and began a steep climb into the next range of hills. The Honda had better muscle going up the hill and had sped ahead two hundred yards by the time they reached a summit marked by an elevation sign and a pull-over for truckers to stop and check their brakes. On the downside of the summit the mountain fell away in a series of acute switchbacks. The Civic geared down to a near-crawl. When the road leveled and widened to allow for a passing lane, the car failed to pick up speed, and stayed in the slower, right hand lane. Travis could see Colquitz watching him in his rear-view mirror. Chances were good he'd been recognized. It seemed to him that Colquitz wanted him to pass, and that's what he wanted as well—to get ahead, cut him off, and make him stop.

Travis put the pedal to the floor and accelerated past. The Taurus at high speed had a slight pull to the right that he had to fight. As he came even with the Honda he glanced over to see Jerrid looking at him, and was surprised—for a moment he'd forgotten that it wouldn't be Colquitz's ugly mug he'd see, but a young kid.

The kid lowered his window as if he was going to shout something. Then he brought up a handgun and aimed it. Instinctively

Travis flinched back into his seat and contracted his neck into his chest. He braked, decelerated, heard a shot, felt the concussion of glass shatter his passenger window, heard the blare of an air horn, and saw the gleaming chrome grill of a huge semi-tractor truck barreling down on him. He turned the wheel sharp to avoid the collision, saw the edge of the road drop away to nothing but air, felt his stomach drop out, his body clench, and braced for impact.

C H A P T E R **9**

"Now you're going to have two on your hands," the deputy warden told Lilia over the phone. "Another inmate's gone into a coma just like the first."

"What's his name?" she asked. But she already knew.

"The one you talked to last time you were out. Travis Pendridge. He's sitting in that same yoga pose like Szymanski was, and no one can rouse him. Just like old George—no signs of life, but no signs of death neither."

"Take the body down to the morgue and lay him out just like you did George. I'll be there as quick as I can."

Forty minutes later in the shabby little room half full of dusty boxes of floor-cleaning fluid, she found Travis lying peacefully on a gurney, with no pulse and no breath. She had some understanding of what was happening—that he was absent from his body proper—but no guesses as to why he hadn't returned. A vague sense of foreboding stirred in her stomach, and she fought the urge to dwell on worst-case scenarios. She looked at his unstirring body and thought, I don't want to have to mourn you. She had half a mind to call an ambulance to come pick him up and have him admitted to the same hospital ward as George. Exhibit B, he'd be. But she hesitated, worried that if Travis was only temporarily absent from this body he wouldn't like it moved without his consent.

She lifted an eyelid and looked into a clear blue cornea, decorated around the vacant black pupil by flecks of hazel. The eyelid flickered of its own accord, and then the other eye opened. She let out a startled, involuntary scream.

The door opened and a guard stuck his head in the room. He saw her standing calmly by the body.

"What was that?" he asked.

"Nothing. I just pricked myself with a scalpel," she said. "It was a bit of a shock, but it didn't even break the skin." She put a hand on Travis's chest to keep him still. "You can go now." The guard hesitated. "Close the door behind you."

He did as told. She went to the door to see if she could lock it. No. When she turned back to Travis he was trying to sit up. "Lay back," she scolded him. "Jesus Christ, don't scare me like that."

"What?"

"Waking up when I'm not expecting it. You look white as a ghost. What happened?"

"I was in a car crash. Thank God for air bags."

"What is going on?"

"Lilia, it's all fucked up. Colquitz is out of jail—he's managed to bilocate out of here," Travis said. "His skill set is better than mine, seems like. He must've followed me to Nellie, right into the house without me even being aware of it." He told her about finding Jerrid in Colquitz's body on Easy C, and Jerrid's story of what had happened. "Switching bodies—there's no way I could pull that off. I mean, I have an inkling, but I really don't know how the fuck Colquitz did it."

"And where is he now?"

"That's the thing. He's with Nellie, in Jerrid's car. He convinced her to run off with him in the middle of the night. She must think he's Jerrid—I mean he *looks* like Jerrid, so why wouldn't she? But he's Colquitz. I'm hoping she'll figure that out—the guy just pulled a gun and shot at me, and drove me off the road. I'm hoping she saw it was me. Even if she didn't, the guy's firing guns at cars and shit, she's got to think he's gone completely psycho. Otherwise she's thinking the whole thing is some weird joyride."

"I'm sure she's got her guard up," Lilia said.

"I hope so. Meanwhile in jail there's Jerrid, a fucked-up kid trapped in an ugly pile of flesh everyone calls Colquitz. And Colquitz is free and easy on the outside in Jerrid's body. And I can't even catch them! Even if I could find them, I can't bilocate to a moving target!"

"Shhh. Speak softly. The guards are just outside."

"I'm an amateur, Lilia. George left me long before he'd given me the full knowledge. Likely George couldn't even bilocate to a high-speed target like that. So what could I do, except chase them in another car? So I went and borrowed my parent's car."

"How did you know where they went?"

"Nellie said the name of the place to my Dad as they were leaving. I had a pretty good hunch that's where they'd be going anyway—I figured Colquitz would be looking for payback. He's on his way to Hawks Nest, a town on the eastern slopes of the Rockies. There's a guy there named Wallace, who ratted him out, and Colquitz himself told me something—that his only ambition in life is to end Wallace's."

"People say those kinds of things. It doesn't mean they follow through."

"Colquitz is crazed enough to do it."

"How do you know Wallace is there?"

"I don't. But he's *from* there. And when people get out of jail they tend to gravitate back to where they have friends and family."

"Why didn't you just bilocate to Hawks Nest, and wait for Colquitz and Nellie to show up?"

"I don't want to wait. Colquitz is a killer. Nellie is my daughter. I can't be waiting. I can't stand it. But I can't bilocate into a moving car, and I can't just bilocate into a town—I need to show up like a real person, in a car, establish myself as having a right to be there. Or so I thought. And now I've wrecked the fucking car. Fuck!"

"Shhh! Keep it down."

"I need to reach Nellie. God knows what he has planned for her."

"Calm down! There must be something we can do."

"Right now I'm going to go look for George. I need some help. I should go tell my parents about the car, but that'll have to wait. George first. Then I'll come back here."

"Not here," Lilia said. "I'm going to transfer your body over to Providence Holy Family, right alongside George's. The experts can poke and prod you too, but at least that way you can stay out of your body proper as long as you need to."

He thought for a moment. "I guess that makes sense."

She heard voices in the hall, and pushed him back down on the gurney. He looked up into her eyes and said, "I feel like crying."

"Don't cry," she said. "There's a lot to do right now."

"You're a cool customer."

"Not really. There's a time and a place to fall to pieces."

"I'm glad I can trust you."

"Yeah, well. We'll talk about that when the dust settles. Let's keep our minds on what needs to be done."

"Right. Okay. You know what? Don't call the ambulance just yet. Let me go see George. He might have a strategy, or know something I don't about how to get Colquitz and Jerrid switched back where they belong."

Dylan Podnovski's hospital room in Tulsa, Oklahoma—under different circumstances Travis would've taken pride in the adroit way he scoped out his landing site and hit it. He came fully into his body abroad, and called out softly to the sleeping figure on the bed.

"George! I mean, Dylan."

No reaction. He nudged gently at a sheet-covered shoulder.

"Hey, I've come for a visit."

The patient rolled over—it wasn't Dylan, but rather an elderly woman who looked like death warmed over. She let out a soft scream, frail and birdlike. He put a hand over her mouth to make sure it didn't get any louder.

"Stop making noise! I'm not going to hurt you," he pleaded with her, doing his best to sound soothing and harmless. The old dear seemed frozen, until she suddenly flailed an arm free and knocked a metal meal tray clattering to the floor. Travis heard footsteps approaching down the hall. There was no time to meditate and bilocate.

A nurse poked her head in the room, and was very startled to see him. "What are you doing in here?" she barked.

"I'm looking for Geor—I mean Dylan. Dylan Podncvksi. Isn't this the right room?"

"Don't you read the news? He was discharged yesterday. He's gone home with his family."

"I do read the news. In fact I write for the papers. I was hoping for an interview."

"You're a journalist? I presume you have some ID?"

"Yeah, sure. Let's go out in the hall, where the light is better. Leave this poor woman to sleep. Sorry ma'am."

The old woman found her voice. "You scared me halfway into the grave, damn fool. What's next?" To the nurse she said, "Put his hand over my mouth like he was trying to suffocate me—"

"Now you're exaggerating," Travis said.

In the hall he pretended to fumble for his wallet.

"You don't look like a journalist," the nurse said. "What are you doing wandering around here in the middle of the night?"

Travis didn't answer. Suddenly he bolted. He sprinted down the hallway at lung-busting speed. He heard her yelling after him but kept going full tilt to the end of the ward, through a door and down four flights of stairs, where he tripped the emergency alarm on a door at ground level, and stumbled out into an unfamiliar town, down a street into a parking garage, down a ramp and into the farthest back corner out of sight, where it was dark and dank, and rank with the smell of urine. It was private, that's what mattered—a quiet place to sit and bilocate. After a couple of minutes to catch his breath and settle himself, he made the journey quickly back to the prison morgue.

Through the nebulous fog of reentry, as he slipped back into his body proper, he heard Lilia's voice. "I timed you. You were gone eight minutes," she said.

"George isn't there anymore. He's been discharged. I scared an old lady."

"Now what?"

"I don't know."

"All right. Lie down. I'm going to get you your ambulance now, and take you to Providence Holy Family."

"I guess. I'm so tired," he said. "George warned me often not to stay in the body abroad too long, said I need to build up stamina gradually. Now I don't have time for gradual improvement."

"If you're going to stay in your body proper, you'll need to stay really still while we transport you. Play dead, essentially."

He thought a moment. "No. I have to go to Hawks Nest."

"You're just going to show up?"

"I have no choice."

"Do you know anything about it? How big is it? Does it have hotels?"

"I don't know. It's got coal mines nearby. It must be fairly big."

"Be careful. Have a look, and come back and tell me what's going on," she said. "Maybe I can do something from this end."

"Yeah. Thank you." He leaned to kiss her on the cheek.

"Promise me you'll check in with me," she said.

"I promise. You're awesome."

"I'll be worried sick if you don't."

"I promise."

The shock of the gunshot rocked like an explosion in her skull, jolting Nellie from her sleep. She thought she heard a screech of tires from another car, but saw nothing ahead out the window but trees passing by in uncountable bunches. Then she saw Jerrid setting the handgun, barrel first, into the dashboard coffee holder. His power window slowly rose to the top, shutting out the sound of the wind and road, and making them alone again.

"I saw a deer, so I took a shot at it," he said.

"What?"

"I saw a deer. So I rolled down the window and tried out my new toy here. It's not bad. I probably only missed by ten yards. That's a joke. More like forty."

She knew he was lying. Something had happened but she didn't know what it was. She started to cry. She didn't care if Jerrid saw the tears, or what he thought of them, she just let them flow.

Jerrid said, "I wasn't really shooting at a deer. I just wanted to try the gun out, and I figured the best way to do it was in the middle of nowhere, while we're driving. If I stop somewhere to do it, someone might notice, but if we're driving, and it's just woods on either side, and there's no cars in sight, it's like a tree falling in the forest. Right?"

"Except me. I hear," she said. "Why didn't you warn me you were going to do that?"

"Because you'd have told me not to, and there'd be a big fight over it, and I don't want to fight with you. I told you I want you to like me."

"Right now, I don't."

"Fair enough. What would make you like me?"

"You can start by putting that away," she said, gesturing to the gun.

"Right. Ugly thing. Let's keep it under my seat."

"I'm going to phone my grandparents."

"Go ahead."

She rummaged through her bag for her cell phone, and couldn't find it.

"Have you seen my phone?"

"No. What's it look like?"

"You've seen it a million times." When she was sure it wasn't in the bag, she unclipped her seatbelt and looked all over and around her seat. Suddenly a thought hit her. "You took it! What did you do with it?"

"I didn't just shoot at the deer, I threw your phone at it."

"What the fuck? That's my *phone*, Jerrid."

"I'm joking. I never touched your fucking phone."

"Where's your phone then?" she said.

"I don't have one."

"Stop messing with me and let me use your phone, Jerrid."

"I don't have it. I must have left it back at the house."

"Great. Stop the car when we see a phone booth, so I can call Grandma. That'll be a first. I've ever used a phone booth in my life."

"Really? Huh. Watch out you don't turn into Superman. Or Supergirl, does she use a phone booth?"

She hugged herself against a sudden chill, and watched the forest slide past. Finally she said, "This is supposed to be an adventure we're on, we're supposed to be into it, into each other, like when lovers used to elope, in olden days. That's what I was expecting."

"You want it to be all, like, romantic. Is that the deal?"

"That's what I thought it was going to be! We'd go to some honeymoon-type place, and hide out, and be totally into each other, and share all kinds of new experiences and stuff, but instead I get you, pulling off onto some gravel road to nowhere, breaking and entering some stranger's house, and stealing money, and guns, and shooting for no reason out the car window, and throwing away my fucking phone."

Colquitz was silent for a minute. "Babe, I'm really sorry," he mumbled softly. "Except the phone part, which I swear I did not do. The rest, I'm going to start making it up to you. Really. I need you. I'm crazy about you."

"Say it without sounding so fake," she said.

They drove all day, through a landscape that had changed from heavy coastal rainforest to a drier, high alpine ranchland of Ponderosa pines. The road rose and fell, and the landscape transformed again by degrees to a nearly desert-like plateau of coppery orange rock outcrops and sagebrush. By evening they had climbed up through a series of high mountain passes. In several places construction crews were busy repairing damage to culverts caused by run-off from heavy rains a few days earlier. The deluge had brought down the last of the snow melt from the tallest peaks. The road in one spot had been reduced to a single lane and they were forced to stop, joining a long line-up of vehicles waiting on a steep grade. Colquitz climbed out, and the closing of the car door woke Nellie, who had spent much of the day fading in and out of a drowsy, dreamy state.

She watched him walk over to a ditch and relieve himself, completely unselfconsciously. Apparently he didn't care who might see him from the line of cars in front or the handful of cars that had already joined the line behind.

Just standing there pissing on the side of the road—she couldn't decide whether she was amused or embarrassed about it, and so couldn't make up her mind what to say when he returned to the car. She decided to be amused. She'd been too hard on his bizarreness. Just go with it, she thought. He was improving. He had let her phone her Grandma from a roadside restaurant, a call that turned out to be strained and weird. Grandma had started crying and saying they had been visited by her dad, who had just appeared in the house, and Dad had been very worried about her, and knew where she was heading, and was trying to catch up with her. "It's none of his business," she had shouted into the phone. The call had ended badly, Grandma warning her to be cautious, and she angrily insisting she was old enough to be out on her own. "And tell Daddy he better not show up at the totally wrong moment," she'd said, and then refused to explain to Grandma what she meant by that.

Jerrid had stood next to her, listening to the whole thing, at least her side of it. "You did good, kid," he'd said afterward. "And I'm not too worried about your dad."

He was on his way back from peeing in the ditch now, wearing a strange complicit smile on his lips, as he crossed in front of the car's blue hood, then climbed back into the driver's seat.

"Did your dinky get cold?"

"Ha. Did you get a good look?"

"I got a good look at the steam rising off the puddle you made."

"I've got a nice one," he said, and she laughed.

"What's funny about that?"

"Just the way you said it. Like a boy with a brand new toy."

"That's pretty close," he said playfully. "Have you had a good look at it before?"

"Jerrid. You know."

"Tell me. Tell me what you've done with it."

"I've stroked it. I've made it spurt."

"How often?"

"A few times. Special occasions only."

"Have you sucked it?"

"Jerrid! That's for later."

"Fucked it?"

"Shut up. But that could change, very soon."

He was silent a moment. With a strange, feigned, nonchalance, he asked, "So it works?"

"You are weird," she said.

He fidgeted restlessly with the settings of the car's air supply, before lighting up another Marlboro.

"You've gone from Mister No Means No to a chain smoker in half a day," she said.

"Pack a day habit. More if I'm stressed."

A big yellow backhoe roared past the long line of stopped cars. They watched the black wheels spin, and listened as the sound of it faded.

"Touch it," he said.

"What?"

"Touch it through my pants."

She gave him a slightly slutty, arch look, her best attempt at play-acting a vamp, then coyly reached over and ran a hand lightly up his thigh.

Colquitz was all attentiveness, waiting for a sign of arousal, of desire. He felt it. He felt his desire stirring, his new cock coming to life. Nellie felt it too, with her fingers she could feel it swelling, and lightly pinched the head through his cotton sweatpants.

"Feel good?" she whispered.

"Feels unbelievable," he sighed. "Feels like it's been forever."

Nellie moved her hand away. "Time to drive," she said, teasingly.

Up ahead a flag woman had turned her red stop sign around to show yellow, and the long line of cars and trucks began to creep forward over loose gravel in a single lane, past a washed out culvert.

"Touch it while I drive," Colquitz said.

"No. Too dangerous," she said. "You might lose control. You might put the car in the ditch."

"Please?"

"No."

"I'm going to get you for that."

After they had climbed up and over the summit the lee side of the mountain showed itself to be forested and lush. Night was falling. By the time they neared Hawks Nest it was dark, and the high hills and mountains, deep green by day, had taken on an impenetrable blackness. The starry night sky above the silhouetted hills looked blue by comparison. It was after midnight when Hawks Nest came into view. They had come over a mountain pass, and descended for some time before Colquitz pulled the car into a lookout on a high ridge. Below them the town presented a pretty picture, a merry twinkle of lights in the shadowed folds of an eighty-mile-long valley called the Skittiketch. Up the valley scattered patches of light marked the open pit coal mines.

Colquitz steered the Honda down into the valley floor, and as it reached town the highway became Main Street, deserted in these late hours. They passed a cluster of sad looking motels, and then a tavern called the Dead Duck Saloon. There were only a handful of vehicles in the parking lot, all of them big mud-splattered four-by-four pickup trucks.

"Looks pretty much the same as ever," Colquitz muttered. "I'm tempted to go in for a drink."

"They'll ID us," Nellie said.

"You can wait in the car."

"I'm not sitting out here in the dark. I thought we were getting a motel room."

"Yeah. You're right. Maybe the Duck can wait for another night. Before we turn in I'm just going to prowl the back streets a bit."

They turned off the main road and passed the neatly kept yards of miners' houses. Most of them were old shacks and cottages, built more than half a century ago, when the mines in the area were underground and wages were low. In the intervening decades union wages had steadily increased, and the houses had been tarted up with additions: some had car ports and huge garages with decks on top that equaled the floor space of the original homes; on others a second story jutted out of the roof line at an odd angle. To Nellie it was just an ugly little corner of an ugly looking town. But Colquitz took it all in hungrily. He had a history to apply to nearly every house, a friend or foe from his fierce, combative past to associate with each front door. The characters might have moved on, but the setting, the stage upon which the play of his life had been performed, was still there intact, and waiting for the next act to begin.

"This is why I've always been partial to small towns," he said. "It's not like the city, where they're constantly tearing shit down to put up new shit. Here there's continuity. It's too small to change much."

"What would you know about this place?" she asked.

"I grew up here, in a past life."

She watched a dog chained to the side of a house, big and part Rottweiler, jump out of the shadows and pad to his restraint's furthest reach, eyeing them with a cool malice, but not barking. "You think reincarnation is true?" she asked, and continued on without waiting for an answer. "I totally believe it could be. But what gets me about people who say they can remember all their past lives— they're always like, Joan of Arc or Alexander the Great, or Cleopatra, or someone huge in history like that. It's never some loser nobody with no connection to anyone you've ever heard of. Like, if you were reincarnated and you're just some housewife in this life, wouldn't it be more realistic if you were like the same thing in your past one? Or some sales clerk, or a peasant in Bolivia or something? Or is it some kind of continuum you're on, where you're improving each time out? Or can you go backward—"

"Can it," he muttered.

"What?"

"Can it. Shut up."

"You shut up."

"I shouldn't even have opened my mouth about a past life," he spat. "It's not like that."

"So what's it like then, Jerrid?"

"I used to live here. This town is small enough I used to know every fucker who lived here. Everyone who wanted coke, that's for sure. I used to deal coke in this town. That's how I made my money."

"What, when you were eleven or something?"

"Not when I was eleven. Are you in with me or not?"

"In with what?"

"I'm going to park you somewhere. For a few hours. Then we're going on a spree, you and me."

"Why can't we just go on the spree, why do I have to be parked? And what the hell is a spree, and what the hell does being parked mean anyway?"

"Parked means you can sit on your ass for a few hours in a motel room. Watch some Real Housewives of Wherever the Fuck and wait for me."

"You said you were done for the night, that we were going to turn in."

"I changed my mind. Some things are easier to do at night."

"Like what? Doing what?"

"Hunting."

"What the hell are you talking about?"

"Are you in with me or not?"

She was silent for a minute. "What's the choice? I don't have any choice."

"You're right about that."

"I don't want to be parked in a motel room. I want to know what you're up to, and go with you."

"You might not like what you see."

"I don't care. I'm not going to sit in some cheesy motel room watching TV, while you're out running around getting into all kinds of shit."

"Good. I like a girl who's loyal. And you'll come in handy anyway. Nothing opens doors like a teenage blonde."

"Whose doors?"

"We're going back to the Duck, and you're going to wait in the car. Give me ten minutes in there, then I'll tell you whose doors."

She sat in the car outside the Dirty Duck, and waited as ten minutes bled into twenty, and twenty into forty. Jerrid had left her the keys, so that she could start the engine and turn on the heat if she got cold, or listen to his Nano or experiment with the radio tuner. Strange stations hundreds of miles away faded briefly in and out.

Nothing lasted. Finally she found one that did, a local station on the AM dial. It was playing the lamest of country tunes, about a wife fed up with her two-timing husband. The singer was a woman with a tenor voice, deep and husky, and she repeated the chorus, *'True love behaves itself, it's not out running around with someone else,'* so many times that Nellie got annoyed by it and shut the radio off. In the silence she wondered what true love really was. A million crappy love songs on a million car radios are driving ribbons round the world right now, she thought. No one really has a clue about what love really is. It's emotions, not definitions. She had thought she loved Jerrid. Now she wasn't even sure she liked him. He'd left her alone in the parking lot of a seedy-looking bar in a strange mountain town, with the time ticking by well after midnight and no arrangement yet made for a bed to sleep in. She could write a country song about that. The chorus would be 'What the fuck is he *doin'* in there?' She started to sing that to herself, impatiently. It sounded more like punk.

A vehicle pulled up and parked two spaces away. It was another mighty pick-up truck, similar to the rest in the lot, ferrying three young coalminers, fresh off shift and hoping to catch last call. She looked at them as they piled out of the truck and they gave her plenty of attention back. She couldn't hear what they were saying but she knew what it was about. They were practically licking their lips. They all three walked toward her in the car, veering from the most direct route to the bar.

"Honey, open the door," one of them said. He had unkempt curly hair and three days growth of beard. His teeth were white and his smile friendly. "Come have a drink with us."

The other two hung back and exchanged remarks between them. What they said she couldn't make out. She didn't feel threatened. They seemed harmless, all three, mixing bravado and shyness like the boys she knew in high school. They attempted a few more lame remarks meant to coax her from her four-wheeled waiting room. She wouldn't roll down the window, but she did smile at them and let them look her over. One of them said, "You're too damn pretty to be sitting in the parking lot," and the curly headed one muttered, "You should be sitting on my face." They watched her for a reaction. She shook her head, as if to say, naughty boy. She felt her power, felt she was up to staring them down.

Curly head opened his arms wide and yelled cheerfully at her, "We tried! Last call, we gotta jet!"

They headed for the tavern. On an impulse Nellie rolled down her window and yelled after them, "Hey! If you see Jerrid in there, tell him I'm getting sick of waiting."

A few minutes later Colquitz came back to the car. His lips were clenched tight. The way he walked gave away he'd been drinking.

"You got looped, didn't you?" Nellie said.

"Did I have time? I don't think so."

"You're acting it."

"I used to be able to drink any fucker under the table. My mind can handle it, it's this body of mine. I didn't go in there to get looped, I went in there to gather information. This was recon. Did I tell you I was in the Marines once?"

"Past life again?"

"Past life. Fuckers kicked me out. Here's to the present." He pulled a pint of rye whisky from under his jacket, unscrewed the cap and took a hefty swig. He held the plastic bottle out to her, arching an eyebrow in expectation. On a whim she took it from him and put it to her lips.

"You sip it like a girl," he said.

"I am a girl. Hard liquor is not my thing."

"That's valid."

He backed the car out of the lot. They cruised the sleepy streets again.

"So did you get it?"

"Get what?"

"Your *information.*"

"Don't sass me. I did find what I needed to know, no thanks to you."

"Me? What did I do?"

"'*Jerrid*, you better get out to the parking lot before your girlfriend gets her panties in a knot.'"

"Well, I was sick of waiting."

"And you had to tell them my name was Jerrid, didn't you?"

"What's wrong with that?"

"Because I don't want people in this town knowing what my fucking name is. The less people know about us the better, you understand me? You're lucky I don't slap you silly right here and now. The only reason I don't is we're conspicuous enough as it is, I'm driving around Testosterone Town with a brand new fucking babe in the front seat beside me, and I'm thinking that the only way we could make even more of a spectacle out of ourselves is if you're battered and bruised."

"You're crossing a line, Jerrid," Nellie said.

"I crossed all the lines there are to cross, a long time back," Colquitz muttered. "Be a good girl and play along with my shit, would you? I told you before to call me Steve."

They were silent for a moment.

"I don't know anything about Steve McQueen, but I doubt he would ever tell a girl he'd slap her silly."

"True enough. Okay. I lost it for a minute there. Now I've got it back. I would never slap you. Ever."

They left behind the streetlamp-lit town, heading back out the same road they'd come in on. Now their headlights were two eyes peering out into pitch black. They made a sharp turn onto a long, narrow, single lane track. A path for each tire, short grass growing between. There was nothing to mark the turn. He had known exactly where it was, even in the darkness. "*Plus ca change*," he said.

"What?"

"Nothing. It's French. You didn't know I was educated, did you? It wasn't all sheet metal classes."

After five minutes the track split. They took the left fork and drove a hundred yards, past a dense stand of pine trees, until they came to a house, a split-level rancher with brown peeling paint. The place had seen better days. A couple of cars were parked to the side on a patch of gravel, and a couple more on what might have once been a lawn in front of the house. As they stepped from the car a dog began to bark in the darkness, and they could hear a metal chain scraping against a hollow metal pole.

"Once we're inside, say as little as possible," Colquitz said.

The door was opened by a fat man with a full red beard that

tumbled down to the top of his belly. Pulled low to his eyes he wore a black leather cap like soldiers' hats Nellie had seen in pictures from the Civil War. He peered at the two strangers through eyeglasses that were murky with dried flecks of dirt. "Uh huh," was all he said.

"Yeah, well, evening and all that. I think you're expecting us," Colquitz said.

"Uh huh."

"Guy at the bar told us this was where we could get some. He phoned. He used the pay phone. He said he was phoning you. And he told us how to get here."

"Nice that he's doing favors for you. What in the Christ is he doing favors for you *for*?"

"He didn't do it for me. He did it for *you*. You're the one making money. I'm the one spending money."

The big man just grunted, and let the door swing open. He crossed the carpet on bare feet, stepped around a kidney-shaped coffee table disfigured with cup rings, and deposited himself on a ramshackle couch, facing a huge television screen, which was showing slow motion shots of a big-breasted, jiggly-assed woman running along a tropical beach, and then the same woman kneeling in the shallow surf and splashing foamy sea water over her shoulders and bikini top, while a 1-888 number scrolled across the bottom of the screen. "Call Sabrina Now! Call Free!" it said. The sound was muted. A radio was playing loudly in the kitchen, tuned to a talk show about visitors from Outer Space.

"That's funny," Colquitz said, gesturing from the TV to Nellie. "Her name is Sabrina too."

"Nice to meet you," said the fat man. Nellie didn't say anything. He invited his guests to sit themselves down. Colquitz went to the couch, and Nellie sat in a plastic patio chair. A mangy kitten strolled in and began to rub against the bottom of her jeans.

"Careful Sabrina," the fat man said. "She's overloaded up with fleas."

Nellie listened as Jerrid made arrangements to buy cocaine. The fat man didn't even have to get up to get it, he just casually pulled a ziplock baggie from the crack between the couch arm and the cushion on which was parked his ample behind.

"So you were expecting us," she heard Jerrid say. Nellie watched the ritual of slicing and dicing the white powder on a mirrored glass tray, and listened to the two men talk of price and purity, of cutting agents and market forces. The fat man kept offering crystal meth, but Jerrid insisted he was a purist for coke. "You look young to be Old School," the fat man muttered. "I got ecstasy too." She watched Jerrid roll up a twenty dollar bill and vacuum a white line up his nose in two parts, one half up each nostril, then tilt his head back, and snort and sniffle snot deep back into his sinuses. He offered to cut her a line but she turned it down. Impulsive, spontaneous, adventurous, sure, but she knew to pick her spots.

"Good girl, eh?" said the fat man.

"Not always," said Jerrid. His face was glowing and his smile was radiantly intoxicated, as if he were watching a cabaret show inside his own head.

"Yes always," Nellie said, just to banter.

"Your face and her tits, that would be awesome," the man said to her, gesturing to the big-breasted phone sex model on the TV commercial, who was stretching out in the sand letting frothy waves lap her thighs.

Jerrid laughed as if that were hilarious.

"She bought those," Nellie said.

"Oh yeah," the big man laughed into this red beard. "Those were a business expense, for sure."

Jerrid said, "You know a guy called Wallace?"

"Uh huh."

"He around?"

"Not today."

"When?"

"For you, likely never."

"She'll be with me, too."

The fat man ran his eyes over Nellie.

"That makes your chances much better. Wallace likes the ladies. But most girls from these parts won't have a lot to do with him."

"So when will he be around?"

"Tomorrow. Come back tomorrow."

"Okay, we'll do that. Back here?"

"Yeah. Tomorrow afternoon. He's due back. He said morning but he usually runs late. He should be here by afternoon for sure."

"Sounds good. Great."

"You have business with him?"

"I'm hoping. I can bring shit up from the coast. Ketamine, GHB, maybe some crystal meth of my own. You guys don't likely see much of that other shit up here. Might be worth bringing some in, just for the novelty. Could catch on. Someone told me Wallace could be interested."

"Oh yeah. Could be. *Potentially*. He's not that ambitious. He's got his client base built up here. Sometimes it's best to give the regulars what they already know and like. He's not as young as he used to be. Likes the same old same old. The problem with new shit is it brings new people with it."

"Tell him I'll be by anyway. Steve is my name. Tomorrow afternoon. I'm offering him exclusive access to a new generation of chemical happiness. It's like any business—demographics change."

"Whatever. The man is always willing to listen."

"One more thing."

"Uh huh."

"Viagra. You got any?"

"Young man like you don't need that shit. Specially with her to help you along."

"What the hell. Double your pleasure, right?"

Back in the car, Nellie said, "What was that all about?"

"Laying plans."

"You made it sound like you have a trunk full of drugs."

"I just needed an excuse to come back."

"Why?"

"Wallace is why. I want a meeting with Mr. Wallace."

"And what's with the Viagra?"

"Just for fun. It'll keep me up all night."

"All night's just about done already."

She was right; it was four in the morning. They woke up the clerk and got a room at the Davey Crockett Motel. It had orange paint on concrete walls, and brown carpet and orange swirly bedspreads on two double beds. The room was cold and they couldn't get the heat to come on. The taps made a noise like a frozen ghost, and the water glasses were wrapped in white paper bags that said "Your guarantee of cleanliness."

Nellie was wishing she'd brought a toothbrush. But she had pajamas. She was glad she had pajamas. She went into the bathroom to change. She didn't realize how cold she was until the water from the tap finally warmed up and she let it splash over her hands. It felt so good she decided to take a shower. A long, hot shower, to wash away the miles and the weirdness.

C H A P T E R **12**

When Nellie came out of the bathroom Jerrid was hunched over, snorting a line of coke off the table top between the beds. He looked up at her, sucked air through his nostrils like a horse, and with a bleary, crazed smile on his face, said, "Don't you look nice, now? All pink and glowing from the shower. The pajamas are cute too."

"No they're not, they're not lingerie or anything like that. They're just pajamas for sleeping in. And I'm sleeping now."

She crawled under the covers of the other bed, dead tired. The sheets felt cool, tucked in tight against her body.

"You can't sleep now," Colquitz complained. "I've just done a couple of lines, and I'm about to get all hyper and jumpy and ready to rock!"

"Rock on, dude," she said with sarcasm. "Alone."

"I'll be back," he said.

"Whatever."

She heard him enter the bathroom, heard the shower running. Almost immediately she drifted off into a strange dream. She was selling cocaine to tourists on a boardwalk in Florida or someplace like that. She had a little uniform like an ice cream vendor, and then she was wearing a sandwich board sign. Then she was naked under it. Her breasts were bigger. They were huge.

She was awakened by Jerrid's voice, calling her name.

He was standing at the end of the bed.

"Look at this thing," he said excitedly. He had his pants off, and he was gripping his penis in a tight fist. "Look!"

"I'm looking."

"It's hard."

"Stop stroking it like that."

"I can't help it!"

She was fully awake now. She turned on her side carefully, so the sheets on her bed wouldn't come untucked. Jerrid went on playing with himself, with a frenzied energy she found disturbing.

"You look like a monkey I saw once at the zoo," she said. "He was like, totally yanking on his little pencil. Just like you."

"You don't understand. There's a history to this."

"I don't need the history of how you jerk off, Jerrid."

"I don't know about Jerrid. Fuck the Jerrid shit!"

"You're grossing me out."

"This is incredible. This is momentous!" he yelled. "I'm ready to go! We're going to fuck now!"

"Shhh! People in the next room will hear. And no we're not. We're not doing anything. You make it sound gross."

"Fuck you! I'm gonna fuck you."

"No you're not! Stop yanking on it like that."

"I don't want to stop working it, jerking it," he moaned. "Sweet Jesus in Heaven, Thank You Thank You Thank You."

"Put it away! You're grinning like a baboon."

Colquitz pulled back the cover on the other double bed and lay on his back. He pulled the covers just over his upraised knees. He could still watch himself stroke, but she couldn't see it. "Do you believe in redemption?" he asked.

"You're weird."

"You don't even know what it means."

"Yes I do," she said. "Redemption is like, when you get a second chance to do something, and you do it right, right?"

"That's right. That is exactly right! That's what I'm doing now. I've got a whole new chance to do it right this time."

"That's good. But there's no hurry. Because I am going to sleep now."

"Good. Good girl. Good plan. Great plan. Great idea."

He got out of bed and made his way toward the bathroom, walking pigeon-toed. He now seemed to be more modest, hiding himself from her, but she caught a glimpse of his penis and thought it had shrunk a little.

"Now what?" she asked.

"I'm shutting down that fucking noise," he said. He went into the bathroom, where a rattling old fan was making a noise like an overburdened airplane trying to take off. "It's like this," he continued. "I never could get it up before. I've never cum. Never in my life. All my friends were jacking off like soap dispensers and I couldn't even get hard." He fumbled for the switch to the fan. It shut off the light too.

He flipped it back on—he needed to see her. Nellie was watching him from the bed, her expression neutral. She'd pulled the covers loose and drawn her knees up; from where he stood it appeared her head was resting atop a little bed-sheet-covered volcano.

"Keep going," she said.

"I tried to do it, at home in my bedroom, with lube and stroke mags, studying pictures of girls with perfect tits and shaved puss-ies—they turned me on in my mind, but my useless prick never did a thing. So much desire, and need, and longing, in my mind—Fuck! Even talking about it is making this thing go down! Don't tank on me now, you sucker! It's going down."

"Fine by me," Nellie said. "It's cuter when it's small."

"Cute? Fuck cute," he growled. "I wanna get it back up to size."

"Making love isn't about the penis anyway," she asserted.

"And how would you know?"

"I just do," she said. She had read plenty of articles about it in women's magazines, where sexy guys and women with perfect skin wrestled playfully on king-sized beds, and the words emphasized touch, and trust, and erogenous zones. If the penis was one such zone, it was expected to take care of itself. "Making love is about creating a special moment," she told him. "It's about foreplay, and arousal, and *sharing*."

"Yeah, I'll share with you," he said. "First I'm going to make sure it works."

"I don't want to watch you whack off," she said.

"You can watch or not."

"Gross! Go in the can. Go do your mastur-perving in there."

"No—I'm going to get there, right now. I'm fucking close!"

She rolled away so she wouldn't have to look. She could hear him muttering to himself in a choked, pinched voice that grew more strained and anxious as she listened. "Goddamn you. Goddamn you motherfucking useless thing. Get there, get there, GET there, *GET there.*"

She rolled back over to look at him. A thought crossed her mind: penises are ugly, that's why you never see them in public. It was half-erect, and looked red and sore. "Just let it go," she said.

"I thought I left all that behind, in my old body!" he snarled, and followed up with a great lung-straining cry of anguish that caught her completely by surprise.

"Shush!" she scolded.

"I'm a sexual fucking cripple!" he cried. "I got myself a new body, but I still brought a shitload of fucked up mentality into it. I'm a cock killer—even sweet horny Jerrid's won't work for me!"

"I wish I knew what the hell you were talking about," said Nellie.

"I'm talking about not getting redeemed. Not getting a second kick at the can."

"Come to bed, and forget about it."

"What do you know about it? You're a kid, practically. I take that back. You're a woman. You're a beautiful, hot, sexy woman, past the age of consent. If I can ever get this thing hard again I'm going to fuck you half to death."

"No you're not. Don't you remember about redemption?"

"Fuck redemption! I just told you I haven't been redeemed!" Then he had a thought. "Where'd I put that Viagra?"

He picked up his shirt from the floor and rummaged in the pocket. "If one is supposed to do it, I'll take two," he muttered. He swallowed them together, without water. "How long do they take?"

"How would I know?"

He lay back on the bed beside hers, naked and spread-eagled, staring at the smoke detector on the ceiling. For a while it seemed he was searching for words, and then he let out a great shuddering sigh of exhaustion. He brought his knuckled fists to his eyes and rubbed hard. "I feel like a dead man, all of a sudden," he said softly. "Look at this limp thing."

Nellie pulled the covers tight up under her chin. He turned on his side to look at her, and saw that her eyes were closed.

"Don't pretend to be asleep," he whimpered. He lay down on his side, still looking at her. For awhile he watched her, naked on his bed, with the bathroom light on, and the bathroom fan rattling and humming its way toward the dawn.

Half an hour later Nellie woke up to the feeling of someone nuzzling her. A hand groped between her thighs. The tearing of fabric shocked her to consciousness.

"What the *fuck* are you *doing*?"

Jerrid's body arced above her like a tomb of flesh, sweaty with strain and purpose.

"Get *off* of me!" she cried.

"Hold still."

"Get *off.*"

"It's hard."

"I don't *care.*"

She crossed her legs tightly against his prying fingers. His face was above hers, malevolent and determined. No love in it. Not even kindness.

She twisted away and rolled from the bed onto the floor, rough carpet against her knees. She jumped to her feet and shouted, "Get the fuck away from me!"

Jerrid kneeled naked in the tangled sheet and blanket on the bed. His face wore the shell-shocked expression of a survivor of a car crash. His mouth formed a self-pitying grimace.

"It's staying hard," he whispered. "Don't make it go soft."

"Jerrid, what the fuck is this about?"

"It's about me giving it one last shot. One last gasp at the fabled redemption."

"You shouldn't do that."

"Shut up and let me get this over with."

"You need to chill." She was shaking as she said it.

"No, *you* need to chill. Come here.

She made a run for the bathroom so she could lock the door on him, but he got up quickly and blocked her path. She backed away to the corner of the room. As he walked toward her, an apparition began to take shape between them.

C H A P T E R **13**

The mystical highways, those Terrulian lines of power, snapped like bright pulsing whips, and Travis felt them pick him up by the scruff of his bowed neck, carry him in haste to the golden cord. He had purpose, resolve, a mission. He transcended the ephemeral air and it became like water, a medium that granted him buoyancy. He had left the limitations of earth and sky, and floated between them along shimmering gold lines of pure energy.

He saw a million people sleep, yet she was not among them. So much to sift through. Focus. Chant. "*The mantra can be written, the meaning cannot be guessed, the faith cannot be shaken, in the one you love the best.*" He had left Lilia in the prison morgue and directed all his love toward Nellie, a pure love, a blood love. "*The mantra can be written, the meaning cannot be guessed, the faith cannot be shaken, in the one you love the best.*"

The golden cord, the caravan of his quest, unerring in its purpose and propulsion, led him where he had never been. A series of mountain valleys, all running north-south, all deep in shadow with the sun long set, with the moon casting only enough glimmer to reflect faintly from the tops of the few tall peaks still wreathed in snow. In the somber valleys, clear-cut patches of trees looked like bald spots on the back of an animal shaved for surgery.

Then the lights of a town, and the lives of the townsfolk. Many were sleeping, some fretfully, some at peace. An insomniac considered whether to swallow a pill to lower the curtain on her obstinate alertness, another wondered if his wife was faithful and feared she was not, a child dreamt of flying over the schoolyard, not for good or evil but merely for the joy of it. In a bar last call had come and gone, and the blinding lights were turned on. All this he glimpsed on the roadside of the golden cord that led him with infinite and resolute speed to his daughter, except where was his daughter? A place he had never been, the Davey Crockett Motel, where all the rooms were at rest, with the lights extinguished, except for that one, at the far end near the outdoor swimming pool, where the bathroom light spilled across the carpet—there was Nellie cowering in a corner, fearing Colquitz, naked and hard in that boy's body. He was coming toward her.

Travis let himself be lowered between them, desperate to reach her, to get in the way, to make a stand. His mindsoul poured into the body abroad, but not quick enough for his need. It flowed as usual, voluptuously, like honey from one jar to another, and he urged it to quicken—hurry up, damn it, hurry up and get to the room, get in the way—he was desperate to fight, but need to be fully there to fight. Then at last he felt himself present, with Colquitz's hard eyes watching him from that boy's face, he'd been waiting for Travis to come, he'd watched him change from a specter to a something real. Colquitz had a handgun, and now he came at Travis with it raised head high, and swung it hard. Travis felt the sharp metal edge explode against his temple, searing pain and blinding stars, his arms came up too late. He screamed, "Stop it motherfucker!" as Colquitz rained down vicious metal punches and Nellie screamed "Daddy!"

"I'm here darling," he shouted, and the hurt told him he was there, and real in the room, spilling forward into pain like a alleyway drunk waking to a kick in the head. He tried to stand, to grab at Colquitz, but his opponent was quick and agile, and deftly slipped out of reach, a matador sidestepping a blood-blinded bull. Travis stumbled past him, felt a blow to the back of his head, then saw only blackness, a shroud.

Colquitz looked at the body slumped at his feet. It was breathing, but unconscious. Nellie whimpered in the corner of the room. "Don't kill him," she murmured. "Don't."

What happens if you kill a body abroad? Colquitz didn't know. Possibly the body proper dies too. Possibly the body proper awakens with a start, and sends out another body abroad, bent on revenge. Possibly it's not possible to kill a body abroad. Or maybe it's just like killing anybody—they die, and now you've got a body to dispose of.

He didn't need that. He decided the current situation was actually the best possible outcome. The best plan would be to keep Travis's body abroad unconscious. In unconsciousness it would lack the awareness necessary to return to the body proper. So Travis would exist in a kind of limbo, with the body proper in stasis back in jail, and the body abroad incapacitated.

"Go out to the car and bring me the duct tape," he said to Nellie. She didn't move.

He brought the barrel of his handgun to Travis's temple.

"Go!"

She was back in a minute. He turned Travis on his side and taped his wrists together behind his back, then wrapped his ankles tightly together too. Then he wrapped tape over his mouth and eyes until he looked like a mummy, with only the nostrils clear. "I told you this tape would come in handy," he grunted to Nellie. She said nothing. "I'm going to put him in the trunk of the car now, before the rest of the world starts waking up around here," he said. "You come with me, so I can keep an eye on you." He sat Travis up and lifted him from under the shoulders, letting his bound feet scrape along the ground as he dragged him outside toward the car. The motel's sign, a giant blue and red retro Davey Crockett, watched over him, and by its light he opened the trunk, shifted to one side the shotgun he'd stored there, then struggled to tip the body in, head and torso first, knees pushed in against the chest, a fetus tucked into gray carpeted uterine walls. That's good, he thought. Even if he comes to, he won't be able to meditate like that, so he can't go anywhere. Then he slammed the trunk lid down, pressing hard on it until he heard the lock catch.

Back in the room he said, "Here's what we're going to do. We're going to wait until light comes—that's only an hour or two, I figure—and then we're going to get up, get showered, have a sumptuous breakfast at this motel's fine coffee shop. Then we're going to play tourist today. Did you pack a swimsuit?"

"No."

"Well then, today we're going to buy swimsuits. We'll steal a couple of towels from this joint. This morning I'm going to take you up to one of my favorite places in the world. It's a mountain lake, called Crystal Lake, where on one side a shale slide runs down into the clear water, and on the other side there's a perfect vertical cliff with a thirty foot drop, and we can dive straight down into super deep water. When the sun's high and the angle's right, you can see all the way to the bottom. Forty feet down. You'll love it. We'll have it all to ourselves, if we're lucky. We might even see a bear, or some bighorn sheep."

"Are you insane? My Dad is locked in the trunk of your car," Nellie said.

"Fuck your dad! Your dad is fine. I didn't kill him, did I? I'll let him go, later. I can't have him meddling right now, is all. Just stay with me on this! Hear me out! We're going to spend a nice morning, and then in the afternoon we'll pay another visit to that place we went last night, and meet up with Mr. Wallace. And I'm going to settle up with him, and after that, you'll get your Dad back, I'll pop the trunk and set him free, and you two can wander on your merry fucking way."

"I said no, Jerrid."

"No more Jerrid!" Colquitz shouted. Getting a grip on himself, he said with strained calmness, "I'm going to level with you. Right here, right now, I'm going to give you the straight goods, no more bullshit. Here's the truth: I'm an old inmate pal of your Daddy's. He came to visit you one night, and I hitched a ride without him being any the wiser. He was in your bedroom with you, and I was just outside, minding my own, wondering what the hell to do next, when who do you think I ran into? Why it was none other than your boyfriend, young Jerrid, half-naked in the hallway, headed to your room! So I tried something out, something George's notebook taught me how to do—I switched bodies with him. That's a stunt even your Daddy can't pull."

"Then where's Jerrid?"

"He's doing my time, back on Easy C. He's got nine years left, if he behaves himself."

Nellie sat down on the bed.

"That's right," said Colquitz coolly. "Now it's all making sense, ain't it? Get up and get dressed. I still need you for one last call of duty. I still need you to come to Wallace's place."

"The blonde that opens doors," she muttered.

"That's right."

"I'm not going."

"I think you will," Colquitz sneered. "I've got what you call leverage, remember? It's tucked away in the trunk of that car. Now do you want your daddy back or not?"

PART IV

George's Szymanski's unliving yet undead body had a new roommate. Lilia had ridden with Travis in the ambulance and come up to the room on the fourth floor with him. She watched as a nurse prepped him and placed him in the bed.

"You should have been here earlier," the nurse told her.

"Why's that?"

"The place was crawling with security people. Not our hospital security—Homeland Security-type people. All these very serious dudes, like detectives, or secret agents or something. They demanded all the files, and took photos of them all, and talked to everyone here like, well, not even *talking*, more like *interrogating*—these guys were not friendly, relaxed people. You'd think George here was some new kind of terrorist or something!"

Lilia felt her jaw tighten. "Strange they haven't talked to me," she said, casually as she could.

"Oh, I'm sure you're on the list. They're the types to leave no stone unturned. They were discussing the best way to move George out of here—I think they're going to cart him off to their own facility somewhere, where they can poke and prod him to their heart's content."

"I hope not," Lilia said. The nurse looked at her.

"I just mean I'd hate to have it taken out of public view, where I wouldn't get to follow what's going on."

"I wonder if it could be a virus," said the nurse. "Otherwise how did two guys get it now? I wonder if I should be wearing a mask and gloves."

"I wouldn't worry about it," said Lilia. "I don't think it's contagious."

"Maybe they'll wake up and be zombies," the nurse said.

"You've been watching too many movies."

"I know. My husband eats them up."

Lilia lingered as the nurse finished up, hoping for a moment to say goodbye to Travis alone. When the nurse finally left she took hold of his hand and studied his face, set in repose deeper than sleep. She worried suddenly that he might never return to her. "Come back to me, sleeping beauty," she whispered, and leant to kiss his forehead. "I wish a kiss would wake you."

A glimmer in the corner of the room caught her eye. She watched as an apparition took shape, a human form, a young man of about twenty. Rather than being shocked or surprised, she waited with curiosity—Travis's visits to her apartment had inured her to being surprised at such things. A body could materialize out of nothing, and it's the new normal.

When the boy was fully present he was the one who looked surprised.

"Who are you?" Lilia asked him.

"A relative of George's."

"I don't think so."

"Yes I am."

"Your name isn't Dylan, by any chance?"

"How did you know?"

"I know all about it, George. I know you've left your old self here—your old body proper—and moved into a good-looking young athlete named Dylan Podnovski."

"Body proper—you even know the terminology. Travis has told you everything?"

"Yes."

"That was foolish! What is he doing here? What is my old body doing here?"

"More to the point, what are *you* doing here?" she asked him.

"I don't precisely know," George said. "I have been quite well enjoying my new life as Dylan Podnovski, yet I've felt a peculiar longing for my old body. I expected Travis to kill my old body proper here—now I can see for myself that it did not happen. This is the very first time I've bilocated out of Dylan, and I felt such a strong pull to this place that I let myself be led here. And here I am." He looked at his body, his true body proper, on the bed. "I hardly know which vessel to pour myself into."

Lilia went the door, made sure it was shut firmly, and stood with her back against it to prevent any sudden interruptions. "Travis was looking for you," she said. "You need to get yourself to a town called Hawks Nest." She told him about Colquitz and Travis's daughter, and how Travis had gone hunting for them. "I'm starting to worry about him. He should have come back by now to tell me what's going on."

"Who are you? What's your relationship to him?" George asked.

"I'm a coroner. I brought your body from the prison to this hospital, and now I've brought his too. You're a medical curiosity, George. The doctors don't know what to make of you, and now it looks like the government is on the case. Homeland Security was prowling around today. Word is they want to take you to their own lab and study you there."

"No! The government must not be involved in this!" George shouted. Lilia thought she heard a Polish accent in the young man's voice. "If they seize this power, if they learn to harness it, they will corrupt it, and militarize it, use it to kill people. History shows this always happens. I will not have it!"

"Too late for that," Lilia said. "Colquitz has already corrupted the power, and he needs to be stopped—get yourself to Hawks Nest, right now."

"I don't know about that," George said. "Right at this moment I'm not feeling well at all. I feel quite unsettled. It must be the proximity to my empty body proper."

"Travis told me he doesn't have the skills," she said sharply. "You're the man with all the knowledge. You're the guru. You made this mess, and you need to sort it out."

He thought for a moment. "I can only do what I'm capable of. I know I can't stay here. I'm being split in two. I'll go home, reunite with Dylan's body proper, get some rest, and think about what I can do."

CHAPTER 2

By the time Lilia got home it was midnight. She had had no word from Travis, and a fear was beginning to take hold of her that something had gone terribly wrong. A plan began to formulate in her mind. She went online and discovered Hawks Nest had only 9,000 people and no regularly scheduled air service; the nearest place she could fly into was Cranmore, an hour down the valley, served by two flights a day. There was a flight early in the morning—she paid for a ticket and printed it up, packed a bag, texted her mother to check on Blizzard while she was away, and tried to catch a few hours sleep. She told herself that Travis was fine, that he would still show up, but hope was overmatched by a looming sense of dread. She slept in fitful snatches.

In the morning she got to the airport early, only to find her flight delayed a couple of hours, so she didn't reach Cranmore until a little after noon. She rented a car and asked for directions for Hawks Nest. An hour later she was cruising into town, past a strip of three motels. The first was fronted by a big neon Davey Crockett in a coonskin cap, with a musket slung over his shoulder. In different circumstances she might have chosen a place like that, something with a hint of kitsch in it, a place with character. But it was shabby-looking enough in the afternoon sun that she thought of bedbugs. She didn't need any more surprises, there was enough going on already. The next place was called the Happy Valley Motel, and like the first it had an air of neglect about it. She chose the third one, from a nationwide chain, because it looked well-maintained.

Now it was nearly two in the afternoon, and she had carried out her plan, as far as it went. Get a car, get a room, and start looking for Travis. And or Colquitz. And or Nellie. A pretty young girl like Nellie would be noticed in a town this size. She told herself it shouldn't be that hard to pick up her trail. She would play detective, and ask around. This trio of motels along the highway was as good a place as any to start.

At her own hotel the clerk shook her head no, she'd seen no one like that. She went next door to the Happy Valley Motor Hotel; the clerk was an older man with cracker crumbs on his shirt. From behind the counter he gave her a haughty, distrustful once-over, and told her, "This place fills at night and empties every morning. That's as much attention as I pay to who's who. You notice the bird houses out back? I built those myself. Ask me about birds and I might tell you of their habits, but with humans, I don't take much interest. When humans get up to no good, I don't involve myself. I like *birds*."

"Jerrid and Nellie are their names. You'd remember them if you saw them. They're teenagers."

"Heh!" The sound was halfway between a grunt and a laugh. "Common species around here."

She pulled her wallet from her purse and flashed her Coroner's ID, to give herself some authority. He looked it over and said, "Spokane's a long way from here."

"Investigations can take us far afield," she said.

"Seems like you're chasing the living, not the dead."

"I need to see your guest list from last night." She said it like an order, not a request. They had a staring contest, and she won. "I'm a lover, not a fighter," the clerk said, and turned the book to face her. "Guests have to show ID and have a credit card in the same name, so there's no hiding behind fake ones." There was no Jerrid Grierson or Nellie Pendridge on the list.

At the Davey Crockett Motel the office was empty, so she wandered up the wrought iron stairs to the second floor, where she could see a cleaning cart parked halfway along the balcony. Through the open door of a room she talked to a chambermaid.

"Blonde and pretty? Uh huh. And with a boy not much older, right?"

"That sounds like them," Lilia confirmed.

"They did seem young to me, to be out on their own like that. Staying in motels and such. I think they left. I know for a fact they left. And it can't have been too long back, because I still haven't cleaned their room."

"Do you know which way they went?"

"Heading that way." She stepped out onto the balcony and pointed along the highway in the direction of town.

"Good. Thank you so much."

The maid was looking over Lilia's shoulder, tracking a car down the highway. "I take that back," she said. "Now they're heading this way."

From the second story balcony they had a sweeping view of the highway and its intermittent traffic. A blue Honda Civic approached and buzzed by, with a boy at the wheel, and a girl in the passenger seat. The girl, blond and slender, noticed the two women observing her. They saw her lean forward in her seat and meet their gaze through the windshield, then the side window, as if she wanted to wave to them, but didn't dare. Lilia did wave, and the girl brought a hand up to touch her face and made a subtle, secretive return of the gesture. The boy never took his eyes from the road. They watched the car turn up a side road that snaked up into the wooded hills behind the motel strip.

"Where do you suppose they're heading?" Lilia asked.

"Don't know," said the chambermaid. "I'm not a mind-reader. But there's nothing up that way, really. A few cabins set back in the forest. Some folks with poor reputations have digs up there."

Lilia thanked her, and hurried down the stairs toward her car.

The motel parking lot was in full sun when Colquitz woke up, and Nellie, fretting that her Dad might get cooked in the heat, pleaded with him to move the car into the shade. He popped the trunk to show her he was fine, or at least alive and unchanged since the last time she'd seen him. Then they headed into town for some fast food from a drive-thru. He had slept late, and there was no time to play tourist, or swim at Crystal Lake. Just as well, he thought, the girl was being sullen and cold to him.

Now, as they made their way back out of town, passing the motel they had stayed in, Nellie noticed two women on the balcony watching their car glide past, watching her watch them, and felt a connection to them. One of them had waved. A strange little jolt of hopefulness surged through her. Someone was paying attention. It was the first optimistic thought or feeling she'd had all day. The rest had been nothing but fear and despair. Jerrid was not Jerrid. He was an escaped prisoner, dangerous and insane.

"What's the matter? You're not hungry?" Colquitz asked. She had a chicken burger and fries spread on a paper bag on her lap, but she'd barely touched the food, and it had already gone cold.

"He could suffocate back there," she said.

"Nah. He's all right. Trust me—no trunk is air-tight. A little bit of air always curls in through the cracks and seams. Especially when we're humming along like this."

They reached the same turn-off they'd taken the night before. In the dark, with low branches overhanging and impinging on the sides, it had seemed like a long tunnel through interwoven tree limbs, a giant snake hole, revealed by the headlights only as far as the next twist in the track. In daylight it looked far more friendly, a country lane through leafy woods, then a sharp turn and climb, ending at the split-level ranch house she'd seen the night before.

Daylight revealed its paint to be peeling. One bedroom window had a Confederate flag for a curtain. Nellie noticed that the cars scattered about the place were mostly wrecks, some up on blocks, others settled in nests of weeds. Many of their windows had been smashed out, and the black rubber seals hung loose and limp like the lips of toothless mouths.

Their car kicked up a dust storm that swirled over them as they stopped. The dog they had heard last night was barking. This time they could see it, a husky-shepherd cross with dirty, unkempt fur, tethered to the side of the house. As he climbed from the car Colquitz shoved his handgun into the waist of his pants and lowered his sweatshirt over it.

Before they reached the house the front door opened and the fat man stepped out, dressed exactly as the night before. He had the

TV remote in his hand. Nellie thought he must have fallen asleep on the couch, with his black leather Civil War cap still on his head. Maybe it was glued on.

"Afternoon, or is it still morning," Colquitz said.

"Uh huh."

"Any sign of Wallace yet?"

"Nah."

A raven croaked from the trees behind the house; for some reason it silenced the barking dog. Then everything was silent.

"I'll wait out here," Nellie said.

"No you won't," said Colquitz.

"What'd she say?"

"Nothing."

"You come on in," said the fat man.

He held open the screen door, which had no screen in the bottom half, and waited for her to come forward.

She stepped past him into the house and smelled bacon and sweat. After the brightness of daylight the place was dark, lit only by the glow of the television, which was tuned to some daytime talk show. They sat down in exactly the same places they'd sat the night before. On TV a woman didn't know for sure which of two men was the biological father of her baby, and now they were all on stage together before a live audience. One of the men was her husband, one had been a fling, a one-night stand many, many years before. The baby was now sixteen, and she was onstage too, looking frail and intimidated by the circumstances, thrust into the spotlight against her will. She looked so exposed they might as well have asked her to strip.

The fat man muttered "Trash," and jabbed the remote toward the television. The channel changed to a show about NASCAR, and he seemed pleased by that.

Nellie almost spoke up, to ask him to turn the channel back. The show had touched her. She wanted to know whether the man the girl thought was her father all her life was really her father. Now she would never know how it ended. Part of her thought it strange that she could find room to worry about that, considering her own Dad was locked in the trunk of a car outside, and she was sitting next to Jerrid, who wasn't Jerrid after all, but a crazy man with a gun and a grudge.

"You brought some stuff?" asked the fat man.

Colquitz nodded.

"Where is it?"

"It's out in the trunk."

"Let's see."

"It's for Wallace."

Outside the dog began to bark again. The fat man listened to it, as if he could read the meaning by the tone. It would bark for a little while half-heartedly, and then stop, then start up again. Then it began to bark continuously, and fiercely.

"Most likely that's him now," said the fat man. He pulled himself up off the couch, and lifted the dark curtain from the window to have a look.

A rental car had parked out front, and a woman was walking up the drive, a good-looking woman, with a style he liked. She was striding right on up to the house like she had every right to be there. He pulled the curtain closed, until there was just a crevice of light to peek out through. She came closer, and he watched as she stopped at the Honda Civic that belonged to the kid on the couch. It almost looked as if she was talking to it. She *was* talking to it. She opened the driver's-side door and reached down along the seat. The hood of the trunk sprang open.

"No, I'm wrong about that being Wallace," said the fat man. "That ain't Wallace. That's some woman I never seen before. Whatever you got in that trunk, she wants some too."

CHAPTER 4

Consciousness. Travis hurt. He remembered the beating.

He was in a dark place. Hot and breathless. Metal. He tried to sit up, and couldn't. He gave up trying. It felt good to give up. Just to rest.

A sliver of air, cooler there. He twisted to breathe it. Sucking air through his nose. His mouth was taped shut. A glue taste.

He remembered he was in the body abroad. His body felt homesick. His legs were bound together tight. Hands too.

A car trunk. Got to be. He stretched his jaw, trying to work the tape free. The top lip pulled away. He yelled.

"Hey. Hey!"

"Open this fucking thing!"

It hurt to yell. The beating was hurting.

"Hey!"

"Hey, somebody!"

"Open this fucking thing!"

A dog barking.

That's good, he thought. The world is out there.

"Hey somebody! Open this fucking thing!"

The dog barked and rattled his chain.

"Hey dog! Get somebody!"

A car was coming. Tires crunched gravel. It was close by now. Then it stopped. A door opened and slammed shut. The dog was going nuts. Travis thought he heard footsteps. "Help me!" he yelled.

"Hello?"

It was a woman's voice.

"Get me out!"

"Where are you?"

"In the dark."

"Wait a sec."

He heard her open the car door. Then the trunk lid popped open like a jaw.

"Travis?"

Lilia pulled at the tape around his eyes. He squinted at trees and a bright blue sky. She heard him mutter something.

"What?"

"I need my body proper."

"No, you need to be here!" She yanked on the duct tape around his mouth, twisting it under his bottom lip.

"How am I going to cut this? You're wrapped like a mummy."

"Sit me up."

She swung his legs over the end of the trunk. Through his one uncovered eye he saw a stranger's yard, like a junk yard. Wrecked cars, a chained dog. A house. The front door opened, and out came Jerrid. "That's Colquitz."

"I know," Lilia said.

"He's got a gun."

"I don't see it."

"Maybe under his shirt,"

"We've got one too," she said. She meant the shotgun sitting beside him in the trunk. But she didn't reach for it. She yanked at the tape around his wrists, but couldn't get it loose.

They heard another vehicle coming—a pickup truck, rumbling up the driveway, kicking up dust, pulling to a stop twenty feet away. The driver climbed out warily.

Colquitz called out to him. "Wallace! You made it."

Wallace was more interested in Travis and Lilia. They made a strange sight—a well-dressed woman, and a guy tied up with duct tape. That couldn't be good. He went back to his pickup and rummaged under the seat for a handgun. He came out with it pointed down at the ground.

Colquitz put his hands up wide and high, a big welcoming grin on his face—Jerrid's handsome young face. "I've been waiting to meet you," he said. He walked right up to Wallace.

"I don't know you," Wallace said.

"I'm Steve. Here on business. Ask the fat man."

Wallace gestured at Travis. "What's with that dude?"

"A practical joke. She'll set him loose now. Put the gun away, you don't need to be waving that thing around."

"Doesn't look like a joke."

"It's not," Travis shouted. "This guy is Colquitz. You remember Colquitz?"

Wallace turned toward Travis and Colquitz leapt at him, and grabbed at his gun, knocking him back against the grill of his truck.

They fell together on the dusty yard, four hands clutching at the gun, fighting for it. Jerrid's young body gave Colquitz the edge—he got on top, straddling Wallace. Their hands pushed the gun barrel around like a Ouija board; it made loop-de-loops between their two straining faces and came to rest at Wallace's throat.

"I should kill you," Colquitz snarled. "I'm sitting on a pile of dead meat."

"I don't even know you," Wallace sputtered.

"Oh you know me full well. Dude's right—you could say Colquitz sent me. Colquitz *created* me, just for this."

Lilia took the shotgun from the trunk and cracked it open. The barrels were empty. She snapped it shut and marched toward the two fighters in the dirt.

"Nobody kill anybody," she said.

"I think we should listen to the lady," Wallace rasped.

"Nice try missy, but the gun ain't loaded," Colquitz said. "Not that you'd shoot it: kill me, and Jerrid doesn't get his body back, right? Kill me and he stays Colquitz forever. So you can't kill me, even if I kill this motherfucking piece of shit who *deserves* to die."

"Where's Nellie?" Lilia demanded.

"In the house with the fat man."

"Nellie!" Travis shouted. "Come on out."

There was no answer.

"Lilia," Travis said. "Go up to the house—get her, take your car and get out of here."

"Not so fast—the fat man's got an arsenal," Colquitz crowed. "I've got a better idea. I'm having a change of heart. I don't actually want to kill Mr. Wallace here—I just got *out* of jail, I'm a free man in a kid's body for fuck's sake, you think I want to go back? No, all I want to do is break every tooth in this motherfucker's head, that'll be revenge enough. Feel better, Wallace? You're not going to die after all. I wish I *could* kill you, but knocking out your teeth with the butt of this pistol will have to do. Then I'll be on my way, and you can have your daughter back, too, Pendridge."

As the fat man parted the curtains to look out at the yard, Nellie watched a storm of dust motes swirl in the slit of golden daylight that spilled across the living room rug.

"What's going on?" she asked.

"Nothing. You just stay back. What's with your boyfriend, anyway? His vibe creeps me out, and that's saying a lot. I'm used to all kinds."

Nellie wanted to see out too, and went to the corner of the picture window to lift back the curtain, but the fat man turned on her grabbing her forearm and yanking her away.

"Not so fast, girlie girl. You stay back out of sight." He twisted her arm hard, taking pleasure in it, and pulled her across the room to shove her down onto the couch. "Now stay put."

He went back to curtains. Nellie heard another vehicle pull into the yard. "Who's that?" she asked.

"That'll be Wallace," said the fat man. "Now maybe we'll see what this is all about."

He watched Wallace go back to his truck for the handgun, saw him talking to the kid. Then they were grappling in the dirt, fighting for control of the gun. The kid came out on top. Then quickly— nimbly for a big man—he let the curtain drop and came over to where Nellie sat on the couch, lifted the seat cushion next to her, and pulled his own handgun from the seam under it. "I'm feeling the need of a firearm about now," he said.

"What's happening?" she demanded.

"Let's just say guns are in play." He went back to the window. "Don't worry, mine's strictly for defense purposes."

From outside she heard her name called. It sounded like her Dad.

"I want to see," she said, and stood up, but the fat man came over and smacked her back down to the couch with his forearm. "Now stay put," he said. He went back to the window.

"My dad's in that car," she said. "He's calling me."

"Well he's all tied up, from what I can see. He's sitting on his ass in the trunk with his hands behind his back."

Nellie stood up again. "I'm going to look," she said defiantly.

"You want me to smack you again?"

"Let me look."

"You enjoy testing my patience?"

"I'm going to look, that's all."

"No you're not." He charged at her like a bull and shoved her back onto the couch. "There's a room down the basement tight as a bank vault—you get up off that couch one more time and I'm lock- ing you in there, understand?"

"You're a bastard," she said.

"You're the one that brought all this trouble."

"Trouble brought *me*."

"Yeah, true enough. I'm not blaming you, girlie girl. But right now I'm all about self-preservation, and you're just another complication. So *sit*, and shut up." He turned away and went back to the window.

Something caught her eye in the shaft of sunlight that spilled over his shoulder down onto the carpet behind him. In the bright swirl of dust an apparition began to take shape. It sat cross-legged, in a meditative pose, and at first she thought it must be her dad come to rescue her, but as the body gained form it was clearly someone else, a younger man, unknown to her, handsome and well-built.

He became whole very quickly, much quicker than her dad ever had. He didn't seem surprised to find himself in this place, but rather gave an aura of confidence and self-assurance. He put a finger to his lips, warning her to stay silent.

She nodded. She watched him get to his feet and tiptoe toward the fat man at the window. With the full weight of his body he threw a punch that caught the fat man blindside at the temple. He staggered sideways but didn't fall. The younger man grabbed for his gun, and the big man straightened up and tried to shake him off. With their bodies close and their hands together on the gun they rocked back and forth like two men in a rowboat. The young man tripped him, but the big man twisted his weight so he came down on top of him, and the younger one's head hit the rug with a muffled thud. The gun fired and sent shockwaves that rattled the picture window. Nellie jumped up from the couch. The bullet had put a hole in the wall not three feet from her head. Outside she heard her dad scream her name.

On the floor the fat man had the upper hand—she looked around and grabbed a table lamp with a wrought-iron base and yanked its cord free from the wall. It was heavy, and the shade made it awkward for her to hold as a weapon, but she found a way to balance it; she swung it up above her head and, summoning an inner warrior, drove the lamp down hard on the back of the fat man's skull. He was stunned—the sharp edge of the lamp's bottom cut him, and blood splattered. She raised it high and struck again, and this time the big man went limp and fell forward on his face. From underneath him the younger man wriggled free and got quickly to his feet.

"Excellent job!" he said. "I came to save the day, and it's *you* who saved my ass, my dear."

"Who are you?"

"My name is Dylan, but your father knows me better as George."

"Swami George?"

"Correct. In a fine new body."

"He told me about it. Next time you pick a body, go for a martial artist."

"Good point. Dylan's a cyclist. A lover, not a fighter. Thank you again for intervening. Mercifully, one doesn't engage in this kind of life-and-death struggle every day."

Nellie went to the window and looked out. "There's another struggle going on out there," she said. She saw her dad sitting in the trunk of the car, arms taped behind him, and a woman with a shotgun standing over Colquitz and Wallace, watching uncertainly as they grappled in the dust.

CHAPTER 6

Travis felt helpless, and *useless*. When the shot rang out in the house he just about jumped out of his skin, but he wasn't going anywhere, duct-taped in the trunk of a car.

Lilia, standing over Colquitz and Wallace, had turned toward the house at the sudden sound of the shot. She seemed frozen to the spot. "Use the butt end of your gun, beat him over the head with it," Travis shouted at her.

She shifted the shotgun in her hands to bring the butt up, and took a step toward them. "I can't," she said.

"Then come and untie me."

"I feel like I need to watch them—"

The door of the house opened and out came Nellie, and right behind her was Dylan. Travis wasn't sure he recognized him. "Is that you, George?" he called out.

Nellie ran to her father and clawed at the duct tape. Then she remembered there was a stolen knife in the car, and she went and got it and swiftly slit the tape from Travis's wrists and legs. "Hold still," she said, as she worked the tape from his head. He tried to lift himself out of the trunk but his legs and shoulders had seized up from being tied so long. He could barely move them. He knew they'd be sore for a long, long time. Nellie took his arms and pulled him out and upright.

George had headed straight to Colquitz and Wallace on the ground, and saw the stalemate of four hands on the pistol at Wallace's throat.

"Gentlemen, time to put your toys away," he said.

"Fuck you," said Colquitz.

Lilia said, "Colquitz, it's all on you. This guy has a gun too. Put yours down now."

Colquitz took a quick glance at the young man pointing a weapon at him. "Who the fuck are you?" he spat.

"Don't you recognize me, old friend? Can you not notice on my lips a hint of the smile that used to drive you insane? It's me, Swami George! You found yourself a fine young body there, but mine's even better."

"George," Colquitz muttered uncertainly, and in his bewilderment loosened his grip on the gun at Wallace's throat. Wallace pushed the barrel up and away—a gunshot cracked and splintered the air and echoed back off the trees. Colquitz was thrown back in a spray of blood. Wallace rose up and pushed him off, and Colquitz lay still in the dirt, a bloody wound at the base of his throat.

"Jerrid!" Nellie screamed, and ran to the body in the dust.

"He's not Jerrid," Travis shouted, limping toward her as she knelt beside him. "He's not Jerrid—Jerrid is somewhere else, and we'll get him back for you!" But the body was Jerrid's, young and beautiful even while dying, and its arms hung limply as she looked down at him, crying out his name. She reached out to hold him, but stopped short—the gaping wound at his throat repelled her, and the look in his eyes made her recoil. Travis came close and saw Colquitz's eyes flickering with an intense, livid glare, saw the fading of Colquitz's raging soul. Blood was running from his mouth as he said faintly, "I'm not—" Then his last words: "Fuck you, little girl."

Nellie's eyes fixed on some distant point, like she was seeing the future. "I want Jerrid back," she said.

"We'll get him," Travis said. "We'll straighten it out. For now, get out of the way. Go wait in the car."

"I hate that car," she said. "I never want to sit in that car again."

"Then Lilia's car," he said, keeping a wary eye on Wallace, who was getting to his feet. He had the pistol in his hand, but he kept it lowered. George had his gun trained on him.

"Now what?" Wallace said. He looked around at each of them, Travis, George, Nellie and Lilia, then he glanced down at himself, as if to make sure he was all in one piece. "Look at me!" he said. His shirt and forearms were splattered in blood. "Look what you made me do! I don't know who you people are, or what you want here, but it's four against one. I surrender. Seems like you weren't on that guy's side, so you won, whatever the game was. Right?"

"Right," said George. "We have nothing against you."

"You're going to get rid of the body, clean up around here?"

"Absolutely."

"I live here, you know? It's gotta be fucking spotless."

"It will."

"Where's Dean?"

"Who?"

"The fat man."

"He's inside. Incapacitated at the present moment. His arms are tied with a lamp cord and he'll have a sore head when he wakes up. He might even be awake by now. He'll be fine," George said. He gestured to the body in the dust. "No one knows this kid around here, no one will be looking for him. You'll have no worries."

"No worries? I just shot some guy dead."

"You've got the gun. Dispose of it," George said. "Now get out of here. We'll take care of this end. There'll be no trace, I promise you."

"You're not setting me up, are you?"

"We don't even know you."

"Seems like you know Colquitz."

"Colquitz is dead. That kid was the end of Colquitz. It's over now. Go."

"There's a creek up from here with a swimming hole. I'm gonna wash all this shit off me."

"Good start."

"So adios then, right?"

"Adios."

They watched him climb in this truck and disappear down the road. Nellie, looking shell-shocked and grim, went and sat in Lilia's rental car. George knelt by Jerrid's body in the dust and felt for a pulse.

"He's definitely dead," he said. "But who is dead? The body is dead, and we can expect that since it contained Colquitz's mindsoul at the moment of death, then that mindsoul is also extinguished."

"Could the soul leave the body after death?" Lilia asked.

"I don't think so. Perhaps Travis has told you of my dear wife, and how I still search for her in the ether. I have hopes she might still be alive there, for she left her body before it died. Colquitz just now would not have had time to make that escape. From all my years of study, I've seen no evidence that the soul leaves the body at the end of life. I've sought out death, to watch it from the ether, to study the mindsoul in that moment, and in every case, in sickbeds and hospital wards, it has flickered and flamed out, and died with the body. So with some confidence I say Colquitz as we knew him is no more."

"And what about Jerrid?"

"Jerrid's conscious mind is alive and well, back in prison."

"Then we'll need to get him out of there," Lilia said.

"First we must dispose of this body," said George.

"No," she said firmly. "You need to go back to prison and bring Jerrid here." She gestured to Nellie in the car. "That girl wants her boyfriend back."

George was quiet a moment. "I do feel a responsibility to put things right," he said. "I'm capable of going from here back to my old stomping grounds on Easy C, but there is a risk of being seen there, in this body, Dylan's body. Perhaps with caution and discretion I could arrive there, then link to Jerrid's mindsoul and bring him back here with me. But the question is: once I bring him here, where do I put him? There is no body for him here."

"Yes there is."

George looked at her.

"Yours," she said.

"No no no," he answered. "This body is mine now."

"It's not. It's the body of a young man. Your real body is waiting for you back in a hospital bed in Spokane, George. You can move back into it anytime. Or if it's too old for you, you can have Colquitz's body in jail, once you take Jerrid out of it."

"Colquitz's? I don't think so."

"Lilia's right, George," Travis said. "Jerrid deserves a healthy young body, and you've got it. Give it up for the kid. Who knows, he might even like it better—Dylan's more athletic, and better looking, I'd say."

"Travis. Please. It's not for us to say Jerrid would be happier," Lilia said. "He'll have to accept it, he has no choice. I only hope Nellie comes to accept him that way, too. This isn't just for him, this is for her."

George looked painfully conflicted. "I've become quite fond of this body," he said. "But in the end we must do what is right, isn't it? I will surrender this body to young Jerrid, and take up residence in Colquitz's, at least for the time being—it will be easier to transfer the two of us from jail to here. If Jerrid does take over this fine young body, I'll have to lead him back to the family home in Tulsa, Oklahoma, so he can play the role of Dylan Podnovski, the miracle coma kid." He gestured to Jerrid's dead body in the dust. "Would it not be better to dispose of this corpse first?"

"No," Travis said. "I think it's better if Jerrid sees it with his own eyes, that his old body is dead, and that there's no choice but to give his soul a new home."

George glanced toward Nellie sitting in Lilia's car. "Will she accept him?"

"That's the million dollar question, isn't it?" Lilia said.

George looked at Lilia carefully. "You're playing a major part in the decision making here. A leading role, one might say. What is your motivation, exactly, for helping us?"

"George," Travis cautioned.

"Are you suspicious of me?" Lilia asked.

"No. I accept you. I'm impressed by you, even. And I trust you. I'm just curious."

"Travis asked me to help."

"And so you would do anything for Travis?"

"It appears that way," she said.

"You are love birds."

"Now is not the time," she said.

"Travis?"

"Yes. We're lovers," he said. "I love her."

"Thank you Travis, but guys, please," she said. "Let's stay on task."

"Good, yes. You're right," George said. "Travis has a very kind soul, he is a gentle man, but a bit of a dreamer. You're good for him, I can tell. You'll keep him on task. Let's get on with it. I'm going to bilocate now and, all going well, I'll be back with young Jerrid in a few moments." He sat down in the dusty yard and began to meditate. Very quickly he began to blur, and fade, and become translucent. Soon enough he was gone.

Travis glanced at Nellie, watching from the car. She turned her head away and stared up into the forested hills. He came toward Lilia and put his arms out to hold her, but she made no move to meet him.

"I'm sorry," he said.

"You should be. This is not like anything I ever imagined myself being involved in. I am so out of my depth here, Travis."

"You're handling it so well. You stay cool in a crisis."

"I'll break down later."

"Me too."

She let him take her hands. "You don't look so good," she said. "Very tired."

"I need to get back to my body proper. I can't stay out as long as George. I'm not as experienced."

"When you go back, you'll be in the hospital. You'll need to play dead."

"I guess so. If not I'll have a lot of explaining to do. Give me a hug."

She let him hold her. It gave him some energy, and strength. He lifted his head and saw Nellie staring at him from the car. He couldn't read her expression.

"Should I go talk to her?"

"Let me do it," Lilia said. "You go in the house and check on the fat guy. Make sure he isn't about to get loose. That's all we need— for him to get up and grab something from his gun collection."

"All right. I love you."

She nodded. "We'll talk about that later. Go."

C H A P T E R **7**

ilia went and sat with Nellie in the car.

"George has gone to get Jerrid for you," she told her.

"Jerrid's dead," Nellie said.

"No, that's not true. He's coming back to you, but in a different body. In the one George was just in. It's a young man's body, like he's used to, and Jerrid will be happy to have it, we hope so, anyway. Right at the moment he's trapped in another one, in jail. George is going to make a switch with him, and bring him here."

"It won't be the same."

"You're right. Not exactly the same. But Jerrid will be alive. And young, and healthy."

And then what are we supposed to do?" Nellie said angrily. "Drive back home to his parents' house? What do we tell them? 'Hey guys, guess what? Here's your boy, for sure he looks a bit different, but it's *him*, he's Jerrid in there, his old body got shot and died.'" She started to cry softly, and rubbed at her eyes with balled up fists, like a child would. "It's too weird, too fucking awful."

"It is awful," Lilia agreed. "And I haven't thought that far ahead, about how we're going to carry on now, or get back to normal."

"There's no normal after this," Nellie said.

"Piece by piece," Lilia said. "We'll take it piece by piece."

Her cell phone, perched in a drink holder on the dash, began to ring. She checked to see who it was. Her mother. She hesitated, then touched the screen to answer.

"Hi Mom."

"Hi sweetie. Are you alright?"

"Yeah. Everything's good."

"I dropped over to check on Blizzard, and found some men here, they're very concerned about you. They asked me to call you and make sure you're okay."

"Men? What men?"

"I'm not sure exactly. Just a minute." Lilia heard muffled voices until her mother came back on. "They're from the government, and seem very official, and have lots of ID. They've been asking me all sorts of questions about prisoners escaping from jail, and whether you've said anything to me about it. That man you took to the hospital, they're very interested in him."

"Which one?"

"I don't know which one. I thought there was only one."

"There's two. Let me talk to them, mom."

"Yes. That's a good idea. I've been no help to them at all, I'm sure."

After a moment a voice came on the line.

"Miss Chambers?"

"Speaking."

"My name is Arthur Tredwell, I'm with a special investigations unit of the federal Department of Homeland Security."

"Okay," Lilia said. She did her best to keep her voice calm. She told herself to pretend there's wasn't a crying teenage girl in the car, and she wasn't parked outside a country crack house with a view through the windshield of a dead body splayed in the dirt. "Homeland Security, that's a big department—is there a specific branch or agency you work for?"

"It's Special Services. Let's leave it at that."

"Why didn't you just call me directly?"

"We would have, shortly, I'm certain. But your mother made the process simpler. Call it serendipity. Apparently you've gone out of town."

"Yeah. Called away suddenly."

"You're in Hawks Nest, Oregon, correct?"

"That's a pretty good guess."

"We have agents on the way there. They should arrive by seven this evening. That's three hours from now. Would you be able to meet with them?"

"What's this about?"

"It's about the two men you've admitted recently at Providence Holy Family. An unusual medical phenomenon like that catches the attention."

"I suppose it does. I suppose you guys track everything these days."

"Exactly. We keep tabs on just all things great and small," he said. His voice was friendly, but to Lilia it sounded too friendly. "This case definitely piqued our interest. In fact we've been over at the hospital, and we've taken over supervision of those two gentlemen now, and very shortly we'll be moving them to a more sophisticated, and secure, facility."

"Where's that, exactly?"

"I'm not at liberty to say. But it's a fascinating case—we only really got on it yesterday, and already we've come across something that made us think we need to pursue this matter as far as we can go. Something highly unusual—it happened last night. Hello?"

"I'm still here," she said.

"Last night you brought in a second body to the hospital, in the same condition as the first. Is that correct?"

"Yes."

"And you were in the room alone with those two bodies, correct?"

"Yes."

"Did anything out of the ordinary happen while you were in the room there?"

"No. Not that I recall," she lied.

"Well you may not be aware of it, but earlier in the day we set up a very small camera, discreet but high-definition, in the corner of the room. Way up where you would hardly notice it."

"I see." The first thing that came into her head was that she had kissed Travis as he lay upon the bed. They would have seen it. Only then did she remember a much bigger event: George, as Dylan, had appeared to her there, out of thin air.

"So we have some footage of what went on in that room."

"I see."

"Now you may think Homeland Security operates like money is no object, but actually, we're on a tight budget like anyone else. I hope you appreciate that."

"I guess. Sure."

"So we can't have an agent watching that camera in real time, just sitting there all night. That would be very expensive, and in most cases a waste of time."

"Uh huh."

"Instead we have software that picks up on the important stuff, the unusual movement, and makes it easy to survey the whole night's worth of activities in the morning."

"That's a good idea."

"So this morning, we saw what went on while you were in the room."

"And what was that?"

"You were there. I think you know."

"Remind me."

"Let's just say someone showed up, without opening or closing a door. And you had a little chat with him, and then he disappeared the same way he came."

"Really? Wow. Okay."

"That's why we want to meet up with you, Miss Chambers. You see, some people might think of the government as a kind of Big Brother, an all-knowing, all-seeing, all-powerful aggregate, but we're really just a collection of human individuals, as prone to human error as anyone else. We installed the camera, and it worked fine, but the microphone turned out to be faulty, which is damned frustrating, as you can imagine, because we couldn't hear a thing you two said to each other."

Through the windshield she saw two figures begin to take shape in the yard.

"I'm happy to cooperate," Lilia said. "I'm a little busy right now, though. Tell your agents to call me when they hit town."

"That's great," he said. "Let's set up a meeting—"

"I'm really busy right now. I've got to go. Have them call me later."

She hung up and powered her phone off.

The fat man was lying like a big old walrus on the rug, with the lamp cord tightly strung around his wrists behind him.

"I'm too heavy to get up," he said.

"Just as well," Travis said.

"I heard a shot out there. Where's Wallace?"

"He's gone. He took off down the road. He killed the boy."

"You mean Steve?"

"The teenage boy that came with the teenage girl. I don't know what he told you his name was."

"Doesn't matter, if he's dead."

"He is dead. And Wallace is the one who pulled the trigger, and now he's taken off. Leaving us to clean up the mess. We don't want trouble. We agreed to pretend Wallace was never here—we let him drive away. The idea is we're going to pretend today didn't happen. We need to get rid of a body—maybe you know the woods around here, know a good spot to stash something like that?"

"Who the fuck are you, and why were you tied up in the trunk of that car?"

"I'm telling you: It's best for everyone if we make it like today never even happened."

"Huh." He thought for a moment. "I'm glad that kid's dead. Trouble with a capital T, from the very beginning. I saw him take Wallace down, it looked like he was going to kill him."

"He wanted to."

"The right guy died."

"You could say. But better if no one had."

They were interrupted then by a voice from outside. It was George, calling Travis. He went to the curtains and looked out at Lilia and Nellie sitting in the car. Nearby he saw that two men had returned from prison.

"Travis. Now I know your name," said the fat man.

"Just stay on the floor until we get this sorted."

"This cord is cutting my wrists."

"Let me go get things sorted. After that we'll leave you in peace."

"You're not going to kill me, are you?"

"No. There shouldn't even have been one killing, it was Wallace who did it. And we let him go. We'll do the same for you, I promise."

Travis went outside and met Dylan and Colquitz in the yard. George's voice was coming from Colquitz's ugly mug. It looked like he'd taken a beating lately. "Come here, come here," he waved to Travis. "I made the switch. Jerrid is here."

Nellie and Lilia got out of the car. Jerrid, in Dylan's body, shouted, "Nellie, you can't believe all the shit I've been through!" He rushed toward her, babbling a story of prison, and of pain; a strange nightmare poured incoherently from him. As he got close to her she backed away uncertainly. "Don't look at me like that," he cried out. "It's me! Jerrid!"

"I'm not ready," Nellie said. She kept her distance. "I've been through a lot too."

"Give the girl a few minutes," said George. "Or maybe a few weeks, I don't know. She'll like you better eventually, but right now she doesn't recognize you as *you*. And now my boy, you need to get a grip—remember I told you what you'd see here? Remember I told you you would need to say goodbye to your old body?" He put a hand lightly on the young man's shoulder and led him toward the body on the ground. "Take a deep breath. Calm yourself. Prepare yourself. See there, in the dust? It's well and truly dead, that body. Your old body."

Jerrid went to the blood-splattered corpse and looked down at his own face, now grey and lifeless. He shivered.

"It's not right," he said. "It is not right! Can't you do something? With all you can do, can't you do something?"

"I wish I could," said George. "But death is final, when it comes. That body is dead, and you will be happy to know that Colquitz, your tormentor, died with it."

"But you're in his body."

"Yes. But his mind is gone—his personality, his thoughts, dreams, schemes—those are all no more."

"Or it could be another trick."

"Time will tell you what is true, my boy. I've freed you from prison, I've led you back here to your lady love. So far, so good, no?"

"She doesn't want me," he said.

"Give her time," George said impatiently. "Besides, there are even bigger fish to fry right now. Travis! Back on Easy C all hell has broken loose. Our secret is out—the place is crawling with security guards and government agents. Coming down through the ether, I could see they had taken One Nut away to interrogate him—he was holding out on them, playing coy, bargaining for special privileges or reduced time, the cagey bugger. Luckily for me their attention was on him, and Jerrid here was alone, in Colquitz's body, in Colquitz's cell—but unluckily they had already interrogated him, and the boy told them everything. So now they know whatever he knows—you and Nellie are thus fully implicated. The fucking government in all its unlimited power and majesty—they are after us, my boy!"

Lilia spoke up. "They're on to me too. They just called me on my cell."

George made a pained face. "This is bad. You didn't tell them where you were, did you?"

"They knew. They have agents on the way. They'll be in Hawks Nest in three hours—that's what they told me."

"God damn it! Turn off your phone! They'll be tracking you right up this road!"

"I turned it off already. They also told me that your body proper in the hospital—and Travis's too—are now under their control. They're moving you to a more secure facility."

"This is bad, bad, bad!" George cried.

"Get a grip, George," Travis said. He gestured to the body lying in the dirt. "First things first—what do we do with this body?"

"We hide the evidence! The five of us need to stick together now," George said excitedly. "We're all implicated—we need to go into hiding! We need to go on the run!"

"Calm down," Lilia said. "Implicated in what? We've done nothing wrong. Wallace killed Jerrid, not us."

"They won't believe that! We need to dispose of this body," he said.

"I have a suggestion," Lilia said. "Why don't Nellie and I go back down to town and wait for the agents to come talk to us, and George, why don't you take Jerrid to his new home in Tulsa, and while we're at it, Travis, why don't you go home to your body proper too? You just told me you need to do it. And most of all, why don't we leave the body right here where it lays, and have Nellie call the local cops about it, and let them come find it? We didn't kill him, George!"

"I'm thinking she's right, George," Travis said. "It would be best for Jerrid to be found and declared dead, otherwise his family will be looking for him forever, and Nellie will be the prime suspect in his disappearance. She'll have to make up a whole bunch of lies to cover herself, and that opens up a whole new can of worms."

George brought a hand up to hold his head steady. In Colquitz's bruised and battered body he looked exhausted and overcome. "I shouldn't have taught you a thing," he said to Travis. "I should have kept my secret."

"It's too late for that, George," Lilia said. "The secret is out. The government is onto all of us—they already know about bilocation from Jerrid, and they have actual evidence of it, because they had a spy-cam installed at Providence Holy and it caught you appearing magically as Dylan when I was there. They saw me speak to you, and saw you disappear into thin air. So if Nellie and I speak to them we won't be telling them anything they don't know already. It's too late to run and hide. Nellie will tell the cops that Jerrid was looking for drugs in town and came up here to get some, and there was a fight, and Jerrid was killed by Wallace. That's all more or less true. And she should tell them whatever else they want to know, about bilocation or anything else. Because that's what I'm going to do. I'm going to have to. There's no other reason in the world for me to drop everything in my life and come racing up here to Hawks Nest, except to save Nellie from Colquitz. And the only way I could know Nellie even existed is through you, Travis."

"I hear you," Travis said. "You're right. You've done nothing wrong, but if you start lying to the authorities, you will have. I've put you in an awful bind."

"All of this is Colquitz's fault," George said. "Why did he have to get wind of what I was up to, and fuck everything up?"

"If it's his fault he's paid in full for it," Travis said.

"Can we go now? Nellie said. "I'm sick of being here."

"I think we all are," said Lilia.

"Yeah," Travis said. "You girls head to town, and call the cops when you get there."

"What are you going to do with the fat man?" Lilia said.

"Just leave him tied up, for the cops to find, I guess," said Travis. "I'm tired. I can't deal. I can't think straight. I need to get back to my body proper."

"When you get there, the authorities will be waiting to talk to you."

"I know. This is only the beginning of complications." Travis turned to George. "And you, my good man, you need to take—"

"Yes, yes," he said irritably. "I'll deliver the young man to his new body proper, and his new home, with the Podnovski family."

"*Where?*" asked Jerrid.

"In Tulsa, Oklahoma. You're an athlete. A cyclist who went into a coma playing hockey, who was declared brain dead," George said.

"No I'm not."

"You are," Travis insisted. "George has been good enough to give up that fine young body so you could move in. Right now you're in the body abroad, but once he takes you home, and puts you back in the body proper, it'll be permanent. It's your new home."

"I don't want a new home! I want my old one!"

"Don't be petulant!" George said. "I explained this already. There's your corpse. It's dead. You've got a fine new body in its place! We're doing the best we can."

"You'll still be you," Travis told him. "With all the same thoughts and ideas, and likes, and dislikes—"

"Shut up!" the boy exploded. "Everything is different! Everything around me will be different. I won't go to premed, I won't see my parents, I won't ever see Nellie!"

"You'll see Nellie," Travis said. "We'll make it happen. You'll be in Tulsa at first, and she'll be back with her Grandma and Grandpa. But you can talk on the phone, which actually might be a better way to start things off. She'll hear your voice, and understand that it really is you she's talking to, and then—"

"You will have a steep learning curve," George interrupted. "I can tell you some things, to settle you in to this new life, and we can blame your renewed lack of familiarity with family and friends as a relapse from the brain injury."

"I do not want this. I did not ask for this," Jerrid murmured.

"Nobody asks for what life deals," George said. "Just play the cards."

"Why don't you take him home now, George?" Travis asked.

"Yeah," said Lilia. "Let's all go where we need to go."

CHAPTER 9

As she drove down the mountain Lilia decided on a slight change in strategy. She coached Nellie on what to say to the Hawks Nest cops; that is, she told her specifically to tell them nothing about Travis, or George, or Dylan or Colquitz—leave out bilocation entirely, in other words—and stick to a straight story: that Jerrid had been eager to score drugs, and she'd gone up the mountain with him, and he'd tied up the fat man and stolen some coke, but then Wallace had driven up the road in his pickup, and there was a confrontation that left Jerrid dead. She had a hunch that when the special agents from Homeland Security arrived they'd be happier if bilocation had been kept a secret from the local authorities.

They followed the highway in the bottom of the valley into town, and found the police station, which housed a sleepy six-man detachment that more typically dealt with fender-benders and domestic disputes; in fact, this was the first murder in Hawks Nest since Colquitz had killed the hitchhiking girl twelve years earlier.

The Police Chief was named Phelps; he was two years from retirement, and a dozen years earlier he had handled the girl's murder. He wasn't at all surprised to learn Wallace was involved in the next killing. He dispatched two officers up the mountain to the crime scene, and another two to look for Wallace, then led the two out-of-town women to his office so he could take their initial statements. Lilia showed him her Coroner's credentials, expecting it would raise his estimation of her, but he gave no outward sign that it did. Nellie told him her version of the story, and he was plainly skeptical, and became even more doubtful after a call came in from one of the officers at Wallace's place. He heard him out, hung up and turned to Lilia.

"Who's Travis?"

"Nellie's father is named Travis," Lilia said.

"The boys up there found Dean—he's local, born and raised, and we've been well-acquainted with him for a long, long time—that boy's been in trouble pretty much since he was eleven and egging windows on Halloween. They found him tied up, all right, just as you said he would be. But according to Dean, someone else did the tying, not Jerrid. In fact, he says there were at least two other guys involved in this thing. One went by the name Travis. And now you tell me her daddy's a Travis?"

"It can't be the same Travis," Lilia said. "He's in a hospital bed in Spokane."

"And how do you know him?"

"He's part of a case I've been working on, as Coroner. A case I'm still on."

"Is that how you know Nellie here? He got you to come chasing after his daughter, after she run away from home?"

"I can't discuss the details, but it was important I find her."

"There's a dead body up there and you can't discuss details?"

"It's a separate case."

"Nothing in this world is ever truly separate, in my experience," he said. He rubbed his face with two big hands, as if waking in a bad mood. "God made it all—he threw everything in a big old pot and stirred it up together."

The phone rang again. Chief Phelps picked it up and listened. He didn't say much, just a few 'uh-huhs' and 'okays.' Before hanging up he said, "Don't touch a thing. I'm coming up the mountain to have a look."

He got up from behind his desk, and said, "I'm not done with you two girls, but I can't leave you here, on account of there's no one left to look after you. I need to lock the place up. I don't think you're any flight risk anyway, you being a Coroner and all. I tell you what—you take Nellie back to your motel room and wait for me there. We'll finish this later tonight. After I've taken a good hard look at that crime scene, I expect I'll have a lot more questions for you."

By the time the Chief came back down the mountain it was late evening. He went straight to the motel to continue his interrogation of Lilia and Nellie, but at the door to Lilia's room he was met by two agents of a special branch of Homeland Security. They showed him documents that declared the case a matter of national security and therefore subject to their exclusive jurisdiction. "This case just keeps getting more and more bizarre. How do I even know those girls are in there?" he demanded.

"Oh they're in there, all right. But under quarantine, so to speak."

"And who's in there with them?"

"They're being interviewed."

"Who's in charge here?"

"He's inside. Interviewing."

Chief Phelps made enough of a fuss that the door was opened, so that he could see that the women were indeed still there. "I'm not done with you ladies," he told them, but in fact he was—two agents blocked him from crossing the threshold, and once the door closed he had no further contact with the two women.

There were two interviewers in the room, and a third, Arthur Treadwell, the one Lilia had spoken to earlier in the day, was on speakerphone. As they resettled after the Chief's interruption, Lilia said to them, "Special Services—I still don't get what you do."

"I'll answer that," said Treadwell, his voice crackling out of the tinny speaker. "You remember a few years back, when Donald Rumsfeld made some major ripples talking about what we know and what we don't know?"

"Vaguely."

"He was talking about threats to America—that there were things we know we know, things we know we don't know, and then, things we don't even know we don't know. He called it the *unknown unknowns*. That's what people like me are assigned to do—find the things we don't even know we don't know, and make sure we get to know them. And we're onto something like that here, something called *bilocation*-- we're now acquainted with that much of it—and we think maybe there's only a half dozen people in the whole wide world who know as much or more than we do—and I'm talking to two of them right now. The local police chief there—we've got him leashed for the time being, but he's chafing at the collar to get in there and have at you two—I hope you haven't added him to the list of people who know what *you* know."

"We haven't," said Lilia. "We kept it simple with him—a straight-up story about a drug score and a robbery turned bad."

"That's good. That's very good. I appreciate that. We're going to keep the Chief in the dark, and settle this thing with as little public fuss as we can manage in a functioning democracy. I'm told our agents have already found Mr. Wallace—he made it no further than his mother's house in Elk Crossing, a tiny hamlet up the valley. His mother swore on a barrel of Bibles that her son had been there for days, but there were traces of blood on the seat of his pick-up truck. You might be aware that Oregon is one of 24 states that allows a Stand-Your-Ground-style defense—Mr. Wallace has already been offered a deal of probation with no jail time in return for a guilty plea to charges of leaving the scene of a crime and failure to report a crime, namely the crime perpetrated upon him by young Jerrid, and he's accepted it, thanks to an added enticement of having no charges being laid in connection to the pile of illicit substances found in his truck. All this will be sorted with the police Chief in due time. What it means is you two ladies will be spared having to testify at a public trial. The only testifying you'll have to do is to me, right here and now, helping your government uncover a pretty damned unbelievable unknown unknown."

"Whatever we can do to help," Lilia said. "We intend to cooperate fully with you. But it seems like you know as much as us, in any case—you know bilocation is possible. We've never done it, so our knowledge is all second-hand, like yours."

"That's fine. You can't tell us more than you know, we understand that. But we've got to go over every little detail. That'll take some time."

And so it did. Lilia and Nellie spent another full day and night in the motel room. Nellie requested Lilia be present as she recounted the strange tale of riding shotgun on a road trip with an inexplicably bizarre Jerrid, who turned out to be someone named Colquitz who wanted to be called Steve. She was glad Lilia was there for moral support as she told two flinty men in suits and a faceless voice on the speakerphone of her near-rape in the Davey Crockett Motel. When it was Lilia's turn she held nothing back in recounting the full story of her encounter with Travis, from their first meeting in the penitentiary, to his visit to her condo, and their subsequent romantic entanglement.

"So you were lovers?" Arthur Treadwell asked.

"Yes."

"Physically?"

"Yes."

"Even though he was only half there?"

"He was in his body abroad, it's true," she said. "But it didn't feel like he was half there. He was fully there."

"I'm not going to pry any further than that," Treadwell said. "Except for one more question: Are you still in love with him?"

Lilia could feel the two agents in the room lean forward. She glanced at Nellie, who was looking at her expectantly.

"Yes."

For the first time in two days, Nellie smiled a little. "That makes you practically like my mom," she said.

"They wouldn't do anything to hurt my Dad, would they? I mean, it's the government, right? The government is *us*!" Nellie said. "It's supposed to serve the people, not hurt the people."

"That is how it's supposed to work," Lilia replied. The two of them were talking on the phone, Lilia from her condo in Spokane, and Nellie back at her dad's parents' house on the Oregon coast. The last time they'd seen Travis was the day they had parted ways in the yard of that mountain house above Hawks Nest. He had returned to his body proper to rest and recover, and Lilia had expected he would then come and see her, but three weeks had now passed without a word from him.

"It worked out pretty awesome for you and me," Nellie said. "I still can't believe how *nice* those special services agents were— they took such good care of us. That local cop wanted a piece of us real bad, but special services, those guys were so smooth, they just swooped in like guardian angels."

"Yeah, they were very good to us," Lilia agreed. "But it was definitely in their interest to be that way."

"I don't get all the subtleties of it, I know that," said Nellie. "All I know is they kicked those Hawks Nest cops to the curb, and thank God they did! I did not want to have to testify in any court."

"Exactly. They didn't want you to, either," Lilia said.

"Jerrid called me again."

"How's he doing?"

"Good. He says the agents have been good to him too, but he's getting a bit tired of it. He told them he wanted to talk to his parents, his real parents, because he saw them online making a big stink in the media over how Hawks Nest handled the case, like they just swept it under the rug, and settled with Wallace so quick. They think there's a cover-up."

"Yeah, well, they happen to be right. I do feel for them—he was their son, after all, and they know better than anyone it was completely out of character for him to suddenly drive all night to some mountain town he'd never even heard of, and then end up being killed there."

"Yeah, I know. I feel bad for his folks too, but it's hard, because they blame *me*, like it must have been all *my* idea," Nellie said. "And I'm not allowed to tell them the true story, so really I've had to lie to them right from the get-go, which I'm not good at, and his Mom especially has some kind of ESP going, she can see right through me."

"Has she told you that?"

"No, but I can tell. The worst was at the funeral, because Jerrid wanted me to record it on my phone for him, so he could see what people were saying. So I was trying to do that, all subtle and everything, but his Mom caught me. She just gave me this *look*, like I was the most *twisted* little pervert she'd ever laid eyes on. I mean, who videos their boyfriend's funeral? And I couldn't say to her, 'Well, he *asked* me to.'"

"So you sent it to him?"

"Yeah."

"I bet the agents didn't like that."

"Yeah, they keep telling us to keep a low profile. They'd like it if we stopped talking, but we're still in love."

"You are? When did that happen?"

"I know! It's weird. It took a while, but when I talk to him on the phone it's the same old Jerrid, who I loved before. We don't Skype or Facetime because it still throws me a little, seeing that new face. Not that he's ugly or anything, he's actually quite good-looking. But it takes getting used to. Eventually I think I will, and we'll get back together. That's my dream."

"I hope it works out."

"Yeah. I'm hoping this eventually all just blows over, and we can get on with our lives. The agents have pretty much left me alone now, so I'm doing my best to pretend my life is normal. They're more interested in Jerrid because he actually experienced it, he bilocated. They're still always taking him in for physicals and tests, trying to see if it affected him. They have a good alibi to do it, because he is recovering from a miracle brain injury. His parents—I mean his new parents—don't suspect anything. They're just happy their boy is back from a coma. The agents keep telling him just to settle in and *become* Dylan, which he's actually trying to do. He likes being more athletic, he says he's got the best of both worlds now—a new jock body on top of getting to keep his geek brain. Nice combo. And his new family is nice, but they're not *his*, and he feels bad for his real mom and dad, suffering like they are, grieving all the time, thinking he's dead, when he's actually still in the world, still alive."

"That must be so hard."

"Yeah. So he keeps getting tempted to call them. He figures as long as they hear his voice, and don't see his face, that would work. He'd make up a story that he's on some secret assignment for the government, real top secret stuff, which is kind of true anyway, and he'll tell them when the time is right he'll see them again someday. And then when he does see them, he's going to tell them he's in kind of like a witness protection program and had to get plastic surgery."

"Do the agents know this?"

"Oh yeah. He asked permission, and they said no. They said it would just add another layer of complication, and they want to keep it simple for now. They're nice and everything, but underneath it, sometimes it feels like they'd get very tough if they had to. Jerrid told them he might still go ahead and phone his folks, and they told him there would be consequences if he did. He couldn't remember exactly how they phrased it, but they told him if they had to, they could make him disappear. They were like, stay below the radar, or we'll take you right off the radar. Which sounds pretty fucking ominous, don't you think?"

"I'd be scared," Lilia said.

"Off the radar—what do you think they meant by that?"

"Maybe we should ask them. I'm pretty sure they're listening right now. I'm pretty sure they have the line bugged."

"That's what Jerrid thinks too. That they're always listening when we talk."

"I think he's likely right about that."

"Hey, whoever's listening," Nellie said loudly. "Where's my dad? When are you going to let us see him?"

"I second that," Lilia said.

C H A P T E R **11**

Two days after her chat with Nellie, Lilia was visited by Travis. She watched as the familiar process unfolded: his body, ghost-like and translucent at first, acquired shape and dimensionality, sitting cross-legged on her couch; then his eyes opened, and he was present. Seeing her, he quickly brought a finger to his lips to tell her to remain silent. He pointed to the walls and the corners of the room as he stood and looked for a pen and paper. He found a pen on the kitchen counter, and a magazine on the coffee table, and scribbled a note across the blonde hair of a shampoo model on the back cover: *"Your place might be bugged. We need to meet somewhere else."*

She took the pen and wrote: *"I think so too. Wait for me outside the Starbucks at South Grand and 13th. I'll cruise by and pick you up. We'll go for a drive."*

He took the pen back and wrote, *"Kiss me."*

She did, eagerly. She felt the crush of his arms around her, felt three weeks of pent-up worry and uncertainty melt into relief.

"I missed you," she whispered in his ear.

"Shhh. Soon."

He held her at arm's length and looked deeply into her eyes. She saw something sorrowful in him, and was troubled. He took the pen and wrote one last thing: "*Don't bring your phone. They'll track us.*"

Ten minutes later she pulled up to the Starbucks, and he was waiting on the sidewalk, looking chilled in the crisp night air. He got quickly into the car and said, "Don't linger. Drive."

"Can we talk now?" she said.

"Wait till we're out of town."

They headed south. A short while later they passed the spot on Highway 195 where young Jordan Summerland had been crushed by a speeding 18-wheeler. A small cross had been erected, and flowers surrounded it, some fresh, some wilted, and some artificial, coated with roadside dust.

She felt an urge to tell him about that case, which had happened the very morning she had met him, but kept quiet. He said, "Take the right turn here," and they started up a side road, until they came to a small State Park, little more than a few acres of trees along a stream, with a handful of picnic tables and a parking lot for a dozen cars. "Pull in here," he said. The place was deserted; a sign said it was illegal to be there after dark. She cut the engine and turned to look at him.

"What's going on?"

"Let's get out and walk."

Among the trees it was so dark she could barely see him. They came to the edge of the stream and a slivered moon reflecting off the water gave enough light to see his face.

"I need your help," he said.

"What do you mean?"

"They're threatening to kill me."

"What?"

"Yes. They've been keeping us in solitary when we're in our bodies proper. They've got us hooked up to monitors and brain scanners, all kinds of machines. At first they tried to stop us from meditating, from getting into the posture, to keep us out of our bodies abroad, but we've managed to overcome that. Now I can do it from any position. George could do it already, I had to practice. He and I have been getting out now, and meeting at a shack in the woods, a special place. I won't even tell you where it is. It's good to get out, it's an escape, because when we come home, back into our bodies proper, we're always hooked up to the monitors and brain scanners."

"Is it painful?"

"It never stops—24-7 we're strapped down and studied—they sit us up to eat, give us a treadmill to walk for an hour a day, that's it. They say it's necessary because we're not cooperating. We won't share. That's the big word—share. They want George to teach them the techniques, and he's refusing. I'm refusing too—I just do not trust these guys. And they've given me a reason not to—they're threatening to kill me if George doesn't cooperate."

"That can't be true."

"It is true."

"Then it's awful. It's wrong."

"No kidding. I'm being denied sleep. They're messing with my brain, putting drugs in my food that do things to me, that make me talk. They're messing George up too, doing the same to him. He's left his body proper again, and hasn't come back. He's looking for another body to occupy, the way he did with Dylan. Ideally it'll be in Poland, out of reach of the American machine. Hasn't found one yet though. It's painful to leave the body proper—when we're out they give us electroshocks to try and stimulate us, and it hurts like hell when we reenter. But they justify it. They tell us they're the good guys of the world, and they see our powers as a tremendous weapon for good—a game-changer in the War on Terror, that's what they keep telling us. We're being un-American, unpatriotic, by not giving it up. But if we give it up, then it's beyond our control how it gets used. They'll start with the best of intentions, purely for good, and then, humans being humans—humans being animals, more like it—before long it'll get used for the wrong reasons."

"You don't trust the government," Lilia said.

"I don't. I don't trust anyone except you."

"What do you want me to do?"

"I want you to help us. Help us get out."

"What does that mean?"

"We've got a plan. You're part of it. We're going to teach you to bilocate."

"What?"

"We figure if we're outside, and free, well not free, exactly, because we'd always be in hiding, but if we were independent from them, we could negotiate with them, and we'd even be willing to accept some of their assignments, on a case-by-case basis, doing only good, and keeping the knowledge contained. Keeping it safe."

They heard cars coming up the river road. Three pairs of head-lights pulled into the parking lot, sending random strobe-like patterns through the trees. The cars stopped but the headlights stayed on, splaying the forest with bright shafts of light. Then came the ominous sound of doors slamming in unison.

"Do you think it's them?" she said.

"Yeah. Too business-like to be anyone else. I've got to go." He pulled her behind the broad, mossy trunk of a hemlock and kissed her on the lips. "Just answer me," he said. "Are you with me? If you're in, you've got to be all in."

She hesitated, but only for a moment. "I'm with you," she said. "I'm all in."

"I love you. I'll see you later."

He let go of her and quickly disappeared. She had never seen him fade away so fast. She waited a few seconds before stepping out from the shadow of the tree, and saw flashlight beams dancing toward her. Squinting into the light, she heard a voice call her name.

"Ms. Chambers? We'd like to speak with you."

"I'm here," she called out. To prepare herself, to steel herself, she whispered softly, "All in starts right now."

the end

of

BOOK ONE
THE GOOD SAMARITANS

ABOUT THE AUTHOR

BRIAN PRESTON is grateful for his sweet and safe existence behind a massive moat called the Salish Sea. That's on the west coast of Canada, if you don't know. Back in the day he wrote non-fiction. *Pot Planet* was a bestseller in Britain and did all right in North America. Then he wrote a book about Martial Arts that is well worth the read. Hilarious in places. These days he writes fiction, top-notch middlebrow escapism. His last book was called *All the Romance a Man Can Stomach,* a romance novel that appeals to men as much as to women.

www.ingramcontent.com/pod-product-compliance
Lightning Source LLC
Chambersburg PA
CBHW031221120726

47905CB00002B/424